A NOVEL

# Bloodstained

## K.B.
## CASIMIR

First published in the United States 2024
This edition published 2024

ISBN: PB: 979-8-9914031-0-8; HB: 979-8-9914031-1-5

Cover and formatting by Books and Moods

*For Becca. You are my Charlotte.*

# 1

"If you want to talk about anything — if you have any questions — please feel free to..."

"I'm fine."

Sebastian walked next to Leona, hoping she didn't continue to press him about what had happened. He was still processing things himself. His senses were overwhelmed with all the new data they were taking in. Perhaps New York City wasn't the greatest place for a new vampire — a reluctant one at that — to learn the ropes of immortality.

"Homeless might be the best option. There's a camp not far from here, near Queens," Charlotte explained as they navigated side streets and alleys together.

"A mass murder *could* raise some eyebrows," Piper chimed in. "Let's just focus on getting Sebastian fed. We can all get our own later. He's the priority right now. And we need to stay together anyway. We don't know who could be lurking and if... *he* is currently on the hunt for us."

Sebastian scoffed under his breath.

"Something you'd like to add?" Piper snapped.

"I think it's pretty fucking likely he's hunting for us. Namely me," Sebastian said. "I'm surprised you didn't have a wooden stake waiting for me when I woke up. How long did it take you to come up with that bullshit story about me being some *chosen* vampire hunter?"

"Sebastian," Leona sighed, a pained frown on her face. "It's not bullshit. You were going to die if I didn't... if *we* didn't..."

"I don't care," Sebastian interrupted. It felt as if his throat were closing in on itself. This hunger — or thirst, more accurately — wasn't like what he felt as a human. His stomach didn't turn into knots or rumble, he just felt... irritated, dry, *parched*. He wondered if he'd forget what things felt like as a human as time went on. Had Leona? He would never be able to experience sunlight again, or alcohol, or sleep, or any of the things he enjoyed regularly.

"Stop," Charlotte said as she put her hand out, making everyone halt in their tracks. She pointed forward, a small light illuminated in the distance. Sebastian could see movement. His eyesight had never been so crisp. They were at least a hundred yards away. "That's the homeless camp," the blonde said, looking at them. "I'm sure we can find some that have broken off from the group for Sebastian."

"Let him hunt," Victor said nonchalantly. Heads turned to him and he folded his arms, shrugging his broad shoulders. "He's already pissed off. Let him do what he wants. We can clean the mess up later."

"Need I remind you we're depending on an element of *discreetness*?!" Whitney hissed, her eyes flashing angrily. "Letting Sebastian run wild is going to draw unnecessary attention to us. If Gid—" she paused, swallowing at the looks she received. His name had garnered too much power in their group. "If *he* catches wind there's vampires here, and he shows up, it won't take him long to sniff us out. We need a plan. No more reckless behavior."

Victor lolled his head to one side, keeping his arms crossed. "Fine. You know best."

"Thank you," Whitney said, before turning to the space where Sebastian was. Her face blanched and her eyes erratically began scanning the area. "Where did Sebastian go?!"

Sebastian was lurking on the outskirts of the camp, watching multiple people gather around a fire, laugh, talk, enjoy life together. He frowned to himself, then rested his head against the wall he was standing by. These people were normal. They were innocent. They hadn't hurt anyone. They didn't *deserve* what his 'friends' wanted to do to them.

He felt like a hypocrite. He had been fine to turn the other cheek to Leona and the rest hunting, feeding, *killing*, but now that he was faced with it, he felt disgusted with himself.

Though, he understood now the pull of his thirst. Even in his horror, he was having to physically restrain himself from walking toward them and ripping each of their throats open.

Was that what life would be now? Misery until he couldn't take it any longer? Leona had mentioned feeding off animals, but that their blood wouldn't fully satisfy any healthy immortal, and that craving would always be present.

If only his father were still alive. He'd gladly travel to the bottom of the country and drain every drop from his worthless body.

"We don't have to do this here."

Sebastian quirked his head, seeing Leona's flaming locks out of the corner of his eye. Turning his attention back to the people, he didn't respond.

Leona approached him, then carefully placed a hand on his shoulder. She tried to ignore the slight flinch from him and chalked it up to him just being in shock. She couldn't afford to think any other way.

There was *no way* she could lose him, not after all this. He was angry, rightfully so, and she wanted to make things better. She wanted to nurture him and give him whatever he needed, no matter how long the transition process took. He wasn't even turning to her, which broke her heart into a thousand pieces. She had barely gotten to touch him since he woke up. He hadn't wanted her near him. The entire walk here was awkward, and if it wasn't silent, it was filled with a snarky and resentful quip from him about how he hadn't asked for any of this. About how she'd betrayed him.

"We can go somewhere else. But you *do* need to feed. Your head will clear and we'll be able to talk about everything. I know this is a huge change — one you never asked for — but this is the hand we've been dealt. *You've* been dealt. Let me help you. I know exactly how you're feeling. And I wish I had had someone who had my best interests at heart holding my hand to guide me," she said, trailing her hand from his shoulder, down his arm, to his fingers.

Sebastian stayed there for a moment, then pulled his hand away from her. "You've done enough."

With that, he went back to the group, who had caught up nearby. Leona closed her eyes and resisted crying out. There weren't many times in her life she'd felt so damn helpless. She more than understood why he was angry, and she knew she didn't have a choice but to let him work through it, but a part of her worried that he never *would* work through it. She worried he would despise her for the rest of their existence.

She felt incredibly selfish for worrying about that at a time like this.

"Charlie," Sebastian said, eyeing his best friend. "I want to go with you."

"We'll all—" Victor started but stopped at Sebastian's expression.

"No. Just Charlie. I just want to be with her," Sebastian pressed.

Charlotte looked between them, her gaze landing on Leona. At the redhead's slight nod of permission, the vampire's light eyes went back to Sebastian. "Okay, Sebby. Let's go."

# 2

"Do you hate me, Sebby?" Charlotte asked as they walked through a quiet and damp street, only the moon and some streetlights illuminating them.

"I could never hate you, Charlie," Sebastian responded, turning to look at her. His red eyes were still jarring to her, and she wondered what it meant. None of their eyes had changed. Gideon had red eyes, and he was all-powerful. Was it reserved for a certain caliber of vampires?

"Don't be angry with Leona. She was weak. She… She didn't want to turn you. She hesitated, knowing you'd be upset. I pushed her aside and did it myself. She couldn't have stopped me if she tried. This is on me, Sebastian. Nobody else."

"Why did you do it? You knew how I felt."

Charlotte's voice wavered. "I couldn't lose you."

Sebastian stopped walking and stared at her, his throat

growing tight with either emotion or thirst. Or both. He couldn't tell anymore. "Now you know how I feel. How I felt when you forced me into a life I never wanted by bringing *them* into our home. Our *home*, Charlie."

"You are our home," Charlotte responded, taking his hands. "Me, you, and Victor. We have always been together. We've always been a family. Our family is just a little bit bigger now. Do you seriously think we can abandon them after all *that*? Leona aside, Gideon wants to kill you for personal reasons now. I believe Leona when she says you come from a strong family. You've always been different, Sebastian. You've never fit in. And now… you have this family. We did enough to get away from Gideon. Now, with you… maybe we can finally beat him. Isn't that what you wanted? What happened to the Sebastian who wouldn't allow us to leave him at home while we rescued Leona? You were so adamant about killing him. Now we actually have a chance! You said you'd die for us."

"I did die."

Charlotte couldn't respond. Sadness tinged her light eyes and she cut her gaze downward.

Coldness washed over Sebastian. He felt perpetually in a horrible mood. He just wanted to scream at her, at the world, which was not like him. He hated raising his voice. His father had always scared him when he yelled, and Sebastian had argued that volume wouldn't get the point across any better. He didn't like to intimidate people for the sake of intimidating them.

"What about blood bags?" Sebastian asked, breaking the

silence.

"We can get some," Charlotte said with a nod. "You will drink from them?"

"I guess I don't have another choice."

"Well…"

"I *don't* have another choice," he repeated firmly. "Just because you're quick to abandon your humanity and suggest killing an entire homeless camp doesn't mean I am."

"You don't think I feel guilt for that?" Charlotte asked, looking at him. "This is the life I chose, Sebastian, and yes, it is difficult to think about killing people, but that's the way things are. I went into this knowing I'd have to end people's lives. And these homeless people, I mean… what do they have to live for anyway?"

"I haven't heard you sound so *aristocratic* in a long time, Charlotte," Sebastian snapped. Charlotte hadn't always been overly kind and generous. He liked to think he had that influence on her, as well as on Victor. They both came from money, whereas he did not, and they had all shown each other empathy in different ways. Charlotte often carried a holier-than-thou attitude when they had first met, but after learning what Sebastian had gone through as a child, she changed her tune over the years. Apparently, the old Charlotte hadn't died completely.

"Get off your high horse," Charlotte quipped back, glaring at him. "Would you rather I go kill children?"

Sebastian answered her with a scathing look. "You're being a bitch."

"*You* are the one being a bitch," Charlotte said, shoving

him. He stumbled a little at the force, but quickly regained his footing.

"What the fuck do you want from me, Charlotte?!" Sebastian said in exasperation. "Forgive me if I'm not so quick to suggest murdering innocent people."

Charlotte sighed deeply and calmed herself down, before speaking in a cool tone, "You mentioned blood bags. We can do that."

Sebastian clenched his jaw, forcing himself to calm down as well. No use in fighting with her. "Where do we go to get those here? A hospital?"

"Yes," Charlotte said. "There's actually a blood bank not far from here. I can get in and out without being seen. I worry you don't have a firm enough handle on your powers yet. I'm happy to get as much as we need. I would ask if you have a preference on what type, but I guess you wouldn't know."

"Leona said that… AB-negative is her favorite."

Charlotte smiled. At least he was coming around. Slowly. A little. "I can find that."

"Just get the one that has the most inventory. I don't want to take away from anyone who might need it."

"*You* need it, too."

Sebastian glared at her. Not what he meant and she knew it. "Let's just go. Can we evanesce there?"

"Yes. I can show you how."

Sebastian pondered that, then shook his head. "I don't want to learn anything right now. Leona says it's hard to do when you're new and weak. I'm both."

"Alright," Charlotte said. She pulled him into her arms.

"Here we go."

Sebastian stared up at the cold, large building. His eyes roamed to the sign. *New York Blood Center.* He closed his eyes for a moment, listening to what he could. Hums of chatter from inside, liquid flowing — which he assumed was people's blood being drawn — and footsteps pattering along linoleum hallways. Inhaling deeply, he could smell different sweet aromas of both fresh and stale blood. He felt a pull in different directions: one toward the building, the other wherever Charlotte went. Opening his eyes, he looked over at the blonde, who was watching him curiously. If he could have blushed, he would have. "Just taking it in."

"Good," Charlotte said, a small smile ghosting her lips. "I'm glad. Continue taking it in. I'll be right back."

Before he could respond, Charlotte had vanished. Sebastian stayed where he was and took the moment alone to just look around. The city felt different than it had when they'd all been in school. He had enjoyed his time in New York more than he'd ever expected and hadn't wanted to come back to New Orleans. Now he couldn't ever imagine leaving Louisiana. New York seemed cold now. Temperature-wise, yes, but culturally and atmospherically, too. Not like it had years ago.

Then again, maybe that was the perfect fit for him now.

He could see the fissures in all the materials used to build the building. His eyes darted to a few bugs flying around, the flaps of their tiny wings sounding like hurricanes in his ears. He could hear full-on conversations, tuning each out as he went through them one by one. Some talking about dinner. Some fighting. Some loving. Some first-time-meetings.

All he could hear was *life*.

One thing he hadn't thought about before and after this entire transition was how much he'd notice about a life he took for granted. There were little things that he was still getting to enjoy and take in. Though he wasn't technically alive, that didn't mean he couldn't *live*.

His daydream was interrupted by a flash of blonde hair. Before he knew it, Charlotte was next to him carrying two big coolers.

"Everything go okay?" Sebastian asked, offering to take the coolers from her.

She handed one off and nodded. "Never even knew I was there. Most of these are O-positive. But I grabbed a few AB-negatives for you. Don't worry," she said quickly in response to his skeptical look. "They won't even notice they're gone. I altered the supply list while I was in there. We do this at home, too. Piper showed me how to cover all our bases. It's the same everywhere."

"I can just do this instead of killing people then," Sebastian said, a glimmer of hope tracing his voice.

Charlotte hesitated, then jerked her head for him to follow her. "Let's just get some blood in you first. We don't have to worry about anything else right now."

"Where are we going?"

"Where do you want to go?"

"I want to go home."

"We can't go home right now. We're going to have to stay here a while. Home's not safe."

Sebastian frowned, feeling like nothing was fair. What a shit show this turned out to be. "Can we go back to your apartment then?"

"The others might be there."

He paused. Deciding that was worth the risk, he met her gaze. "I still want to go."

"Okay. Hold on."

"Stop staring at me."

Sebastian held the blood bag in his hands, the warmth feeling stark against his cool palms. Charlotte had thrown the bag in the microwave, insisting it was better heated up. He wouldn't know the damn difference. At least he didn't have to worry about getting cancer with the warmed-up plastic.

"I just feel honored to be the one to share in this experience with you. I'll stare all I want, Beliveau," Charlotte grinned, propping her chin on the heels of her hands. She was sitting on a barstool at the kitchen counter. "Go on then!"

"Do I just... bite?"

"Sebastian, the fangs aren't straws. They're just to pierce the skin. Or... plastic. Open your mouth."

He did as instructed, and as if on cue, he could feel his teeth expanding. His canines grew elongated and sharp. Bringing his finger up, he poked the bottom of one, puncturing a shallow hole in his skin. A small droplet of blood formed, before healing almost immediately. Carefully, he closed his mouth, not wanting to make a new lip piercing.

"You just bite down and drink. Swallow like usual," Charlotte continued.

"What does it taste like?"

"Mmm..." she hummed, leaning back in her chair thoughtfully. "Metallic. I think it tastes like black licorice, but nobody seems to agree with me."

"There is no way blood tastes like candy."

"Only one way to find out," she said, pointing insistently to the bag in his hand. "You're stalling. Aren't you thirsty?"

"Yes, but... I'm not exactly sucking down a milkshake," he snapped. He *was* stalling and he knew it. "You weren't freaked out at first?"

"Not at all. I was excited."

"You are definitely made to be a serial killer."

"Drink, Sebby!"

Sebastian grunted under his breath, then brought the bag up to his mouth. He needed to just go for it. If he hated it, he could just spit it out. No harm, no foul. Teeth first, he pierced the bag, thick, red liquid gushing into his mouth. The moment that first drop touched his tongue, his red eyes darkened and he was sucking the bag dry as if he would die otherwise. Technically, he supposed he would. He squeezed whatever remnants he could, before grabbing another bag nearby. Ignoring Charlotte's quick offers to microwave it, he drained that one, too. And another. And another.

After thirty bags were crumpled on the floor around him,

Sebastian took a break. His frenzied eyes looked down at the scene of the crime, blood smeared around his mouth and cheeks. Some had dripped down his chin and blended into the material of his pants.

"How do you feel?" Charlotte asked, keeping a close look at the color of his eyes. "Sebastian?"

Coming out of his reverie, he lifted his head and looked at her. His eyes were still red, but brighter now. The color of a blazing fire.

"I feel better," he admitted. "A lot better."

"And you didn't even have to kill anyone. Did you like the warm blood better?"

"I… I didn't notice," he confessed. He had been too focused on getting as much as he could into his body. "Is thirty bags normal?"

"For someone who has never fed and needed nutrients, yes. But it might go down later. It depends on how hungry you are. After sex, I always want more. The most I've taken down is two grown men. That's about… twenty bags. I don't do that on a normal basis though. Usually, one person is enough. A human carries about ten units in their body. Or ten bags."

"Glad you got two coolers."

"I knew you'd go through a lot. I wanted to be on the liberal side. Should've still gotten another cooler."

"I'm alright for now. Leona was right, my head does feel clearer. I'm in a better mood. I felt fatigued, but… vampires don't get fatigued."

"It's like a fog. I know what you mean," Charlotte said reassuringly. She quickly gathered the soiled bags and threw them away. When she came back, she had a damp rag. "Here. Clean your face up, hellion."

Sebastian huffed in response and got up, going to the mirror in her half bathroom.

This was the first time he'd actually seen himself.

He backed up a step, then gathered his thoughts. Coming back toward the mirror, he touched his messy face. He truly did look terrifying. Every blemish he'd had before was gone. His facial hair was still there, which bewildered him. What did the body see as imperfections? He shed his coat and looked down at the pale, perfect skin exposed on his arms. Skin that hadn't been bare since he was a teenager. His scars were gone. He looked better than he ever had, but also... not. He looked like himself but didn't. It was the strangest sensation he'd ever known.

"Sorry," Charlotte said from the doorway. "I guess I forgot you haven't been looking at you like I have the last couple of hours."

"It's alright," he murmured. Charlotte gently pried the rag from his hand and began carefully cleaning his face and neck up. Soon enough, he was as good as new. He turned his head toward the mirror again and opened his mouth, his fangs still extended. This was something out of a dream.

Or a nightmare.

"You grew taller during the transformation."

"I thought it was because I was wearing some of Vic's heels."

"That, too," Charlotte laughed, glancing down at the lifted boots he had on. All of his clothes from Gideon's had been ruined. "You've got to be seven feet now."

"I noticed when I nearly hit the fuck out of my head walking in here," he said. "I think I'm bigger all the way around," he muttered, running his hands over his clothed chest and down his biceps.

"*All* the way around?" Charlotte asked, stepping beside him to look at him through the mirror. She raised *one* cheeky, blonde eyebrow.

"Oh, now that I'm the epitome of a hot vampire king, you want in my pants?" Sebastian said, a smirk bubbling from him. It was the first time he'd really smiled since all this started. "I haven't checked that. We don't go to the bathroom, do we?"

"No," Charlotte said. "If we eat any kind of human food, we absorb it. It doesn't feel like blood though and doesn't do anything for us nutritionally. It's sort of like... when humans eat lettuce. Yeah, it goes in, but it doesn't contribute a whole lot. Nothing comes out the bottom end though. The blood we drink, of course, also just absorbs back in our system."

"That makes no sense," Sebastian said.

"So werewolves and vampires fighting is totally normal, but you draw the line at undead bodily functions?"

Sebastian did chuckle at that. He shook his head. "Guess you're right. Someone ought to write a book on all this. Do some research."

"They have. Humans just can't access the texts. Piper has a few copies in her room. Victor and I read them. It's interesting. She said there is more information all around the world. It's part of the reason she travels so much and searches for friends. To learn. Gideon seemed to have a lot, too. While we were running for our lives and trying not to get killed, I noticed his library. When we do kill him, I'd love to spend a few days in there."

"I don't want to spend *any* time in his house," Sebastian muttered. "But leave it to you to notice the books when a psychopath was disemboweling me. When did you turn into such a nerd?"

Charlotte smiled sympathetically, before tugging him out of the bathroom. "The others will be back soon, I'm sure. I assume they're hunting. Probably best we went on our own," she said, grabbing the last few bags of blood to warm them up.

"Will that be enough for you?"

"I had some when the others returned from Gideon's. This will be enough until the next time we all hunt. Don't worry."

Sebastian watched her. She moved so fast, but slow. It was something he never would have noticed as a human. It's something he *didn't* notice as a human. It only dawned on him how blissfully ignorant he'd been to the world. There was an air of elegance and poise to her that hadn't existed before, and that was saying something. Was he the same?

Charlotte's apartment was luxurious, but not overly big. There wasn't an abundance of space in the city. But it had a kitchen, a walk-in closet, two bathrooms, and a washing machine and dryer, which was more than most people could even hope for in New York.

"So we share a bond now," Sebastian said, moving to lean against the kitchen counter.

It was a statement more than a question. Charlotte turned from the microwave and met his intense stare. She nodded. "Can't you feel it?"

"Yes," he answered. "It's deeper than anything I've ever felt. Even love."

"This might be a good time to remind you I'm married and Victor is *also* immortal."

Sebastian smirked. "I think I could take him."

"Sebastian!"

"You know I didn't mean deep in *that* way. I feel like our friendship is just stronger. The thought of someone touching you, harming you…"

"That's not going to happen," Charlotte said. A trio of beeps from the microwave interrupted her, and she opened the door to get her dinner out. Sucking the bags dry, she spoke between each one. "You're already super protective…" Bag. Slurp. Toss to trash. "That's all just amplified now…" New bag. Slurp. Trash. "I feel the same about you, you know. I'll rip Gideon apart if he so much as looks at you."

Sebastian felt that in his bones. In his *cells*. "I'm glad it was you."

"You're glad?" Charlotte repeated in confusion. "I thought you didn't…"

"I mean I'm glad you're the one who did it. If it had to be done."

"I would've thought you'd preferred Leona. Since you two are…"

"Look at what happened between her and Gideon."

"You're not Gideon."

"I know. But we already share an intense bond. Or at least… we did. I don't know what's going to happen now. What if a creator bond somehow ruined that? I have never wanted incentives to run our relationship and dictate our love."

"You still love her, don't you?"

Sebastian sunk onto the sofa and looked down at his hands in his lap. "I am angry."

"I told you to be angry with me."

"It's complicated," Sebastian said. "I'm angry, but… not necessarily at anyone. I just wish things could be different. I'm scared," he added. "Really scared."

"That's normal," she said, tossing the last bag in the trash. She joined him on the sofa and placed a hand over his knee. "But we've got you. We can be scared together."

Sebastian slowly slid his hand over hers and squeezed. "Don't ever leave me, Charlie. The world would burn without you."

Charlotte smiled and shook her head. "You couldn't get rid of me if you tried, Sebby. But arson *does* sound fun."

Sebastian laughed and rested his head against hers, leaning into her side. If anyone could ruin a moment, it was her.

But he wouldn't have her any other way.

3

"He's going to be fine, Le. The transition is different for all of us. You of all people should know how it feels to be forced into this life," Piper said as she watched her redheaded best friend pace around. They fed on a few different people in a square-mile radius. Not too far from each other, but far enough that hopefully they wouldn't draw attention to themselves. It was a big city full of crime and murder. They were good at covering their tracks now after centuries of practice.

For a city brimming with millions of people, it was eerily quiet in that location at that time of night. It was good for them, given their element of discretion, but since shacking up in New Orleans for the last several months, Leona found herself missing the constant hum of music and chatter the Crescent City offered.

"He hates me, Piper. He's never going to look at me the same again. I know it's selfish but… what good is this life if

I can't have him to share in it with?" Leona said dejectedly.

"I'm going to not take offense to that," Piper said, rolling her eyes. "He's with Charlotte. He's in good hands."

"He really is," Victor added. "He and Charlie have a bond that's unlike anything else, and that was *before* she changed him. They're soulmates in every sense of the word. Platonically. They get each other. Honestly, I'm not surprised she was the one who ended up changing him. She's going to take care of him and talk him off the ledge. She's done it so many times before. I have, too. But I've learned that sometimes she can do it better than any of us ever could. No matter how close we are to him."

Leona didn't respond. Frowning, she stopped her pacing. Perhaps it was rather dramatic to be reacting the way she was, but this was a situation she'd never found herself in. It made her feel almost as bad as Gideon, making Sebastian into a monster when she promised she would never do that to him. She just prayed that Victor was right and Charlotte was able to get through to him.

She took a few steps away from the group and seized a moment for herself and her thoughts.

It made her think back on when she'd been turned by Gideon. She had been betrayed, hurt, led on… Some of those days still haunted her memories. Gideon was a vindictive, evil son-of-a-bitch and she cringed at the thought of ever setting sight on him again. When she'd turned, she had been overcome with grief and fear. All of a sudden, her entire world shrunk down to revolve around her creator. She had lost all of her life and family in one fell swoop and she hadn't even had time to process it before Gideon was yanking her by the arm to go wherever he beckoned. She never wanted to become a ball-and-chain for Sebastian, or anyone, for that matter. She hoped with everything in her that Sebastian would calm down and see that she *had* respected his wishes. She was going to let him die, she…

"Do you want to head back?" Whitney asked, placing a hand on Leona's shoulder. "I bet they're there."

"Not just yet," the redhead answered with a slight shake of her head. Her treacherous thoughts slowly dissipated from her mind. She wasn't ready to face the music. If he wanted nothing to do with her, if he just wanted to get trained as an immortal and be on his way, she was going to respect that decision. She would not hold him hostage.

She just hoped he could remember all the wonderful times they enjoyed with each other. And the fact that they had been madly in love just a week ago.

How quickly things could turn to absolute shit.

"I'm sorry, Le."

Leona turned to Whitney and frowned at the look of utmost sadness and guilt on her friend's face. "What?"

"I feel like this is my fault. When I left Damien to come back for the ball, I… That was the whole reason Gideon came back. He found us because of me. I should never have done that. I don't know why I keep going back to Damien. He has this pull that I just can never bring myself to ignore. I need to be stronger because what happened *cannot* happen again. I will not put you or anyone else at risk again."

"Whitney," Leona said, taking her hands in hers. She

squeezed her fingers, then pulled her in for a tight hug. "Nothing that's happened has been your fault. We both know Gideon would have found us eventually. He probably knew where we were the entire time," she murmured against her hair, before pulling back. Stroking some of her dark brown curls away from her face, Leona gave Whitney a reassuring smile. "I love you all the same. I want you to be happy. Gideon aside, Damien just needs to treat you better. Sometimes I wonder if he really loves you or if you're just a convenience to him."

Whitney sighed sadly and cut her eyes down. "I know… I don't know why I value myself so little. He seems to be more bothered by Theodore at any given time than me."

Leona had seen this look a hundred times and had this conversation even more. They all knew that Damien and Theodore had a history, one that caused everyone around them strife at some point or another. Leona thought carefully about what to say in response to her.

"Any man, wolf, vampire, *creature* who doesn't see that you're everything anyone could ever hope for doesn't deserve to lick the bottom of your shoes, Whit. You know that."

The brunette gave a tearful smile, and eventually, she nodded. "I know. I know."

"Good." Leona hugged her close once more, then stroked a hand down her hair. "I don't know what I'd do without you and Piper."

"I think that every single day."

Leona's throat tightened and she kept her eyes closed as she and Whitney continued embracing. She relished this quiet moment with her friend. It was giving her a small reprieve from the histrionics plaguing her head. She had never had a panic attack before, but… this felt like what people described.

Leona and Whitney broke apart, then rejoined the group nearby. Piper and Victor were engaged in conversation but stopped talking when the other two vampires came by their sides.

Leona hoped their stalling gave Charlotte more time to talk to Sebastian and calm him down. It did hurt her a little that he picked the blonde over her, but if Victor didn't feel jealous over it, perhaps she shouldn't either. Leona trusted Sebastian implicitly and knew the relationship between him and Charlotte didn't go further than best friends, but she also knew how powerful the bond between sire and fledgling could be. Sometimes things happened and they couldn't be helped.

"How are you feeling?" Piper asked Leona, tilting her head. "A little better?"

"Not really, but…" Leona trailed off, shrugging.

Piper frowned and glanced at Whitney, then back to Leona. "We really do need to get out of the open. I know you aren't ready to go back yet, but… the apartment is safer."

Leona knew that. She knew them being out here *at all* was a major risk. Gideon was probably terrorizing all of New Orleans looking for them. He was an exceptionally skilled tracker, and based on his history, Leona knew it wouldn't take long at all for him to trace them back to New York. They *had* to be gone before he got this far.

"We can go back," Leona said with a deep breath. Three hundred years of being immortal and she still had human habits. "I'm ready."

# 4

eona could smell blood the moment they evanesced into the apartment.

She looked around, fearing the worst, but after a few seconds of processing, realized there was no danger inside the home. Loosing a breath, Leona let her eyes dart over as Piper, Whitney, and Victor walked past her to go find Charlotte and Sebastian.

"Was wondering when you'd come back," Charlotte's voice sounded from just down the hall. The blonde hugged her husband close, pressing a few kisses to his lips. "Were you able to get fed?"

"Yes, my love," Victor said with a nod. "We all ate. How is Bas?"

"He's fine. Better," she nodded. "He's on the roof practicing evanescing. So he claims anyway. I think he just wanted to be alone."

"You left him alone?" Piper asked, her eyes wide. "What

if he gets hurt? What if someone sees him? What if he goes on a killing spree?"

"If any of that happens, feel free to set me on fire," Charlotte snapped back. "He's fine. Sebastian isn't one to be hovered over."

Piper looked over at Leona for backup, but the redhead was lost in her own world of thought. "Leona," Piper said, catching the woman's attention. "Sebastian is on the roof."

"Okay."

Sebastian sat on the edge of the building, his long legs dangling off the side. He could hear and see so much from this vantage. The shimmering lights of the cars illuminated the streets beyond. The moonlight shimmered against the reflection of the Hudson River and he could swear he'd never beheld beauty such as this before. It was quite ironic, only seeing the beauty in life when he would never experience it the same way again. The cold weather licked his skin and he looked down at his exposed arms and hands. How strange to not be susceptible to the elements any longer. What else wouldn't bother him?

His stomach turned and he inhaled slightly, catching a familiar scent. Then, like clockwork, he heard the door creak open behind him. "Just you? No army to tell me not to jump?" Sebastian called out without turning around.

Leona stared at his back, then shut the door behind her. Slowly, she approached him and perched down next to him on the ledge. "Fresh out of armies, I'm afraid."

Sebastian smiled weakly, then looked down at Leona's hand next to his. Slowly, he moved his pinky to brush against the side of hers. Fingers froze, then crept toward each other in an embrace.

"Charlie said you were practicing evanescing," Leona said, feeling infinitely better just by *touching* him. "Were you?"

"Not really," Sebastian said. "She told me how to do it, and we tried it once, but I just wanted the excuse to be alone."

"Do you want me to leave?"

A few moments of silence settled between them, then Sebastian looked out toward the cityscape. "No."

Relief flooded through Leona. She kept a vice on his hand and joined him in looking upon the beautiful scenery. "Though I miss the sunlight and everything that comes with daytime… this life forces you to appreciate the nature of the dark, too. Nighttime is a truly beautiful thing."

"It is," he agreed. "But I think I've always been a creature of the night."

"You are an angel sent from heaven," Leona said, turning her head to look at him. "You are my savior. I'm so sorry I couldn't be yours."

Tearing his gaze from facing forward, he met her eyes. "You saved me the minute you walked into that party."

Leona felt her throat tighten with emotion. He *did* still love her.

"Did you feed?" she asked instead of bringing up anything to do with their relationship. It didn't feel like the right time.

"Yes. Charlie stole some blood bags from some blood

center. I drank thirty. She said that was normal."

"For a man of your size, and the fact you were probably starving at that point, I agree. You definitely got taller though."

"That's what Charlie said. Almost seven feet. There's a little mark on the doorframe of the bathroom to prove it," he teased, his legs swinging slightly in the cool air. "Why do I have red eyes? Why didn't mine stay the same? Gideon has red eyes, too."

Leona was trying not to internally cringe at the name every time someone said it. They needed to go back to avoiding it. Even in the last few hours, everyone seemed to be relaxing. That was *not* an option for them. "Everyone is different. He's the only other immortal with red eyes I know. Mine were green from the start. They never changed. I wondered for a long time if it had to do with morality, evilness, power... But you're not evil. You're *good*. So perhaps it truly is power. It's in your blood."

"Really," Sebastian said in a monotone. "'It's in your blood?'"

"How else am I supposed to say it?!" Leona laughed, leaning over to nudge him with her shoulder. "It is. I wasn't lying when I told you what he told me. Perhaps..." she trailed off, her teeth worrying her lip in thought.

"Perhaps?"

"You two were enemies before you were ever even a thought. Maybe those things being intertwined has something to do with it."

"Like fate?"

"Yeah."

Sebastian thought about this, then looked down at his thighs. "I'm going to kill him."

"Sebastian…"

"Not today, not tomorrow, but I will. I'm going to go to his home and rip him out of it. I'm going to take everything he holds dear and watch him choke on it. I want to be the last thing he sees before the light leaves his eyes."

"There is no light in those eyes," Leona muttered. "He will kill you."

"You said my great, great… whatever, almost killed him. I'm going to finish the job," he said. "Do you believe in divine intervention?"

"Not necessarily. I thought you were an atheist?"

"My perception of what's true and what's not has been skewed over the last six months," Sebastian said. "Maybe you're right. Maybe it is all connected. My ancestor almost kills him, so you and he kill my ancestor. Hundreds of years later, you just so happen to come to the home of my best friends. We meet. Everything changes. That can't all be a coincidence. You and I both said it: we were drawn to each other the moment we met."

"I recognized you that night. Or at least… something made me want to speak to you. I couldn't figure it out. I chalked it up to both being hungry and horny."

Sebastian smiled slightly in amusement, then looked at her again. "You and I will find each other in every lifetime."

Leona felt her emotions reach a crescendo. Tears pooled in her eyes and she brought her hand up to cup his cheek. "And I'll love you in all of them, too. But now we get to have *this* lifetime… forever."

"I told you when we walked by the river back home that I would never let him harm you again. I broke that promise when he took you," Sebastian said. Searching her eyes, he shook his head. "I will *not* break it again."

"I love you," Leona whispered, her voice shaking.

"I love you more."

Sebastian closed his eyes as Leona dove forward and kissed him. Sebastian, keeping his balance so they didn't plummet to the pavement, wrapped his arms around her and held her close. Their kiss deepened and tears rolled down both their cheeks, mixing together.

After a few moments, Leona pulled back, but only just. She pressed her forehead against his, her eyelashes fluttering with his. "I thought you… I wasn't sure…"

"I thought you knew I was an asshole. This never came up?"

"*Asshole*," Leona hissed, pecking a few more kisses to his lips. Hers were puffy from the effort. "How silly of me."

"Silly indeed," he purred, nudging his nose with hers. "Nothing could make me fall out of love with you. Not even becoming a corpse."

"You grew, like, six inches. And you have abs now."

"I had abs before."

"They're… *abbier* now."

"Not a word."

"Definitely is a word. You need the vampire dictionary. It's in there."

"Now you're *lying* to me? Not a very good way to start our

new relationship as star-crossed undead lovers."

"I'm considering pushing you off this building."

"So violent," Sebastian said, their laughs melding together as they kissed again.

Maybe everything wouldn't be so bad.

# 5

"**Y**ou know, I was majorly holding back when we had sex before. I mean *majorly*," Leona said as they walked across the rooftop back to the door.

Sebastian laughed under his breath and looked at Leona, his eyebrow raised. "You think I didn't know that? I'm just happy you didn't end up murdering me while you had me tied up. I was helpless."

"I try not to murder my partners. It *has* happened though…" Leona said sheepishly.

Sebastian scoffed in amusement and moved to open the door for her so they could go back down. "Seriously? You fucked someone to *death*?"

"I didn't mean to! It was a while ago, the first human I had bedded after I escaped from *him*. The bloke was nice, handsome, tall—"

Sebastian made a gagging noise.

Leona nudged him and went to the elevator, pressing the button to go down. "Stop being jealous. Anyway, to make a story you don't want to hear *very* short, I may have gotten a little carried away whilst on top and… well, I like to think he enjoyed his last moments."

"Ugh," Sebastian grimaced as the elevator began its descent. "Remind me to stop asking you about your exes."

"Unfortunately, I don't think we're going to stop hearing about one anytime soon." As the elevator dinged, her expression faded from mild amusement to intense concern.

"What is it?" Sebastian asked, his hackles up. "Jesus," he then groaned, putting his hand up to his face. "What the hell is that horrific smell?"

"A werewolf," Leona said, cautiously stepping out of the elevator when the door opened. She looked around, scanning their surroundings. If there were werewolves there, they were there for one reason. Was Gideon nearby? She couldn't feel or smell him, but that didn't mean they were safe. She was always unpleasantly surprised by the tricks he always seemed to have under his expensive sleeves.

Sebastian reached out and took Leona's hand to stop her from walking any further. "Stop. We need to be careful."

"What about the others?" she hissed, her eyes flicking to Charlotte's apartment door. "It's definitely coming from in there. One of *them* is in there. With our friends. With our *family*."

"Well… then we go in together," Sebastian said. "Together in *everything*, remember?"

Leona nodded and squeezed his hand. "In everything."

The pair stepped up to the door, their shoes clicking against the stone flooring. Sebastian, for a moment, felt like a human again. He felt fear. The last time he'd gone into the unknown, he'd practically had his heart ripped out of his chest. He had new abilities now, of course, but he wasn't in tune with them. He didn't even know what he *could* do. He had been strong before, and knew that was enhanced now, as well as his speed, but… did he have anything *special*?

"Do we just bust in there? Like the movies?" Sebastian whispered as they closed the distance between them and the door.

"Shut up," Leona snapped, her eyes peeled forward. "I need you to be serious."

"Our entrance is an extremely serious matter of discussion," Sebastian retorted in a hiss. "If I'm going to get my shit rocked again, I at least want to look cool doing it."

"Just be quiet," Leona said, reaching out for the door handle. Turning it, she opened the door and looked around, scoping out the situation.

Things seemed normal and nothing looked to be in disarray. The kitchen seemed untouched, and even the throw pillows on the couch were perfectly fluffed and unbothered. Leona crept forward, Sebastian practically glued to her backside. She appreciated his support, but she was worried about both herself and him. She wasn't sure what he would be like in a fight without any training, and she wouldn't be able to focus on protecting herself if she was distracted by his vulnerability.

"You're back."

Charlotte appeared from the doorway that led from the living room to her bedroom. Sebastian focused on her, trying to suss out whether something had happened and she was trying to cover it up. She looked normal, and didn't seem hurt, but… he could tell by her body language that there was something she wanted to say, but didn't know how to say it. She had the same look on her face when she'd broken one of his cameras on accident by knocking it off the kitchen counter where he'd left it. His fault, technically, but he still hadn't been happy. She had bought him a new expensive one to make up for it, as well as a few new lenses, and his anger had magically dissipated.

Though he knew Charlie like the back of his hand, he had even more insight into her feelings. It was like a whisper in the back of his head, twisting through his neck, to his ears…

"Theodore is here," Sebastian said, which made both Leona and Charlotte snap their heads to him. "He just arrived. He's with the others in the bedroom."

"How did you…"

"We can discuss this later!" Leona interrupted, throwing her hands up. "It's just Theo? How did he find us?"

"He—"

Leona moved past Charlotte before she got another word out and disappeared into the bedroom, leaving Sebastian behind. The blonde vampire rolled her eyes and jerked her head toward the bedroom. "Come on, Sebby, let's introduce you to a werewolf."

Sebastian wasn't quite sure what he expected from a werewolf, but it wasn't the man in front of him.

Theodore Selwyn was a taller man, but nowhere near the height of Gideon. Closer to where Sebastian had been as a human. The man seemed almost too… *normal* to be anything supernatural. He had shaggy, longer, light brown hair, and a large scar from his temple, down past his right eye, and down to his jaw. His eyes were a light brown and not cold like what Sebastian expected. His clothes were casual — jeans and a thick sweater — and for all intents and purposes, he seemed like a regular man. Minus the stench.

"Leona," Theodore was saying when Sebastian walked in, "I'm so sorry. Damien told me there was a big fight and… I just had to come find you. I can't deal with it anymore. Dame is pissed and I…" he trailed off, glancing at Whitney. "I just can't do it anymore."

"How did you find us?" Sebastian asked.

Theodore seemed to only just notice the man's presence in the room. "Who are you?"

"How — did — you — find — us?" Sebastian repeated firmer this time. If he found them, who's to say he wasn't leading Gideon straight to them? The monster was probably waiting to pounce as they spoke.

"I'm part dog," Theodore said dully. "Not hard to track people," he said, looking him up and down. "Are you Sebastian?"

"Yes," he said. There was nothing to hide anymore, nothing to be afraid of. These creatures were going to find him whether he liked it or not. Before, he had hated people recognizing him in the streets or the store and had actively avoided the interaction. Now? There was no form of camouflage. He had attracted the attention of the most powerful vampire in the world. His face was probably plastered on a 'wanted' sign in whatever Transylvanian hovel Gideon crawled around.

"Damien told me you were human. You're not," Theodore observed.

"Recent development," Sebastian muttered. "Who else is here? Who else have you brought with you? If you think for one *second* I'm going to let you and your pack of mongrels take Leona away—"

"Calm down," Theodore interrupted, putting his hands up. "I'm not here to cause trouble. The opposite, in fact. I want to be here with you. Protect you. All of you."

Sebastian scoffed and looked around, hoping for similar reactions. When he got none, he shook his head. "You can't be serious… He's part of Gideon's crew. He can't be trusted!"

"We've known Theo for centuries, Seb," Leona said, placing her hand on his bicep as a comfort. "I trust him. I trust him more than Damien."

Whitney rolled her eyes at that comment.

Still not convinced, Sebastian eyed Theodore so hard, that he half-wondered if lasers would come out and singe a hole in his forehead. As he glared at him, that little whisper came back, but it was in a different voice this time. A deeper voice. Theodore's voice? It was so… *slight.*

*Damien can't find out where I am… He's going to be so pissed… Whitney doesn't deserve him… She's done nothing but glare at me the entire time I've been here… Does anyone else see how awkward this is? What does he see in her? Does he truly love her, or…*

Sebastian pulled out of whatever trance he'd been in, then blinked a few times. Strange. So strange. Shifting his gaze, he went to Leona, focusing the same way on her.

*Theo wouldn't sell me out. Would he? No, he wouldn't. He cares too much about Damien… But then again, if he cared about Damien, wouldn't he be worried about going to the other side? If Damien found out he was here, consulting with the enemy… he would lose his shit. But Theo hasn't been the same since Whitney came along and stole Damien. Will he betray us because of that? Maybe I don't trust him as much as I thought…*

Blinking, Sebastian gave a minuscule shake of his head. So weird. So…

He moved his sights to Charlotte, who was leaning up against the wall, her arms folded. She seemed to just be listening to everyone's banter, waiting for the right time to chime in.

As he focused on her, he was rather startled when she snapped her head over to him. His eyes rounded in embarrassment. How had she known he was doing this… *whatever* it was? Could she do it too?

"Sebastian got telepathy," Charlotte announced suddenly.

The conversations in the room stopped, and Leona was the first one to speak up again. "What?"

"His power. He got telepathy. He can read minds. He just tried to do it on me."

"Damn," Victor swore. "And what the fuck did I get? Nothing."

Sebastian ignored the man. This wasn't as much of a shock to him as it probably should have been. He had always been rather good at reading people growing up, which was why a life of crime had come easy to him. It hadn't been hard to work out the ones who were too trusting or careless with locking up their things. A few well-placed questions and lingering smiles made a world of difference when it came to ripping people off. He supposed that talent translated into his immortality and he was rewarded for it.

"Charlotte can read minds, too," Piper said. "As can I. It's possible to pass gifts down to the people we change. It doesn't always happen, else Le would be one kickass immortal with all of Gideon's good parts. But maybe the gene is strong with me. I thought it was a lucky break when I changed Charlie, but now that it's happened twice, I can't help but think it's a pattern."

"What about Victor? He said he didn't get anything," Sebastian said.

"It can take a while for powers to show themselves," Whitney said with a shrug. "Sometimes the basic powers are all we get. Sometimes we can do things better or easier. Leona doesn't have any *outright* special abilities beyond our usual ones, but she's able to evanesce further and quicker than any of us can."

"What can you do?" Sebastian asked her. "Other than the usual stuff."

"Glamouring is my ability. Shapeshifting. I can't look identical to other people, like a twin, but I can change my hair color and eye color at will. You'd be surprised how little people pay attention to someone they know if you just change a few key parts of the body," Whitney explained. "I've heard some vampires can see the future. Some can shapeshift completely into animals and whatnot. Bats," she said with a small smirk. "That's a fun legend the humans came up with. Some are adept at swimming and can breathe underwater. I've even heard of some that aren't as susceptible to the sunlight. I'm sure there are countless abilities we haven't heard of, too. Gideon has… a plethora."

"No shit," Sebastian muttered. Not that he needed any of that shit. He could probably kill anyone he wanted to without breaking one of those sharp nails of his. He looked at Leona. "You told me before you couldn't read minds. Why can I?"

"Just because *I* can't do it doesn't mean you can't," Leona murmured. "I told you I can sense feelings, sense thoughts. Your ability is more developed than mine. That's all. We can all sense feelings, as far as I know, but some of us, like Piper and Charlotte, can actually hear every word that goes through people's heads. It's annoying when you're arguing," she said, rolling her eyes.

"Only because you're too coward to say shit to my face," Piper snipped back, shaking her head.

"What can a werewolf do?" Sebastian asked.

"We change when we like," Theodore said. "But our transformation is most powerful during a full moon. Just like all the stories say. We don't howl outside or bark," he said, cutting his eyes to Piper, who innocently put her hands up. "I can't read your mind or see the future. But we are fast, strong, and as far as I know, immortal as well."

"As far as you know?"

"I mean… I've been alive for over five hundred years and I haven't turned into dust yet. Maybe I'm over the hill."

Sebastian's eyes widened and he decided he didn't want to ask any more questions. He felt so inadequate. He was new to all of this and didn't know *anything*. He should have asked Leona more questions when he'd been a human. Not that he ever thought this would happen to him, but…maybe he wouldn't feel so overwhelmed. He was trying to control his thoughts because now he didn't know who was listening. Would he be able to notice it like Charlotte obviously had? What would it feel like?

A hand on his elbow brought him out of his panicked daydream. Looking down, he met the pale eyes of Charlotte. "What?" he asked, worried she'd said something and he'd completely ignored her. Anything to avoid her usual question of—

"You look like something's on your mind. We can let them talk if you want to have some space."

Sebastian shook his head, then slowly pried his elbow from her hold. "I'm fine."

He was not fine.

Sebastian was going back and forth from embracing this new life to shitting bricks that this was what he had to live with forever now. There was no changing it, so he didn't know why he wasted any time feeling concerned over what was happening. If their impending doom with a God-knows-how-old vampire wasn't looming over their heads, maybe he'd feel a little more excited about all this.

"Damien doesn't know where I am," Theodore said. "I plan to keep it that way. You're safe for now."

"Safe?" Leona scoffed, her eyes as fiery as her hair. "We're never safe. *I'm* never safe. And now, Sebastian will never be safe. We're going to have to look over our shoulders for the rest of our lives. Why are you *here*, Theo?"

"Because I'm tired of being their lapdog. Damien keeps me at arm's length at *his* convenience, and Gideon only tolerates me for Damien. I'm never the first choice. And if I'm going to be the second choice, I might as well pick the side that isn't psycho."

"Speak for yourself," Piper said with a smirk, laughing under her breath as Whitney nudged her in the side. "That's all very sentimental, Theo, but we really don't care. You've known how Gideon is for half a millennia. Why the fuck are you having such a change of heart now? And don't feed me that sob-story bullshit again. I ain't buying it."

Theodore clenched his jaw, then shook his head. "I'm tired of lying down. I want to stand up for once."

"The sob-story bullshit was better," Piper said with a groan. "Whatever. But if you're planning on betraying us, I'm going to bite off your dick and send it wrapped in a bow to Damien myself."

Theodore paled slightly, then looked away from the blonde.

The subject changed after that.

# 6

"Your eyes are red like Gideon's."

"Are you always this astute?" Sebastian snapped as he glared pointedly at Theodore, who had looked at him at least a thousand times in the last two minutes. "What's it to you?"

"You are *so* sweet," Theodore exhaled as he raised his eyebrows and shifted uncomfortably on the couch. "I'm not going to hurt anyone. I've known them a lot longer than you."

Sebastian stood up and lunged toward him. His fangs extended with his anger and he was so close, he could smell whatever filth this dog had for lunch. "I don't give a shit if you've known them since the dawn of time. I can hear what your mutt brain is thinking, so if you so much as *breathe* in a way that irks me, I'm going to drain every drop from you. Understand?"

Theodore didn't flinch or retreat. He stared up at the man and exhaled. "They told me you've been refusing human blood. *Fresh* human blood. You really think you have it in you to come after me?"

"You're not human."

Theodore's eyes darkened and he swallowed. "Werewolves kill vampires."

"Not this one," Sebastian growled.

"*Ooookay*," Piper said as she tugged on Sebastian's shoulder to rear him back. "That's enough of the pissing contest, boys. Sebastian wants to protect us, Theo wants to protect us, we're *all* lucky to have big, strong men here protecting us," she drawled, rolling her eyes. "We need to do something worth our time like work out a damn plan to keep us all *un*dead instead of dead-dead."

Sebastian shrugged from her grip and shook his head, going over to Leona, Charlotte, and Victor. "You have the worst friends," he muttered to his girlfriend.

"Behave," Leona said sternly, but quietly. She squeezed his bicep, then raised her eyebrows. "That's new."

Charlotte's giggle died as quickly as it was born at Sebastian's look. It could have killed Satan himself. The raven-haired man shook his head and rubbed a hand down his face. "As much as this is going to kill me to say, Piper is right—"

"Well, *finally*. Wait, someone record this. Say it again," the blonde vampiress teased.

"*Anyway*," Sebastian continued, his disdain obvious on his face, "we need to figure out what we're going to do. As much as I am eternally grateful for Charlotte's never-ending hospitality and generosity, I want to go back home eventually.

So let's talk about the actions we need to take to kill Gideon."

Theodore scoffed, and Sebastian turned to him. "Something you want to say, Rougarou?"

Victor burst out laughing at this and earned a mixture of confused looks and glares from everyone in the room. Sebastian bit back his smirk.

"Rougarou?" the werewolf said, then pushed on his knees to rise from the sofa. "I don't even want to *know*. You are so bloody charming, you know that, leech? Leona, you have a type." Theodore rolled his eyes. "You can't just roll in there and kill Gideon. I don't care that you're the size of a door. You need strategy. You need *training*. You hearing thoughts is an advantage, I'll give you that. As far as I know, Gideon doesn't attain that ability. He does, however, have countless others. Speed, strength, night-vision, glamouring, scent, persuasion, shapeshifting... and probably ten more I don't even know about. But there is one weakness I know of."

"Look at you, starting to be useful. Bravo," Sebastian said in a bored voice. "Go on then."

Theodore's gaze swiveled to the redhead beside Sebastian. He lifted a hand and pointed at her. "You, Le. His inhibitions are lowered around you. You are a distraction to him, a drug he can't quit. In all the years I've known him, I've never seen him get so... *frenzied* over anything before. When it comes to Leona, everything else ceases to exist."

"Are you suggesting we use Leona as bait?" Charlotte scoffed, finally chiming in. "Have you lost your fucking mind?"

"We should do it," Leona said before anyone else could

get another word in and speak for her.

"What?" came from every voice in the room apart from Theodore's.

"I can make my own decisions," Leona continued. "If me offering myself to him is our only good shot at killing that bastard, then we need to go for it."

"Leona—" Sebastian started to plead, but the redhead merely snapped her head at him and gave him a look that pierced right through his core.

"I said I can make my own decisions, Sebastian. And that's final."

Piper frowned and looked between the couple, then at Theodore, then the Labasques, then back at Sebastian and Leona. "Well… if that's the way it's going to be then we need to go somewhere where Sebastian can train. Otherwise, we aren't going to stand a damn chance."

While Piper, Whitney, and Theodore made arrangements for their group to travel abroad once more, Sebastian, Leona, Charlotte, and Victor stayed behind to keep an eye on each other in the apartment.

They were planning to go to Spain where a couple of the coven's friends lived. Sebastian thought it was rather random, but then again, Spain is where Victor and Charlotte had met Piper, so maybe it wasn't random at all. It was a hell of a lot further away from anywhere Gideon could potentially find them, and he wasn't mad at the idea of having more immortals surrounding them to protect Leona. And… honestly, Sebastian was eager to get some reps in and find out the true scope of his new immortality.

"We aren't just going to evanesce to Spain?" Sebastian asked, perched in an armchair situated by a window overlooking the life below. Lights shimmered in the distance, the hum of chattering within the streets below sinking into Sebastian's ears. He hadn't missed the city too much in recent years, but was thankful he knew his way around from college, especially now that he solely operated in the dark. It would make any need for a quick exit that much easier.

"We are, but we still need to make calls to our friends overseas," Leona explained. "We also need to make sure *he* isn't waiting on us anywhere nearby. There are a handful of people we can trust, and most of them are in Barcelona," she added. "Just trust me, Seb. Trust them."

"Alright," Sebastian nodded, appeased for the moment. "Is it safe for our friends to be walking around in the open? What if Gideon catches their scent?" He paused when Leona winced out of instinct. "I'm not afraid of his name."

"I know," Leona sighed. "I wish you were more afraid. You'd probably still be human."

"Well, I'm not," Sebastian muttered. "You didn't answer my questions."

"Nowhere is safe. I'm honestly surprised he didn't come straight after us. As far as we know, he might have. He is an exceptional tracker and it won't take him long to hunt us down if he's so inclined. We've already walked around in the streets, our scent is already out there. Theodore found us, it's only a matter of time before he does, too."

"Why wouldn't he just follow us to Spain then?" Sebastian asked.

"There are ways to mask our scent. He usually doesn't get fooled by them, but… it's the only chance we have. And Jules and Lucinda's protection measures are fairly extensive."

"Jules and Lucinda?" Sebastian repeated in confusion.

"We trained with them in Spain," Victor chimed. "They're nice, Bas."

Leona's eyes moved to Sebastian, who looked rather uneasy. He had never been very trusting, even she knew that from how hard she had to work to win his favor. She smiled sympathetically and placed a hand on his cheek. "You trust me, don't you, my love?"

Sebastian stared into her eyes, then nodded. "With my life."

"Good," she said, patting his face gently. "You'll like them."

"What are they like?" Sebastian asked.

Leona sighed and began packing up a few things as she spoke. "They're both women and are quite old. I don't think they're as old as Gideon, but… they're pretty close. Jules can affect moods and is wicked fast. She's *so* sweet and loves to make sure everyone is taken care of. Lucinda was a fisher before she was turned and can now breathe underwater. She's like Jules in that she wants to ensure everyone has what they need. She'll ask you a hundred times if you got enough to drink," she chuckled gently, moving quickly around the room. "They're very easy to get along with. We're lucky to know them. I certainly wouldn't want to be on their bad sides."

Sebastian nodded, not saying anything else. His eyes followed her as she rapidly folded up some more articles of clothing and placed them neatly in a suitcase. Luckily he and Victor could share clothes, and the girls could all share too. They would be able to pick up more things and establish a temporary residency in Spain.

He hadn't had much time to get his head around everything that had happened. It was all still so… mind-blowing. He had thought his friends would become these demons, but now he could see all his worrying was for nothing. Of course, he was still trying to come to terms with the fact that he had to drink blood to survive, but he dealt with those units from the blood bank well enough. He could just do that. He didn't have to kill. He didn't have to resort to a life of crime again. He could be a *good* vampire. He would train, get strong, hone in his new abilities, and go back to England to turn that piece of shit Gideon into *ash*.

The coven evanesced together across the Atlantic down to Spain. It had been a long journey, but a necessary one. Sebastian had briefly wished they had more time to explore, given it was difficult to see any sort of scenery while you were a plume of smoke. With Leona fully recovered from her imprisonment, she was able to travel quicker and more efficiently. Though she was the fastest of the coven, Whitney and Piper were no slouches, and they all were able to get to Spain in a matter of hours with the newest vampires and *one* werewolf in their arms.

They'd arrived at a large home reclusive to other dwellings in Castellví de Rosanes just outside of Barcelona. The home had a cobble-stoned exterior flecked with greys, beiges, and whites. It was situated atop a hill and surrounded by dense forestry. The doorway was rounded and made of a dark stone, the door's wood matching the earthy tones. Plants grew thick along the edges of the house and cascaded over. It had just reached dusk and the lighting from within the home began sparking to life.

It was breathtaking.

Piper knocked on the door and they were greeted almost instantaneously, the door flinging open.

"Piper, my darling," an olive-skinned woman with shoulder-length black ringlets said with a thick Hispanic accent, her arms outstretched. "I am so relieved you made it here safely."

Piper moved into her embrace and inhaled her deeply, before pressing a few kisses to her cheek. "Us, too. Thank you for hosting us. We are more grateful than you could ever know," she said, pulling back to look into her eyes. They were a rich purple when they hit the light just right. The rest of the coven (and Theodore) shuffled inside and shut the door behind them to get out of the open. "I want you to meet our newest member of the coven, Sebastian Beliveau."

"Ah…" the woman said, looking past her to the tall, black-haired immortal. "I have heard so much about you. You're what's been causing all this trouble, eh, cariño?"

Sebastian shifted and set down the small suitcase he'd been commanded to carry. He folded his arms. "I'm not the problem."

The woman huffed and stepped close to him, and suddenly Sebastian felt like he was a prize-winning pig getting judged for first place. He did not wilt under her gaze, but he did feel a pull. Cutting his eyes to her, he tilted his head. "I don't know your name."

"How rude of me," the woman said, before holding out

her hand. "Julia Martinez. But you can call me Jules. Julia was my grandmother, and I like to think I'm much younger-looking than her," she said with a light laugh. The sound sent chills down Sebastian's spine. It was the first time he'd felt… *warmth* since all of this started.

"I can influence moods," Jules explained, her hand still clasped in Sebastian's. She pulled him toward her, forcing him to close the distance between them. "It makes meeting people so much easier, especially humans. We tend to make them uneasy. Have you noticed that?"

Sebastian didn't answer. He focused on her, trying to repeat his earlier trick of reading minds. His brain was a little foggy, and he assumed it was due to the mood control, or whatever the hell this Jules woman did to him. Or maybe he just wasn't very good at telepathy. Flexing his fingers, relief washed over him when she finally released him from her grip. "We are here to train," Sebastian added, not wanting to dilly-dally.

"I need to get to know you first," Jules said. "You're safe here, Sebastian. I know you only just met me, and you've no reason to trust me, but I wouldn't let harm come to the people I love. Which is everyone in this room, and quite a few *not* in this room. And if they love you, then that extends to me as well. You are part of the coven, our *familia*. We will protect you. Always."

Sebastian would believe it when he saw it. Instinctively, he hovered over to Leona and stood just slightly behind her as she wrapped her hand around his arm. Leona glanced up at him, trying to reassure him with a mere look, then she turned to Jules. "Where is Lucinda?"

"She's out fishing—"

"What is that phrase? Speak of the… devil?" a different woman with another thick Hispanic accent interrupted as she came into the home, carrying a basket full of fishing supplies: a pole, line, bait, and hooks. Heads turned as she nudged the door closed behind her with her hip. "I apologize I wasn't here in time to meet you when you came in. I forget how fast you travel, Leona," she said, moving to the redhead. The fisherwoman was tall, broad-shouldered, and looked older physically than Jules. Her hair was pin straight and dark, with a few wisps of silver strewn throughout. Skin darker than the other Spanish woman, her eyes were a light violet, a perfect complement to Jules's irises. She pulled Leona in for a hug and kissed her right cheek, showing the same affection Piper and Jules had shared. "It's so wonderful to see you, amor. I am so sorry for all the heartache you have endured. Jules told me everything."

"We're alright now," Leona reassured quietly, rubbing her back. "Lucinda, this is Sebastian. He's here for training. Sebastian, Lucinda Santos. She is Jules's partner and wife."

"Your mate," Lucinda said in recognition. "Yes, Jules mentioned him briefly too, from what Piper told us. He sounded special, and I can tell from just looking at him that he is. It's wonderful to meet you," she said, outstretching her hand.

Sebastian took it slowly, wondering if she had more powers than breathing underwater. He focused closely on her, and felt a whisper in his head once more, this time with a Spanish lilt.

*He is exactly as Piper described. Those red eyes… I wonder if he knows how powerful he truly can be. With the right guidance, I'm sure he could be even stronger than Xavier. Maybe even—*

"You know about Xavier? My heritage?" Sebastian asked, causing all heads to turn.

Lucinda blinked twice, then her eyes softened. "You inherited telepathy. Is that right?" As Sebastian nodded, she sighed and began putting some of her fishing supplies away. "I didn't just know about Xavier. I ran into him many times, much to my chagrin. He didn't share in the same sentiment we do: that vampires and humans can coexist peacefully someday."

Theodore huffed and Whitney nudged him so harshly in the side he wilted.

Lucinda ignored the werewolf and gestured to the living room, which had three dark blue sofas and an armchair to match surrounding an ornate, circular, dark brown coffee table. Sebastian noticed all the windows in the house almost immediately, finding it odd that so much sunlight could potentially make its way in. The windowpanes were covered with dark curtains, of course, but… it wouldn't take much to singe them all.

"Please, sit. Are you thirsty? You have traveled all this way. We have plenty of blood stored. We also have O-negative stew, I think I have a *bit* of B-positive ice cream left, but—" Lucinda started, but Sebastian interrupted her.

"Wait… what?" Sebastian gawked, looking around to see if anyone else was as confused as he was. "What the hell are you talking about?"

"Lucinda is a chef, too," Jules explained, giving her lover a look that could make anyone's toes curl with warmth. "She believes that just because we gave up our human side does not mean we should not be able to enjoy other parts of *life*. There are many ways to prepare blood, you just have to know how to do it. We're limited on recipes for now, and at the end of the day, it all really does taste the same, but… it's nice for a change once in a while. The ice cream we have is fused with oranges, ground up into a perfect paste, and frozen. Would you like some?"

"Uh…" Sebastian said, glancing around. Nobody seemed perplexed. "Okay."

"Splendid," Lucinda said with a clap, before disappearing into the nearby kitchen.

Sebastian looked around the interior of the home again in the interim. It didn't look as big as it was from the outside. It wasn't bigger than the Labasque Manor, but it didn't have to be. He wondered how old these vampires were. He inherently had to trust them, because everyone else around him did. Well, everyone except maybe Theodore. Sebastian wasn't sure what his stance was on vampires. But either way, Sebastian still saw him as an enemy and was keeping *very* close tabs on his thoughts when he was able.

The house was a cream color inside, had deep, rose-colored hardwood flooring throughout, and was immaculately decorated. Everything seemed to be part of a set. It was all impeccably organized, and there were so many grand paintings hanging on every wall that he made a mental note to go exploring later. There were a lot of plants scattered throughout, all of them vibrant and thriving. Just like the Labasques', this place *reeked* of wealth. He didn't even want to *know* how much the property was worth. But money seemed to be a very common theme among vampires; perhaps that was why Charlotte and Victor fit right in.

"Here we go," Lucinda said as she brought out a tray with bowls of red ice cream. Sebastian took his and peered into it, poking the dessert with the spoon leaning against the rim of the bowl. It looked normal enough, if not a bit... off. He supposed if she wasn't using milk or any kind of cream, it wouldn't be exact. It was innovative, he'd give them that.

Slowly, Sebastian took a bite and made a face. But, being the Southern boy he was, he quelled that expression and became neutral once more, swallowing it down. His mother would be turning in her grave if she knew he offended a lady by insulting her cooking skills in her own home, vampire or not.

"You don't like it," Lucinda said with a frown, her hopeful shoulders slumping.

"No, it's just... it tastes like blood," Sebastian said, realizing how stupid that sounded the second he said it out loud. "I'm— I've only fed once and my brain wasn't even thinking straight because I was starving. I didn't really notice the taste, but I couldn't stop. Now that I'm not so hungry, I guess..."

"It's alright," Lucinda said as she waved her hands. "It has been so long since I've tasted blood for the *first* time that I forget how much it takes to get used to. But you saying it tastes like blood *is* indeed a compliment."

Sebastian nodded and forced himself to continue eating. He would have to get used to it, given it was all he had. Perhaps the stew would have been a safer choice.

"How does this not make you sick? Or at least… give you the nutrients you need?" Sebastian asked, looking down at the bowl. Everyone else seemed to be doing just fine with it. Perhaps it was the remnants of his human mind convincing his stomach to turn.

"It wasn't easy to get right at first," Lucinda sighed, crossing a leg over the other once she sat down. "We couldn't get the ratio correct. We were using ingredients we shouldn't have been. We've found that fruit doesn't affect us as much as other artificial ingredients with preservatives do. There are some foods that we have difficulty processing, despite it all being broken down by our bodies. We have an orchard in the back," she explained. "If you grind your ingredients down enough, the chemicals inside the fruit — or blood — fuse and coagulate. They become one. Our bodies recognize the platelets from the blood and can break them down inside our bodies. It's a fascinating science, really."

Sebastian nodded in agreement. He thought back to his first real *night* with Leona when they walked along the river and he pondered aloud what her body looked like from the inside and how all the mechanics worked in her organs if she was a walking corpse. He should have taken her advice not to think about it so hard. None of this made any real *logical* sense.

"What is your favorite?" Sebastian asked. He was *trying*

to be polite.

"Oranges," Lucinda nodded. "That," she said, gesturing to the bowl. "Oranges and other citruses maintain the ability to eat away at certain bacteria and other things. Pineapples can eat you from the inside out," she explained. "Their chemical properties mesh with ours quite well. One day, I'll show you our blood and some orange pieces under a microscope and let you see how they coexist. Blood oranges are not called that just because of the color."

Sebastian huffed humorously under his breath. He supposed if he had been around for... however long, he'd start experimenting too.

It went against all of his manners, but her comment about tasting blood for the first time had intrigued him, as well as her experimentation and his earlier inner monologue, so he asked, "How old are you?"

"Mmm..." Lucinda sighed, tilting her head. "What year is it now?"

"Twenty-fifteen."

"Ah... so..." Lucinda said slowly, glancing at her wife. "You're about two thousand now," she grinned. "As for me, about eighteen hundred."

Sebastian's eyebrows shot up into his hairline and his spoon clattered back into the bowl. He gawked at Jules now. "Two... thousand?"

"And four," Jules piped up, perching on the arm of the sofa Victor and Charlotte were commandeering. She folded a leg over the other and looked down at her red-painted nails. "I think I look great for my age."

"Wow," Sebastian said. They had to be some of the oldest in the world. Leona had mentioned that to him, but… still. Even Gideon was… what, three thousand? Give or take? Did they know him? The geek in him couldn't help but internally gush about how much history they undoubtedly experienced. What was their favorite era? How different was today from when *they* were humans?

"I can see all those questions in that pretty head of yours," Jules teased. "You finish up eating and all of you get settled into your rooms. Take whichever ones you like," she said, standing up. "We'll prepare dinner for everyone in the meantime. You deserve a proper meal after all you've been through. What would you prefer, Theodore?"

The werewolf tore his disgusted gaze from Whitney's near-empty bowl of ice cream and settled it back on the Spanish vampire. "I can go out and hunt."

"That is not what I asked you," Jules said, a bit firmer this time, but her smile was just as sweet. "These are our lands and have been for millennia. You will abide by the rules set by *us* under our roof," she said, holding his gaze for a few threatening and terrifying seconds. "Now then," she said, her tone back to being bubbly. "What would you prefer, Señor Selwyn?"

"Uh…" Theodore started, knowing better than to piss off a house full of vampires. "Just… any meat is fine."

"Perfect," Jules said, her eyes glinting. "Rare, I assume?"

"Blue."

Sebastian watched the exchange in awe. Now he understood why these women had been around for thousands of years.

Sebastian went upstairs to find a long hallway with four doors on the right and four doors on the left. There was a long, simply patterned blue rug running along the length of the dark, hardwood flooring of the hallway. The walls were painted a coral color, different from the motif present downstairs, and all the doors were white. He stepped forward and opened the first door on the right. A bedroom. He didn't go inside, then opened the door on the opposite side. Another bedroom. Before he could open another door, Piper groaned and shoved past him into the room he was about to scope out.

"Ugh, Sebastian, get the hell out of the way," Piper muttered when she breezed by. "For a vampire, you're so bloody slow."

"I was just exploring," Sebastian snapped. The other members of the coven were in the hallway behind him, laying claim to their rooms.

"The first two doors on either side are bedrooms. The next door on both sides are bathrooms, and then the last doors are more bedrooms. Jules and Lucinda's bedroom is the last one on the right. The rest are fair play."

"Thanks for ruining my tour," Sebastian muttered. "What if I wanted this room?"

"You're shit out of luck," Piper swore, kicking off her shoes. "I'm going to shower. If I come back and see you've set up camp in here, I'm shaving your head. Clear?"

"Crystal," Sebastian mumbled, stepping aside so Piper could leave the room to take up one of the bathrooms. He turned to look at Leona, who merely raised her eyebrows and shook her head. Charlotte and Victor stopped staring at the scene and quickly busied themselves by disappearing behind the first open door to the right, and Whitney picked the room opposite Jules and Lucinda's. Sebastian looked at the doors next to Piper's room and the Labasques' room. They were caddy-cornered from each other, and he wasn't sure if he wanted to be next to Leona's irritating best friend or *his* irritating best friends.

Ultimately, they went for the room next to the Labasques. Theodore could have Piper as a neighbor.

Sebastian walked inside and looked around. The room was a neutral cream color, similar to the living room, and had one window decorated with dark blue curtains. No sunlight would be creeping in on accident. A bed sat in the middle of the room, the headboard against the wall with the window. Two dark blue, wooden nightstands were on either side of the bed and there was an en-suite bathroom on the opposite side of the room. Sebastian raised his eyebrows and briefly eyed the multiple bookshelves lining the wall adjacent to the window. "Wow," he said, looking down at Leona. "They really like blue. I don't know what I expected. Why is there a bed?"

"I'm sure they have non-immortal guests sometimes, or werewolves," Leona said, walking past him and into the room. She set down the bag they'd packed on the bed, then sunk onto the mattress. "Beds can also be used for other things."

Sebastian's mind immediately went to activities he really

shouldn't have been thinking about. Surely they were too busy and scared for sex? He could feel his insides twist with desire and quickly squashed any dirty thoughts out of his brain. "I'm sure," he responded, smirking at her. "You said vampires rest but don't sleep."

"I did," she nodded.

"So you can rest here."

"If you'd like. It's not necessary. Piper prefers bathtubs when she rests."

"What?"

Leona laughed and leaned back on her hands, the mattress dipping slightly. "Yeah. She's strange. I've found her curled up in the clawfoot tub back home more times than I can even remember. She said she likes the coolness of the porcelain against her skin."

"Strange, I think, is an understatement for your partner in crime," Sebastian muttered, shaking his head. He walked over and sat down next to her on the bed, their hands immediately finding each other. "You're sure we can trust these vampires?"

He didn't have to mention Jules and Lucinda by name for her to understand. Leona brought her free hand up to cradle his cheek and first answered him with a gentle kiss to the lips. When she pulled back, her head nodded. "Yes. I promise."

8

After everyone got settled into their respective rooms, Sebastian took a brief respite later that night to stand outside and stare at the beautiful Spanish countryside from the upper deck. The sea was glimmering in the distance, barely visible with all the other buildings scattered along the land. The water was a good twenty miles away at least, but his newfound scope of vision was coming in handy. Did Lucinda do her fishing closer to the city or in some mysterious body of water near the house? Closing his eyes, he inhaled deeply, letting his senses wash over him. He could smell the salt from the ocean, different foods families nearby were cooking, and even the rich aroma of the dirt surrounding them. Giving himself over, he basked in the beauty this new life provided him. From hearing the rustling of animals prancing around however far away, to the buzz of insects exploring the city, to the sound of children's laughter ricocheting throughout the air. It made him feel heat the sun could no longer provide.

"Do you want to be alone?"

Sebastian jumped slightly and whipped around to face the woman he'd come to love deeper than anything he'd ever felt. "Even as a vampire you manage to sneak up on me."

Leona smiled and leaned in the doorway, her eyes roaming over him carefully. "I'll teach you all the tricks, don't worry. I just came to check on you. You've been fairly quiet this whole time. You barely said a word during dinner. Are you doing okay?"

"Yeah," Sebastian sighed, sidestepping a foot to invite her out on the terrace with him. Leona slid the glass door shut and took her place by his side.

"Just 'yeah?'" Leona asked, curling her hands around the railing of the balcony. She looked up at him, her expression laced with concern and worry.

"This is all very overwhelming," Sebastian confessed. "And I have questions about myself. My heritage. There are so many mysteries surrounding who I am. I always thought I was just this poor boy who got lucky meeting a rich family, but… it all goes so much deeper than that. I never expected to be launched into this life. My world was this big just six months ago," he said, holding his forefinger and thumb a few inches apart. "Now? It's so big I don't know which direction to even start walking in."

"I know the feeling," Leona said with a sad smile. "That's why we're here, Sebastian: to get answers. And ensure everyone gets some training reps in to fight off whatever war we have coming to our doorstep. But we're going to figure everything out. Together. I promise."

Sebastian nodded and turned his head forward to look at the scenery again. His hair whipped gently around his face and he wondered why he'd never been to this country before. He had gone on several family trips with the Labasques when he was younger and had seen more of the world than he ever thought he would as a child, but… this was different. It was almost like he had been blind before.

"How did you meet Jules and Lucinda?" Sebastian asked without looking away from the view.

Leona sighed and mimicked Sebastian, her eyes scanning over the trees swaying in the wind. "I met them through Piper. As usual. Though we're basically the same age, she traveled much more than I did. She met them not long after she was turned. She met Jules first, who, as I'm sure you noticed, was quick to vet her and take her in. She and Lucinda are very hospitable, generous immortals. It's not common among our kind. They want a better world for all of us. One day, they hope we can reveal ourselves to humans across the world and live in peace among them."

"I don't think humans will take too kindly to a group of people who kill for survival."

"They wouldn't. Jules and Lucinda survive off human blood, but strictly through donors. Vampires are rich in this culture, much like New Orleans and Louisiana. Though there will always be those who do not believe, the ones who do can offer themselves as donors in exchange for protection. At least, that's the arrangement they have with their townspeople."

"So they're like Batman?"

"Batman?" Leona repeated, looking at him in confusion. "Is that some kind of joke about us turning into bats?"

Sebastian laughed under his breath and shook his head. "No. He's a superhero. He's this rich philanthropist whose parents were murdered in front of him when he was a child. He turned his grief into a life of fighting crime, using his fortune to create super-suits and gadgets to protect him. In turn, he defeats bad guys in Gotham to protect the townspeople… even though he isn't properly appreciated for it."

Leona regarded him thoughtfully, unable to hide the smile that crept over her lips. She loved this boy so much it *hurt*. "Yeah. They're kind of like Batman then. You'll have to teach me more about your world's superheroes."

"He's not real," Sebastian chuckled. "But I'll let you look at my comic collection whenever we go back home. *If* we go back home," he corrected, his expression falling.

"We *will*," Leona reassured, reaching out to touch him.

Sebastian nodded and cut his eyes downward. "So… Piper introduced you to them?"

"Yes," Leona said, getting back on track. She looped her arm through Sebastian's and moved closer to his side as they resumed admiring the landscape. "Piper was part of their relationship for a long time. A few decades at least. She grew popular within this community. As you know, I met Piper during a hunt. When *he* was out of my life for the time being, she took me here for refuge. I learned how to use my powers properly, for the right reasons. Not for hate and murder and bloodshed like I was used to."

"When did you kill my ancestor?" Sebastian asked.

"Mmm…" Leona hummed. "It was near the beginning of my new life as an immortal. I was still wild and unpredictable as a baby vampire. My impulses could not be controlled. *He* used that to his advantage and took me with him to kill Xavier. If I had been a little smarter, I would've refused and let Xavier do him in."

"So how did *you* kill Xavier when he was so close to killing Gid—" he paused, noting her wince. "*Him*, as it was?"

"Well…" Leona sighed. "I didn't technically kill him, and I didn't exactly know at the time he was a vampire slayer. I just thought he was someone he wanted dead. Questioning him wasn't something that came easy to me. Our bond was so fresh and strong. We were in France. As I said, it wasn't long after I was turned. A decade at most. It's all so fuzzy now, the years just blend together for me. Many memories from that period with him are. He abused and starved me so often when he'd get angry, I lost a lot of years. But France was facing an economic crisis at the time, and vampires took the opportunity to kill humans and disguise it as famine or plague. Often, I would seduce humans or other immortals to get their guards down. That way he could easily go in for the kill. It was like clockwork.

"The first time I met Xavier was at a tavern vampires and courtesans were known to lurk around. You didn't go there unless you were another immortal or you had a death wish. I've heard stories of some vampires going for sex and a meal, but… I never partook in any of that," Leona explained. She turned against Sebastian's arm and slid her hand up to hold his cheek. "It may be easier if I just show you. Focus on me."

Sebastian did as he was told, and his eyes glazed over as Leona's memories swept over his consciousness.

*Leona pushed the hood of her cloak down as she walked inside a dimly lit tavern. Gideon had given her a description of this human, but not much else: tall frame, long, black hair, black facial hair, and a voice that sounded like churned gravel. Gideon had told her to watch her back, which she found to be out-of-character, considering this was* just *a human. He'd never told her that before. Perhaps he* really did *care about her and was starting to show it more.*

*She wandered to the bar and ordered a glass of wine, her eyes scanning the room. Her night-vision was honed and the bar might as well have had bright floodlights lining the ceiling. Eventually, her gaze settled on a man sitting alone at a table nestled in the corner of the building, nursing what appeared to be just a glass of water. Strange. Why come to a pub if you weren't going to drink anything that made you feel good?*

*He matched the description Gideon had given her. Her hackles were up and knots formed in the pit of her stomach.*

*Something just didn't feel... right.*

*Gideon's 'concern' for her — more like himself — aside, it almost seemed too easy. Gideon claimed he would be there should she need assistance, but was it all an elaborate trap? Yet another lesson she needed to be taught as an immortal? She didn't think she needed* more training, but... *Gideon knew best. Surely her creator wouldn't put her in* serious *danger, would he?*

*Would he?*

*Slowly, she crossed the room, cradling her glass in her hand. The man didn't even look up when she got to the edge of the table.*

*"This seat taken?" Leona cooed as she pointed a slender finger down at the empty space across from the man.*

*"I'm not interested," the man said gruffly, not looking at her. "Move along. I don't have any money to give you."*

*"I'm not looking for money. Just some good company. Good conversation," she said, her voice dripping with seduction. "I don't know anyone else here. Please?"*

*The man finally turned his gaze upward at Leona. He looked her over, then arched an eyebrow. "What's a lady like you doing in a tavern where she doesn't know anybody?"*

*"I like to travel. I'm going to rest my head at the inn here tonight, then be on my way to the next stop," she explained, not waiting for him to formally include her in his space before she slid down opposite him. "I'm Leona."*

*"Xavier."*

*She was sure this was the right bloke.*

*"I like that name," the redhead said. "So what brings you here tonight, Xavier? Why would a handsome man like yourself be drinking water all alone in a pub? Surely there are a few female suitors you could occupy yourself with."*

*Xavier didn't respond. He merely kept his eyes scanning around the bar, his glass of water untouched. Leona frowned. Usually, this worked much quicker. Why was he so... standoffish? No wonder Gideon wanted him killed. He probably pissed him off for being rude. Why he couldn't do it himself was beyond her, but... she wasn't in a position to challenge his decisions. She merely did as she was told.*

"This is a nice place," she said, trying again. She'd get under his skin. "I've even heard vampires frequent it. Is that true?"

That got his attention. Xavier moved his head to look at her. "What do you know about vampires?"

Leona resisted smirking triumphantly. Perhaps Xavier had found out about their kind and Gideon wanted the threat of exposure wiped out. It still didn't explain to her why he couldn't do it himself. But she didn't mind killing a random man — at least she'd get a meal out of him.

"Oh, nothing much… I like to think we aren't the only beings in the world. I mean, it can't just be all humans, can it?" she laughed, fluttering her eyelashes. "Who's to say there aren't vampires or witches or whatever else people come up with? The world would be terribly boring with just us around, don't you think?"

"It would be safer," he muttered. "You should go. This bar isn't safe for someone like you."

"Someone like me?" Leona pouted. "You don't like me? I thought we were starting to be friends."

Xavier's jaw clenched. If Leona knew how to do one thing, it was annoy a man. "I said you need to leave."

Leona frowned and rested her head on her palm, eyeing him closely. "You're really serious, aren't you? There are vampires here?"

"Ones that want nothing more than to rip your throat out. You should not have come here alone. Or at all."

"Have you ever met a vampire? A real vampire?" Leona asked, focusing on him intently. She wanted to sway him just enough that he didn't notice, but would still give her the information she needed to finish this job. Gideon had insisted that she make quick work of this, using her body to distract him and fulfill her mission, but…

something told her it wouldn't be that easy. She would just use all her best assets and act dumb as a stump. That usually seemed to work wonders with men.

Xavier hesitated, blinking a few times. "Yes. A few."

"Wow!" Leona gasped, covering her mouth. She'd play along. "What were they like?"

"Evil," he answered. "Cold. Dark. Unnatural. Demonic."

"Sounds scary," Leona agreed with a nod, her eyes wide. "How'd you get away?"

"I killed them," he said, eyeing her levelly.

Leona's blood ran as cold as her skin. Gideon's insistence on the death of this human made perfect sense now. Why would he send her straight to a vampire slayer? She had heard of deaths in Europe of their kind but thought it was just vampire-on-vampire crime. Never... the likes of a human.

"You must be pretty strong to be able to kill one of them," Leona said, her voice calm as she grappled with how to proceed. This was going to be much more complicated than seducing and murdering a regular man. Her hackles were up and she was suddenly acutely aware of everything in the room. Did he have others with him? Where was Gideon?

"You just need to know where to hit," he said. "Like between the ribs, for example," he said, pointing at her chest. "Or between the eyes," he said, lifting his hand. "Or just chop the head clean off. Set them on fire."

Leona swallowed once, then let out a light giggle. "Wow," she said for what felt like the hundredth time. Sometimes she wanted to gag herself when she had to play these parts. "You should take the night off," she suggested. "Maybe you could keep me company in my room and tell me all about those evil, nasty vampires you killed. Good riddance, in my opinion."

"Perhaps," Xavier said, shifting in his seat. Leona's eyes were glued to his every movement. "That would make things easy for you, wouldn't it?"

"Easy for... me?" Leona repeated, tilting her head. Dread filled her to the brim; she felt like it would pour out of her if she even opened her mouth again. Gideon surely knew everything that was happening and was just waiting for the right moment to pounce. Maybe he was in her room. If she could just... convince him to come...

She swallowed thickly again, her chest tight. As if someone were stepping on it with all their weight.

"You think I don't know what you are?"

Leona stared at him. He stared back. They sat for a few moments of nearly unbearable silence.

"What am I then, Xavier?"

The dark-haired man released an amused exhale. "Playing dumb doesn't suit your kind. I prefer being upfront about everything," he said. Slowly, he reached for his glass of water, then splashed it straight on Leona, who let out a cry. She was incapacitated for a moment, long enough to give Xavier the chance to slide out of the booth and rear a wooden stake up behind his head. Before he could drive it down into Leona, she shot her hand up to grab him, her grip so tight Xavier wailed in pain.

Leona blinked angrily, her porcelain skin red. "What the fuck was that?!" she hissed, glaring at him.

"Holy water," he grunted. "You're going to die tonight, Leona."

"Like hell I am," she growled. "Gideon!"

*Xavier's eyes widened and before he could react, an arm crunched through his back and out his chest, his heart twitching from the removal.*

*"Like my distraction, insect?" a dark, sinister voice cooed from behind him. "You'll be the only one dying tonight," Gideon said, yanking his hand back through the way it came. Xavier crumpled to the floor, blood pooling around him. Screams and chaos erupted within the tavern.*

*Leona stared down at the man, then back up at Gideon, who was licking his hand clean. His eyes glowed a searingly bright red for a second, then faded to their usual crimson. She blinked a few times, then realized the magnitude of the situation. "You fucking bastard," Leona hissed, shoving at his chest. "You sent me into bed with a* vampire slayer*?! How stupid are you?" she cried out, moving to hit him again, but Gideon caught her hand.*

*"Careful with your outbursts, flower. Remember: think before you speak. You were never in any* real *danger. I had it under control. I just needed him to be distracted for a while. That's all. I knew those tits would do the trick."*

*Leona frowned and wrenched her hand from his grip, then instinctively crossed her arms over her chest. "Well... next time, give me a bloody warning."*

*"Noted," Gideon drawled, before gesturing to the body and gore on the ground. "Someone come clean this. This is a* fine *establishment," he called out. Then, he stalked out of the building, Leona closely in tow behind him. So much for keeping their kind a secret.*

*"Why didn't you tell me what he was?" Leona asked.*

*Gideon kept walking. "Because you wouldn't have wanted to*

*do it. Better to let you think it was just another person I hated who you could kill."*

*"Why do you hate him so much?"*

*Gideon scoffed. "Is being a vampire hunter not enough for you?"*

*"Well, yes, but… You usually just take care of these kind of things yourself. Why did you need me? Why not just go after him and kill him?"*

*"Because…" Gideon said, sighing sharply, "he is an especially irksome pest to get rid of. Or at least, he was. But he's a red-blooded human just like the rest of them. Pretty eyes and a good body are always their undoing."*

*Leona frowned, feeling used. She* had *been used. Over and over and over. "What if he had killed me, Gideon?"*

*Gideon quirked his head back to glance at her. "He didn't."*

*"But what if he* had*?"*

*"Then… you entertained me for a while," Gideon laughed, putting his hands up in a shrug. "What do you want me to say, Leona? I thought you were done with all the empty compliments. You know what you mean to me. You're my creation, my* mate.*"*

*Leona frowned and jogged closer to him, then tucked her arm through his. She leaned her head against his bicep and stared ahead as they walked together. She didn't feel safe at all.*

The scene fizzled from Sebastian's vision and he was brought back to the present. Leona had a pained look on her face that mirrored Sebastian's.

"That was the beginning of the end with… him and me. I felt so betrayed, so used… and I realized that I was just some pawn in his game of gaining power."

It was difficult for her to recall that memory because Xavier really *did* look like Sebastian. It reminded her of when he'd nearly died, and she felt her insides turn at the mere thought of losing him. She regarded Sebastian carefully, unable to decipher his current expression. "It was so long ago, and such a brief encounter, it makes sense to me why it wasn't at the forefront of my mind when I met you. And after all the abuse I endured from *him*, my memories aren't as intact as I'd like them to be."

"Why didn't he just kill me at the ball? Surely he recognized me," Sebastian said, at a loss.

"He said he didn't. At least, not fully. He told me when I was chained up in his dungeon that he returned home to do research. Then I suppose he just… capitalized on the fact that we were all clueless. He used it to his advantage and hatched his plan."

"He really likes to kill people by shoving his hand through their bodies, doesn't he?"

Leona grimaced and shook her head. "His signature. It's disgusting. So unnecessarily messy. Shows what kind of psychopath he is."

"Yeah," Sebastian said. "What is Xavier's full name?"

"Xavier de Bellevau. Which… now makes me feel like a fool for not having seen it sooner."

"How did it go from him, in France, to me, in New Orleans? My father is a drunken piece of shit without a penny to his name."

Leona shrugged. "I don't know Xavier's history," she paused. "… Gideon," she said, tensing, "showed me few documents, but I was so out of it, I could barely read what they said. Many of them were in old French, a language I am fluent in but… it's been a while. He didn't give me time to *pore* over them or anything. He assumes Xavier had a wife or perhaps… a lover, who furthered the bloodline and immigrated to the States. New Orleans is full of French culture, and supernatural culture. It's not a stretch that someone related to him ended up in Louisiana. Over the years, I suppose the lineage diluted and things… moved on. Beliveau *does* mean drunkard, though."

"Of course it does," Sebastian muttered while rolling his eyes.

Leona smiled sadly and pushed a hand through his hair. "You are not your father and you are not Xavier. You are Sebastian."

"Lucky me," he muttered.

"Lucky *me*," she reassured, leaning up on her toes to kiss his lips. They stayed joined for several seconds, their embrace strengthening.

When they pulled back, Leona stared at him, her eyes hooded with lust. It was a look Sebastian had never seen on her before, even in the throes of ecstasy in his bedroom back in Louisiana. Sebastian arched an eyebrow and pulled back a little. "You look like you want to eat me. You said vampires can't drink other vampires."

"Mmm," Leona hummed, giving him a once, twice, *thrice*

over. "'Drink' is not the verb I have in my head."

Sebastian raised both his eyebrows this time. *Oh.*

"Well then," he said, not missing a beat. "Show me how much you were holding back before, Abrin."

# 9

Leona and Sebastian burst through the door of their assigned bedroom in an explosion of hot kisses and inappropriate touches.

"I'm not human anymore so— that means I get to be in charge, right?" Sebastian moaned against Leona's lips as her hands frantically roamed over him.

"Not a fucking chance, darling," Leona laughed. "Now be a good boy and get on the bed," she said, pushing him down onto the mattress with so much force, that the headboard splintered. Sebastian stared at her wide-eyed, seeing a completely new side of his girlfriend.

He had never been more turned on in his life.

Leona had always been dominant in the bedroom, which he had absolutely *no* complaints about, but this was something else entirely. They didn't have to sleep, they didn't have to stop and rest, and from how ravenous she had been toward him over the last several months, he could only imagine a vampire's libido was leagues above a human's.

Thank *God*.

In a flash of movement, Leona was straddling him. Her fingers moved to his buttoned shirt, and with little more than a tug, she ripped it apart. Buttons flew to every corner of the room, and Leona pulled up on the fabric to make Sebastian sit up so she could shed the clothing from his arms and chest.

Desire coursed through Sebastian's veins like never before. Though Leona had always been powerfully tantalizing, this was opening his eyes to a newfound... *feral* version of her. She wasn't reserved in fear that she would hurt him. She wasn't holding back. She was loving him how she was meant to — how *they* were meant to.

"You're overdressed," Sebastian rasped as Leona worked to rid him of the final piece of clothing covering his hips. "Please."

"You know I love it when you beg," Leona purred, rocking her hips against his to tease him to the point of breaking. She could feel how excited he was and it made her mouth water. Raking her hands through his hair, she curled her fingers around the locks and tugged his head to the side harshly. "I will miss tasting you," she breathed, dragging her tongue up the cool skin of his jugular. "But I won't miss battering and bruising you."

"I didn't mind the bruises," Sebastian murmured, his hands caressing whatever he could find of her body. Taking a page from her book, he pinched the fabric of the top she was wearing and harshly pulled each side in opposite directions, the material immediately giving way. Leona laughed against his cheek, pivoting her body so the tattered rags came off her arms. She reached behind her and unclasped the thin lace bra confining her chest. It joined the rest of their clothes on the floor. Both vampires mirrored the other as they pulled their underwear off, and finally, no layers stood between them.

Sebastian moaned as their skin finally made contact. It was charging him to the point of near-combustion. He had never believed in soulmates before he met Leona — at least, not that he had one. Watching Victor and Charlotte together would make anyone believe in love, but… he never thought it was in the cards for him. Now he knew this woman was always meant to be his, and he was always meant to be hers.

"I want to taste you," Sebastian moaned, his fangs extending from his excitement. His jaw fell slack as her center rubbed against his in the most delicious way.

"As much as I want that — and miss that — I need you to get more used to your new teeth before I let your mouth down there," she laughed, nuzzling her nose against his. "Just enjoy this and let me make you feel good."

"Yes ma'am," Sebastian said, emphasizing his southern drawl in a way that made Leona giggle and hold him tighter. The thought of never getting to hear that sweet sound ever again had he died made him feel grateful Charlotte had been selfish.

And getting to feel Leona sink onto his length again. He had nearly forgotten how wonderful she *always* felt. Now that his senses were heightened, the feelings were multiplied a hundred times over.

Sebastian's hands settled on Leona's hips as she rode him,

her knees digging into the mattress. Her arms looped around his neck as her fingers teased the fine hairs at the nape of his neck. Both their moans, heavy breathing, and dirty and sweet nothings mixed together in the air of the bedroom. Though they didn't *need* air, it was taking moderate exertion, even as immortals. And… Sebastian was still panting out of habit.

"I love you," Sebastian said, staring into those beautiful green eyes as their bodies continued melding as one. "I love you for eternity, Leona Abrin."

Leona's eyes watered and she cradled his cheek with one hand as the other grasped his back for support, her hips never stopping. If anything, they moved with even more purpose. "And I love you, Sebastian Beliveau. The rest of time won't even be long enough."

Their lips joined in a passionate clinch of tongues and teeth. Leona nipped at Sebastian's lower lip, blood drawing and disappearing almost instantaneously. The man's hands clawed down the woman's back, making Leona moan loudly in his ear. Settling on her ass, Sebastian squeezed and used the leverage to flip them over. The bed creaked in protest at all the harsh and fast movement, but neither of them noticed. They were the only two people in the world.

"More," Leona commanded, her heels hooking around each other and digging into Sebastian's asscheeks as his hips thrust furiously into hers. She squeezed his sides with her thighs and her hands held onto his hair for dear life. "Bite me."

Sebastian's movements slowed but didn't still as he processed what she asked of him. "But vampires don't drink—"

"Just do it."

Sebastian didn't have to be told twice. It was his first time ever doing this to another person, but… it wasn't as if she was human. This wasn't for food. Dipping his head to the juncture of her neck, he bit into her skin without another thought. His sharp teeth pierced the barrier and liquid gushed into his mouth. Leona moaned loudly and clamped her hand behind his head to press him even further into her embrace. "*Yes,*" Sebastian heard her breathe, his skin prickling from how much he enjoyed that sound, this *sensation.*

Pulling back, his mouth glistened crimson, and the puncture wounds soon disappeared from Leona's skin. The redhead grinned up at him, then pulled him down to return the favor. It was Sebastian's turn to moan now as she bit into him. He had never felt something so pleasurable, so erotic. It was as if they were connected on a level that went deeper than anything physical or mental. It was molecular. Instinctual.

Once Leona had released her vice on him, their lips joined again, the moisture of blood between them making everything slick. Their hips resumed their blurred pace.

There might as well have been angels singing from the heavens when they each reached their orgasms. Warmth coursed through him and he realized again, in that moment, that being outside in the day was not the only heat he could experience. He all but roared his release, Leona reaching the same peak of ecstasy right there with him. They fell together off the cliff of pleasure, clutching each other so close that nothing could squeeze its way between their bodies.

"Now you see why vampires are so horny all the time,"

Leona said quietly, laughing under her breath. Sebastian had since collapsed against her chest and had his face buried in her cleavage as he recovered. He grunted out a muffled response she couldn't understand, which made her smile contentedly.

Leona carded her fingers through his hair until he was ready to ravish her again. And again. And again.

# 10

"Surprised you two stopped long enough to grace us with your presence," Piper said as Leona and Sebastian came into the sitting area where everyone was gathered the next morning. Charlotte was reading a book that suspiciously looked like some sort of trashy, Spanish romance novel, and Victor was sipping from a coffee mug. Sebastian assumed it was *not* coffee inside. Jules and Lucinda were leaned in close, discussing something he could not quite make out. It seemed like a relaxed conversation, and though he was tempted to listen in mentally, he controlled himself. It was none of his business. Piper was still eyeing them teasingly from her position against the wall, her arms folded. Whitney was just staying out of the conversation altogether, shaking her head disapprovingly at her friend's cheek. Sebastian did not know where Theodore was, nor did he really care.

The shutters and curtains were drawn and Sebastian

could feel the warmth from the daylight outside. He did miss it. Maybe he should have appreciated it more when he was a human. He hadn't known he *needed* to appreciate it.

"Grow up," Leona responded, sticking up her middle finger as she dragged Sebastian behind her by the hand. The man sat down in a vacant armchair near the Labasques first, Leona curling up sideways on his lap once he was settled. One of her arms looped around his shoulders, the other gently holding his hand. "What's the plan for today?"

"Training," Jules said. "And lots of it. I am eager to see what your abilities are. Other than telepathy and strength," she added, looking at Sebastian. "Are you ready? You should feed first. Get your strength up. What blood do you prefer?"

Sebastian glanced at Leona for help, but when it was obvious she wouldn't speak for him, he cleared his throat. "Any kind is fine. I… do not want to kill anybody. You have blood in bags or containers, right?"

Jules smiled and nodded. "Do you prefer it warm or cold?"

"Warm."

His eyes followed her as she got up and was gone in a blink to fetch his breakfast. Turning his attention elsewhere, his eyes settled on his two best friends. "What was your training like?"

Charlotte looked over at Victor, then smiled. "I kicked his ass."

"Overstatement," Victor immediately defended, shaking his head. "There's a large basement area that serves as a training facility as well. It's so we can do whatever we need no matter what time it is. We went down there, and basically just…

sparred with everybody. Lucinda, Jules, Piper, Whitney. We were exploring any potential abilities we had and were getting used to our new bodies. I definitely think we would have died at Gideon's had we not had that preparation. I just didn't know we'd have to use it so soon. I think we could all use as much tuning up as we can manage. That bastard cut through us like syrup in a snowball."

That was the truth.

Jules came back with a large insulated cup, steam rising from the top. "Here you go," she murmured, handing it to Sebastian. "It's O-positive. Hope that's okay."

"It's fine," he said, staring down at it. Would he ever get used to this taste? Slowly, he brought the cup to his lips and began sipping. His pupils dilated from the contact with his tongue, and his fangs extended. After a minute or so, the whole cup was downed and he licked his lips clean. "I feel better."

"I'm sure Leona worked up your appetite," Piper said cheekily, sitting down and hiding her smirk behind her hand as she rested her chin against her palm. "Okay, okay, I'm done. Promise," she said in response to Leona's glare.

"We all did it," Leona snapped. "Quit embarrassing Seb."

"It's alright," Sebastian reassured. He looked around, noticing they were now short one immortal. "Where is Lucinda?"

"She's downstairs prepping everything," Jules answered. "If you're ready, we've already eaten. We can go down there now."

After they descended the *many* steps into the basement, Sebastian looked around the room. Smooth stone lined the flooring, and bricks of dark rock surrounded the walls. There were sparring dummies, multiple platforms of varying heights scattered throughout, what looked like a rock-climbing wall on the other side of the room, and a table full of instruments: knives, swords, whips, nunchucks, throwing stars, guns.

"Holy shit," Sebastian blurted out, taking it all in. "How deep does this place go?"

"Deep enough. Hundred meters… give or take," Lucinda said, joining the group. "It's a good bunker, too, in case things ever go south. Thankfully we haven't needed to use it for anything like that. Yet."

"Are you ready, Sebastian?" Jules asked, gesturing to the clearing in the middle of the room. The dark-haired vampire nodded and joined the woman out in the center. Looking around, all eyes were on him. He didn't know what to expect — or what *they* expected, but he was going to do his best to impress. He was curious, too, and wanted to know what splendors this new life afforded him.

"Alright," Jules said, clapping her hands together. "Go get that ribbon," she instructed, pointing to a hanging ribbon wrapped around a bar. The bar was bolted to the wall near the ceiling. The raised platforms led to it, but it was obvious he'd have to jump to each one. "Go on," Jules encouraged, waving her hand toward the platforms. "You won't get hurt if you fall. Trust your instincts."

Sebastian nodded and almost asked if he needed to stretch first. Probably a stupid question. He glanced back at Leona, who gave him a grin and two thumbs up. Motivated by her support, he turned back toward the training area and clenched his fists together. Dust exploded around him as he broke out into a run toward the first one.

But he tripped right over it and went flying into another platform's sidewall.

Collective groans sounded from the other immortals in the room, and Sebastian pushed himself up to try again.

"You're not used to your speed, that's all. You're thinking too much. Just let go," Lucinda said.

Sebastian went back to the starting point and sprinted again, jumping up onto the first platform. He stopped, gathering himself. First one down... five to go. He stared at the other one, which was at least thirty feet away from him, both in distance and height. The first one was only a few feet in height and hadn't been hard for him to get atop. He could only imagine how both badass and goofy he looked parading around at the speed of light. His eyes darted from platform to platform and he mentally mapped out his trajectory. That ribbon seemed a world away, but he could get to it. He had to.

Sebastian jumped with such force that the flat stone top of the platform he'd been standing on cracked under the pressure, and in a second, he was pulling himself onto the next platform. Maybe he hadn't judged his jump *that* well, but he hadn't wanted to go flying again. Steeling his nerves, he repeated the process and landed on his feet on the next platform. He jumped again and landed gracefully on the next. And the next. Only one remained, but he could tell he wouldn't be able to just jump straight ahead to it. The wall would have to bolster him. His eyes moved to a small indentation within the bricks on the wall, and he had the plan clear in his mind.

Jumping to the side, his foot hit the tiny ledge, giving him enough leverage to push off the wall and up onto the last platform. Smiling triumphantly, he snatched the ribbon and then looked down. "Now what?"

"Jump down," Jules called out with a laugh. "Don't tell me you're scared?"

"It's got to be over a hundred feet," Sebastian responded, peering over the edge. "I'll just come back the way I came."

"No. Jump down," Jules insisted, her voice firm. "Trust. Your. Instincts."

Sebastian clenched his jaw, then stuffed the ribbon in his pocket. He was immortal. He couldn't be killed. Right?

He hopped off the platform and gave into the air rushing around him. Internally, he relaxed, but physically, he braced himself. Landing on the ground in little more than a thud, his knees only bent marginally. A few plumes of dust blew around him, and he looked around. Not dead. Thank God.

As Jules came over, he took the ribbon out and held it out to her. "Wasn't so hard," he said with a sloppy smirk.

"Pretty good for your first try," Jules teased, before eyeing the ribbon. "Why are you handing that to me? Go put it back."

Sebastian's face fell and his shoulders slumped. Ignoring the light laughter coming from his friends, he rolled his eyes. He should have known. Walking back to the first platform, he repeated the exercise with more fluidity to his motions this time around. It only took one try. When he was far above them, he tied the ribbon back on the bar and flew back down without any hint of nervousness.

"Now you look like you're one of us," Piper said, her arms folded over her chest. "Dibs on sparring with him first."

"Why?" Leona asked.

"Well, he's my best friend's new beau. He needs to know how he's gonna get his ass handed to him if he ever decides to hurt you," she grinned. "Though, if he does, he'll meet Death *again*."

"I don't want to hurt you, Piper," Sebastian answered. "But I appreciate your faith in me. Makes me feel good."

Jules smiled and glanced at Lucinda, before looking back at the coven's newest member. "You'll start with me. Don't worry, you won't hurt me. I want you to give me all you've got."

"Be careful," Victor chimed in, heads turning to him. "Sebastian knows how to fight."

"Do you?" Jules asked whilst raising her eyebrows. "This should be fun then."

Sebastian was going to lean into this completely. He knew how to fight physically, but that was as a human. Perhaps Jules could teach him some new moves as a vampire, given he could jump off walls now. It felt like he needed to be in a franchise with laser swords and a masked, asthmatic giant claiming to be his father.

Jules ran toward him and he barely had time to think before he was knocked to the ground by a punch. Staring up at her incredulously, he almost didn't register her words.

"I thought you said you knew how to fight?"

Shit. Sebastian frowned in frustration, then swept his leg against Jules's, knocking her down with him. In a blur, they were both on their feet. His mind was racing, but he willed it to calm. He had powers now, ones he didn't have before. What could he use? Physical strength wouldn't help him in this arena, nor speed.

He sidestepped another lunge from Jules and heard her voice faintly, but her lips weren't moving. He focused on her and realized it was her jumbled thoughts planning her next move. He smirked to himself and felt like he'd won already. It was obvious now.

Jules seemed to note the shift and her smirk mirrored his. She moved forward, Sebastian dodging and parrying every one of her attacks. She wanted to lead him in a direction where he latched onto those abilities and used them to their full potential, which he seemed to be doing. And now...

*Thwack!*

Sebastian grunted and slid down the wall he'd just been thrown into. "But you—"

"Thought hard about a move I never intended to make. I'm glad you used those abilities as an enhancement for your skills but don't rely on them completely. It will be useful to those who don't know what powers you possess, but those who do... will be expecting it. They will want to flank you and misguide you. Always be three steps ahead."

Sebastian nodded and stood up again, brushing dirt and dust from his clothing. "Okay. Let's go again."

"It's *my* turn," Piper said, stepping into the ring. Jules acquiesced this time and let the blonde go. Piper's smile was feral and Sebastian momentarily felt fear. "You ready, Beliveau?"

"Bring it on."

"I'll remind you I can hear thoughts too, so don't even try to use that against me," Piper said, before barreling toward him. She was nimble and slender, which helped in her pursuit. She jumped over Sebastian's punch and wrapped her legs around his neck, yanking him down on the ground. Holding him there, her ankle locked around the other, she grabbed his hands and held them in place. "Wow, you suck," she taunted with a laugh.

"Not fair," Sebastian muttered as he struggled against the hold. "You're ancient. I'm a baby."

"Poor baby," Piper cooed as she kept her vice tight on him. "Leona deserves someone stronger."

"Pipe," Leona warned, but Jules silenced her, her eyes still locked on the pair fighting.

"Shut up," Sebastian said, thrashing to try and get the upper hand. What the fuck kind of chokehold was this? Where did she *learn* this?

"Taiwan," Piper said, his thoughts loud and clear. "I knew you weren't good enough for her. Turning you was a *waste*," she hissed. "And she almost died because of you. We all did."

Sebastian was growing angrier by the second. Each word she spewed out of that hateful mouth fueled his rage. He grabbed onto her arms, and when he couldn't pry her off, he felt fury explode from him. Sparks whizzed between them and suddenly, in a burst of static and light, they were blasted apart from each other. Sebastian felt dazed, and Whitney immediately went to check on Piper, who had smoke permeating from her body.

"Seb!" Leona called out, immediately by his side. "Are you alright?"

"Yeah," Sebastian said, sitting up. "What... was that? What happened?"

"Exactly what I wanted to happen," Piper grunted, sitting up as well. Her hair was sticking out from the static shock he'd given her. "Burned my clothes up, dickhead."

"I didn't mean to," Sebastian said. "I got so angry..."

"Electromagnetism," Lucinda interrupted. "Another ability. A rare one."

Sebastian looked down at his hands. He could faintly see a glowing hue fade from his fingertips. Glancing over at Piper, who was brushing off her clothes, he felt relieved she was okay. "So I can... electrocute people?" he asked, looking at Lucinda.

"Yes. A very useful gift," she said, her accent thick. "Sometimes our abilities shine through when we're emotional."

"No hard feelings," Piper said as she patted his shoulder in passing, then jerked her hand back at the quiet pop. "Ouch," she hissed, shaking her hand out. "Somebody get Sebastian a rubber suit or something."

He stood and opened and closed his hands. He felt as though his entire world had expanded to an infinite level.

What else could he do? Could he shapeshift? Fly? Breathe underwater?

"Let's keep working," Jules suggested. "All of us."

"**G**ood to see you're embracing the dark side."

Sebastian looked up from his mug of steaming blood and met the pretty, light eyes of Charlotte. They had all returned from training and were mingling on their own. He was enjoying his peace and quiet alone in one of the sitting rooms, trying to get used to the metallic drink in his hand, but Charlotte was a welcomed distraction. He smirked and took another sip, licking the crimson from his lips. "Well, considering I possess the powers of Emperor Palpatine, you're not far off."

"As long as you don't choke me from across the room with your hand in the air, we'll be good," she laughed, perching down next to him on the sofa. She peered into his mug and arched an eyebrow, then sniffed. "What *is* that?"

"Blood."

"No shit."

Sebastian chuckled under his breath and swirled the

thick liquid around inside the mug. "B-negative mixed with O-positive. I've been experimenting. I think I finally got the ratio right."

"Always a bartender at heart," Charlotte cooed, taking the mug from him. She stole a few sips, then cut her eyes to him. "That's yummy."

"I think so," he shrugged, taking the mug back from her. "But you have to go get your own, Baldwin."

"*Baldwin*," Charlotte gaped with a smile. "Oh my *God*, I haven't heard that in forever."

"Really? You've only been married to Vic for, like, seven years. It hasn't been *that* long. And you grew up with that name your whole life before that."

"Yes, but the night I went to sleep after meeting Victor, I was doodling 'Mrs. Charlotte Labasque' in my notebook. It was *supposed* to be for chemistry class, but…"

"Well, you failed that class, so this is all starting to make sense," Sebastian said, laughing as Charlotte elbowed his ribs. "So violent. As usual."

"You like my violence."

"Sometimes," he deadpanned, taking another sip. "You met me that day, too, you know. What about 'Mrs. Charlotte Beliveau?'"

"Doesn't roll off the tongue as easy."

"You don't know *what* rolls off my tongue," Sebastian muttered in a huff.

"I don't, and I never plan to. But given your performance last night, I think we all have a pretty good idea. You sounded like a gorilla. I thought you were *killing* Leona!"

Sebastian felt like blushing. "You never had sex that makes you feel like you can die and go to heaven right then?"

"I mean…"

"Listen, with the number of times I've either walked in on or heard you and Victor fucking, you were well overdue hearing me have sex. You didn't *have* to listen, you know."

"Believe me, Sebby, people in Australia could hear you two. I'm not saying it's a bad thing, it's just like… knowing your kid is having sex, you know? It's weird."

"I am *not* your kid," Sebastian groaned, lolling his head back against the cushions of the sofa. "Sorry that we disturbed you."

"Don't be," Charlotte shrugged. "I'm sure it was great. God knows it was when Vicky and I both did it as vampires for the first time. I didn't think we were ever going to stop. You ought to be glad you didn't walk in on any of *that*."

"Believe me, I am," Sebastian muttered.

"Seems like yesterday you were just a little baby virgin, scared of seeing a girl naked," Charlotte purred at him, poking his cheek. Sebastian grimaced and waved her hand away, swearing at her. She laughed and continued poking his cheek, then his ear, then his closed eyelid. "Widdle Sebby-baby is all gwown up," she said in a baby voice, puckering her lips up and making kissing noises.

"*Okay*," Sebastian groaned, shrugging her off. "Just because I didn't have sex at, what, *four* like the whore you are doesn't mean my first time was anything less than ordinary!"

"Excuse me, I was four-and-a-*half,* thank you," Charlotte scoffed, putting her hand up at him. "I'm surprised you didn't come to ask me for help before you and Leona slept together. Or did my tutelage the first time sink in that much?"

"Here we go," Sebastian said, glaring at her.

When he had been in college, he had taken an interest in a girl who sat next to him in his creative writing class, and Victor had *pleaded* with him to make a move, but he had been too nervous. Sebastian also hadn't been completely convinced the girl even liked him, despite both Victor and Charlotte reassuring him that he was overthinking and that she was into him.

Eventually, his crush had made the move and they had gone out for ice cream one night. It ended with a kiss, and Sebastian had all but kicked himself when he got home that he hadn't done more. Not that he was anything other than a perfect gentleman, but looking back on the incident made him cringe. He had been completely oblivious to her longing gazes and her telling him she 'needed help with her faucet at home' and Sebastian responding that he 'had no clue how to fix a faucet.'

Idiot.

Somehow, she had found it endearing and they went on a second date. Then a third. However, upon Charlotte finding out he hadn't done more than make out and have a quick, clumsy fumble over the bra with this poor girl in three dates, she had taken matters into her own hands.

*"Sebby, we need to talk."*

*"Okay... Am I in trouble?" Sebastian asked, putting his pen down on his notebook. He had been in the middle of some homework, but Charlotte sounded like she meant business. They*

*were in their shared apartment, him living in one room, Charlotte and Victor inhabiting the other.*

*"When are you going to have sex with this girl? You know she isn't going to stick around forever if you keep being shy."*

*"I... I don't know!" Sebastian blurted out, his cheeks as red as the cover of his notebook. "I don't even know what to do!"*

*"You've never..."*

*"I... No," he finally admitted. "I mean, I* know *what to do, but... only in theory. What if I'm not good at it? What if I can't make her feel good? What if—"*

*"Calm down," Charlotte laughed. "I'll show you."*

*"What... are you... doing..." Sebastian asked slowly, horror spreading across his face as Charlotte shed her cardigan and began to pull her blouse over her head.*

*"I just told you. Go to the bed and lie down."*

*"Have you gone insane?!" Sebastian gawked, rolling his desk chair back and away from her. "Get out of my room!"*

*"Listen, you need to learn one way or another. I'm just going to show you where everything is and what to do."*

*"I know where everything is!"*

*"You just said you didn't! Come here," she said, walking over to him. Sebastian lurched up and stumbled over things as he backed away vehemently from her. "Sebby, stop being so dramatic!"*

*"Victor is going to* kill *us," Sebastian said, stepping across his bed and to the other side on the floor, just to put some distance between them.*

*"Huh?" came Victor's voice from the room next door. "Did you call me?"*

*"No! Stay out there!" Sebastian yelped from his room.*

*Victor did no such thing, especially at how strange Sebastian sounded. When he came into the room, he arched his eyebrow at the scene before him. "Should I come back later?"*

*"Get your psycho girlfriend some clothes and* away from me!" *Sebastian hissed, pointing at Charlotte.*

*"You didn't tell me Sebastian was a virgin," Charlotte said to her boyfriend, ignoring Sebastian's near-seizure on the other end of the room. "He's too scared to sleep with… what's her name again?"*

*"Eleanor," Sebastian said.*

*"Right. Anyway, I wanted to show him what to do so he wasn't so nervous."*

*Victor regarded her carefully, then shrugged. "Makes sense to me."*

*"Victor!" Sebastian whined helplessly. "Why?!"*

*The blonde teenager laughed and shrugged. "Why not? Charlie's good at what she does, you couldn't have a better teacher."*

*"She's* your *girlfriend," Sebastian said, shaking his head. This was absolutely some kind of trap. Satan was coming to test him. That was definitely what it was. He had to be strong. "Will you please put your fucking shirt back on or something?"*

*"I'm wearing a bra," Charlotte scoffed. "Do you need to watch me and Vic do it instead? We can talk you through it."*

*"No, I absolutely do* not *need to see that, thank you very much," Sebastian said, his tone desperate.*

*"Okay, okay, Charlie, ease up. He's going to go into cardiac arrest," Victor laughed, moving to pick up her shirt. He handed it to her, then walked over to Sebastian. Clapping a hand on his shoulder, he smiled. "Always so loyal."*

*"I hate you both."*

Sebastian smirked at the memory and shook his head when Charlotte questioned him. "I was thinking about your *tutelage* that first time is all."

"Hey, I think I did a fine job getting you ready to unleash your inner sex demon. It never sounded like she was complaining when you brought her home! What was her name again?"

"*Eleanor*," Sebastian laughed, shaking his head. "Did you *ever* learn it?"

"Probably not," she said with a sheepish smile. "What ever happened to her?"

"She said I was too clingy," Sebastian muttered, rolling his eyes.

"You *are* kind of clingy…"

Sebastian gave her a look that said it all.

Charlotte grinned and leaned her head on his shoulder. "You were so skinny back then."

"I had yet to discover the wonders of the campus gym."

"Now the world is better for it," she teased, poking his hard chest. She smiled up at him, then slid her arms around his torso, hugging him so close to her. "I was so scared when I thought I was gonna lose you."

"I know," Sebastian murmured into her hair, then he pressed a gentle kiss to the top of her head. "But I'm right here. And I'm not going anywhere. I promise."

"Good," Charlotte smiled, closing her eyes. "I don't know what I'd do without you."

"Probably die."

Charlotte snorted a laugh and smacked him on the back,

then burrowed further against his chest. "Asshole."

"*There* she is."

He stroked his fingers gently down her hair, and eventually, she pulled back from his embrace. He stared down at her, then closed the distance to press another kiss to her forehead. "We're never going to be apart now. Any of us. You saved me."

"Letting you die was *not* an option. It never will be."

Sebastian loosed a small breath, then nodded. "I'll return the favor by keeping your ass out of trouble for the rest of time."

"Deal," Charlotte grinned, before pushing off him. She snagged his mug and chugged the rest down, then dashed into the kitchen before he could catch her.

# 12

hile Sebastian and Charlotte talked, Leona was upstairs watching Whitney paint Piper's nails a pastel blue color.

"Since when do you get manicures?" Leona asked the blonde with a quiet laugh. She was lounged on a chaise in the corner of Piper's room, her long legs extended. She propped her head against her knuckles, her elbow resting against the arm of the furniture.

"Hey, I like getting dolled up as much as the next girl," Piper defended with a scoff. "I just haven't had much use for mani-pedis is all. Blokes like them anyway."

"You've been really enjoying men lately, Pipe, what gives?" Whitney asked as she carefully glided the brush over the woman's thumbnail. "Not gay anymore?"

"That's not how it works," Piper muttered, rolling her eyes. "Just because I'm sleeping with men a lot doesn't mean I don't still appreciate the female form. Isn't that right, Le?"

Leona smirked and shook her head. "Dunno what you're talking about, love."

"That hurts," Piper whined, moving her hand. Whitney hissed and yanked her hand back to her, inspecting the polish. She grumbled under her breath and began to carefully clean up the smudges. Piper giggled under her breath and flexed her fingers again, causing Whitney to swear.

"That's it, you're on your fucking own, Pipe," Whitney snapped, throwing her hand away from her.

Piper burst out laughing and held her hand out again. "No, come on, Whit, I'm *sorry*. I was just having a laugh. Please?"

Whitney stared at her for a few moments, then slowly scooted closer to resume painting her nails. "You never really answered my question," the brunette said, her dark eyes flicking up to meet Piper's blue ones. "No girls?"

"I've had my heart broken one too many times. Men are easy," Piper murmured nonchalantly, careful not to move her hands again. While Whitney focused on her hands, the blonde glanced over at Leona, who was giving her a sad look. Piper frowned and shook her head just a fraction as if to say, *Don't do that.*

Leona relaxed a little and settled back on the chaise, tuning out Piper and Whitney's new subject of conversation. She thought about when she first met Piper and the first time they escaped Gideon. It had been scary and they had fled to New Orleans. It seemed like a lifetime ago. She had thought they'd be safe there, that they wouldn't have to run anymore.

## 1760.

*Leona walked barefoot into her shared bedroom with Piper in nothing more than a nightgown. Piper was on the bed with a lantern lit, reading a book.*

*"What is it this time?" Leona asked as she pulled her side of the covers down and crawled into bed. "Romance?"*

*"As usual," Piper laughed, closing her book. "I don't know why I bother. These women deserve better. It's barely entertaining," she sighed, setting the book down on the small table next to her side of the bed. Turning a knob, she dimmed the oil lantern and turned back over to face her best friend. "Any word from Whitney?"*

*"She wrote, she's safe," Leona nodded, turning on her side. She fisted the pillow beneath her head and frowned. "I wish she would just leave Damien. He's the worst."*

*"Maybe not the worst, but close to it," Piper said with a nod. She reached up and gently fingered Leona's fist, urging her to unclench her hand and relax. "You have me, Le. He isn't going to touch you. I'm going to keep you safe. You're everything to me."*

*Leona smiled and clutched the blonde's hand tightly. "I don't know what I'd do without you, Piper. It's silly of me to keep getting upset over all of this. There's more to life than a happily ever after."*

*"You aren't silly for wanting happiness or a companion. Those are both great things to dream for. I know the feeling," Piper said, her thumb gently stroking the back of Leona's hand. Her skin was so soft. "I know Margery isn't anything like Gideon, but… I still feel for you. I know what it's like to be used and thrown away. You know I'd never do that to you, right, Leona?"*

*Leona smiled tearfully and looked into her blue eyes. "I know, Piper. I know. Sometimes I get so wrapped up in my foolish daydreams I forget to look at the gem right in front of me."*

*Piper smiled bashfully and slid her hand from Leona's up to her pale cheek. She cradled her face and searched her eyes, their bodies close. "You're my lifeblood, Leona."*

*Leona blinked and focused on Piper's eyes, both their pupils dilated. Slowly, Leona slid her hand along the sheets and up to Piper's waist. Her fingers gently trailed up her side and Piper couldn't help the shiver that tore through her entire body. Leona smiled slightly to herself at the reaction, her eyes raking over what she could see of Piper. They stayed that way, merely looking at each other, admiring each other for what felt like an eternity. It could have been a few seconds, it could have been a few minutes, Leona wasn't sure.*

*Leona's hand gently trailed further up Piper's body, and when her thumb carefully brushed the underside of one of Piper's breasts, the blonde's restraint snapped like a taut wire.*

*Piper crushed her lips to Leona's, moans sounding from both women. Piper weaved her hand into Leona's thick, auburn locks and pulled her tight against her body. Their legs tangled together as any free hands desperately clawed at whatever piece of flesh they could find.*

*Piper had been waiting for this day from the moment she met Leona. She never thought fighting over draining a man would ever bring her together with her... what was Leona? Her soulmate? Maybe? Hopefully?*

*Piper's thoughts fizzled as Leona broke their kiss and leaned down to bite her neck. The blonde cried out in ecstasy as she felt*

*Leona's fangs break the skin. Clenching her thighs together to relieve* some *of the tension in her core, Piper anchored Leona's head against her neck, urging more, more,* more.

*"Fuck," Leona blurted as she pulled back from Piper's neck, her mouth and chin stained with blood.*

*"That's the plan," Piper grinned, leaning forward to lick Leona's face clean. It was an unusual thing for a vampire to taste their own blood, but Piper loved every drop. When finished, she pushed the covers off them and moved in a flash to straddle Leona. She pinned the redhead's hands back by either side of her head, their fingers laced together. "I've wanted this for a long time," Piper breathed.*

*"Really?" Leona whispered, staring up at her. "With me?"*

*"Yes, with you," Piper laughed, shaking her head, her blonde locks tumbling prettily down her shoulders. "Why do you sound so surprised?"*

*"I wouldn't think you'd... want..."*

*Piper tilted her head at Leona's stammering and leaned down to kiss her, putting her out of her misery. After a slow, deep kiss filled with tongues and moans, the blonde pulled back just enough where she could speak. "You are everything I've ever wanted. I'm lucky to get to call you mine for even just a night."*

*Leona let her eyes fall closed and she craned her neck up to kiss her again, her knees bending slightly with how hot and bothered she was. She had never been with a woman before — truthfully, she had only ever been with Gideon. She had been too afraid to pursue someone else when she lived with him and in the years after her escape. This was invigorating every inch of her body.*

*Piper broke the kiss once more and leaned back on her heels, her thighs keeping Leona's hips in place. She harshly ripped open Leona's nightgown and pulled the tatters from her, letting them hit the floor. She pulled her own nightgown over her head, leaving them both naked. Piper sighed and ran her hands up Leona's body, stopping at her breasts. She had seen Leona naked before, and vice versa, but never in this context. Usually it had just been when they were changing or she was helping her recover from Gideon's abuse.*

*Piper leaned down and hastily took one of Leona's hardened nipples into her mouth, her left hand coming up to palm the other one. Leona was nearly in tears with how much she was enjoying herself, her body squirming and aching for some sort of release. Piper continued showering Leona with any affection she could: kissing, sucking, biting, all of it. While Piper's mouth worked, one of her hands snaked down Leona's body and stopped at the apex between her thighs. For a moment, she waited for Leona to open up and let her in — which, she did. Piper gently explored Leona, her fingers becoming slick with the redhead's arousal. Leona was crooning, begging for anything Piper could give her. Piper leaned up from Leona's chest and put her focus on fully pleasing her.*

*Piper easily slid a finger into Leona's core. As she curled it inside her, Leona whooshed out a breath and something that sounded close to Piper's name. A feral grin spread across the blonde's lips as she continued pumping her finger in and out, her thumb caressing Leona's clit. She watched her best friend carefully, wanting to memorize every second of this encounter. Piper had heard horror stories from Leona about what Gideon did to her both inside and outside the bedroom, either against her will or with reluctant consent. It broke her heart and she was thankful for the opportunity to show her it didn't have to be that way. She was* allowed to be happy.

"Piper," Leona rasped, her back arching off the bed. She curled her fingers into the sheets, piercing the mattress. Raking her hands up, causing a tattered trail, Leona abandoned the ruined mattress and instead clutched onto the woman above her for dear life.

"Yes, my darling?" Piper whispered gently, using her free arm to hold Leona close against her. She breathed against the red locks strewn across Leona's back as she curled into her embrace. "You're so beautiful like this, Leona. So beautiful."

Leona was incapable of thinking straight, let alone responding in a verbally coherent way. She merely let out another cry of happiness as a crescendo built deep in her stomach. Piper took this as a sign to continue what she was doing, and the moment another finger worked its way inside Leona's body, the redhead's breath hitched in the base of her throat and her body froze. Piper hissed a soft encouragement into her friend's ear and Leona's entire body quaked as she let go. Piper held her close, her fingers eventually slowing, then retreating from her body. Leona's face was buried in the crook of Piper's neck, and eventually, they were both lying side by side, tangled in each other's arms.

"I thought we weren't supposed to get out of breath," Leona laughed, breaking the comfortable silence between them.

Piper joined in her laughter and traced patterns on Leona's soft skin. "I take that as a compliment."

"You should," Leona said.

Piper was in no hurry to do anything else. She could have just held Leona for as long as she'd allow it.

"I wish I could fall asleep right here," Leona murmured.

"Tired of me already?" Piper teased.

Leona propped herself up so she could look into those pretty blue eyes. "Never."

The corners of Piper's lips quirked up and she moved to run a hand through Leona's tangled hair. Words weren't coming to her, so instead, she kissed her with everything she had. It seemed to be enough with the way Leona immediately folded into her and returned her enthusiasm. Piper shifted her other arm so she could snag Leona around the waist and press their bodies together again. Leona's fingers slowly skirted down Piper's body and the blonde broke their kiss with a moan. Spreading her legs, Piper gladly let Leona explore her. She'd be happy to give her any advice if needed.

"I've never done this before," Leona said.

"You're a virgin?!" Piper gasped.

"Piper," Leona hissed. "I'm serious! Don't make jokes!"

"I know you've never done this before, Le. What you're doing is—" Piper started, but was interrupted by a small squeak hitching in the back of her throat when Leona suddenly pushed two fingers inside her. Piper swallowed thickly and fought to keep her eyes open. "...fine."

"Just fine?" Leona smirked.

"Thought you were nervous," Piper breathed, kissing over what she could reach of Leona's cheek. "Right there."

Leona continued thrusting her fingers just as Piper had done to her minutes before. She had enjoyed herself when Piper's hands were on her, and she was enjoying seeing the blonde melt against her now, but... her chest felt tight. What if she lost Piper? What if Gideon had been good before he met Leona, and she was the reason he turned evil? What if Leona was the one who was cursed to ruin anything she touched? Could she do that to Piper?

*Piper was too engrossed in Leona's movements to notice the shift in her best friend. Mere seconds passed and Piper's moans died on her throat as ecstasy overtook her.*

*"I love you," Piper cried out in a strangled voice, her body bending ever closer while riding wave after delicious wave.*

*Leona froze and promptly removed her fingers. She stared at Piper, her eyes wide, as the other woman came back down to Earth. Piper immediately tensed and sat up, her orgasm forgotten. "Leona, I—"*

*"No," Leona interrupted, her voice wavering. "Piper... You can't love me." Her green eyes were big as saucers and her eyebrows were furrowed deeply together, a firm line forming between them against her skin.*

*"Of course I can," Piper scoffed. "How can you say that? After* this?"

*"It's not... It's not about* this, *or you. It's about me," Leona said, frowning as Piper's face fell. "You* know *what he'd do if he ever found out about... I just... I can't be with someone like that again."*

*"You seemed to manage just fine about ten minutes ago," Piper muttered.*

*"Please, don't be cross with me. I love you, Piper, just..."*

*"Not in the way I love you," Piper finished for her. At Leona's silence, Piper slowly nodded, her throat tight. She clenched her jaw and cut her eyes from the other woman. "I'm such an idiot."*

*"No, you aren't," Leona reassured quickly, reaching out for her hand. Piper quickly snatched it away. "Please, Piper. You must understand... That was a mistake."*

*Piper let out an incredulous laugh laced with defeat. "A*

mistake," she whispered, swaying while she sat as if Leona's words had physically pushed her back. "Loving you has never been a mistake."

Tears pooled in Leona's eyes. "I am broken. You do not want me."

"Do not *tell me what I want*," Piper snarled, her eyes now dark as an ocean. "Do not presume to know my desires better than myself!"

Tears poured down Leona's cheeks. She was lost. "I cannot lose you."

Piper wanted to walk away. She wanted it to be easy, to stand up, get dressed, and leave her forever. She stared at Leona, never blinking. Slowly, she reached up and cradled Leona's cheek in her palm. "You burn me in ways I can never mend."

Leona let out a mangled sob and rested her forehead against Piper's. "I'm so sorry. If he comes after you, I'll never forgive myself. I am not worth the risk."

Piper closed her eyes, a few tears absorbing into her long lashes. She shook her head and brought her other hand to hold Leona's opposite cheek. "A life without you is no life at all."

"Do you hate me?"

Piper let out a quiet, sad breath, then shook her head. "No. I don't. I understand."

"I want to make you happy. I want *to want this*, I don't know why..."

"It's alright, Le," Piper reassured, kissing her cheek. She lingered there for a moment, then in another move, she was off the bed and pulling some clothes on. "I'm going to go find someone to drink."

*"Piper…" Leona said in little more than a whine. "You'll come back?"*

*Piper looked at her for a few seconds, then nodded. "I'll always come back to you."*

Leona came back to the present and looked over, again tuning into what the two women across the room were saying.

"You aren't going to let me do yours now?" Piper asked, huffing.

"I'm alright," Whitney laughed, shaking her head. She looked between her two best friends, sensing tension. Leona had been rather quiet ever since Piper made her comment about women earlier. The brunette cleared her throat, then stood and stretched out. "I'm going to go get a snack. Then probably think of some way to annoy Victor while I'm down there."

"Seb can help with that," Leona said with a smirk. Whitney left the room and Leona turned her head to look at Piper, who was now sitting on the edge of the bed next to Leona's seat. "Surprised you want to be so close to me," Leona muttered.

"What?" Piper gawked. "Why would you say something like that?"

"Why would *you* say something like that? 'I've had my heart broken one too many times.' We've talked about this time and time again. I thought you understood," Leona said with a frown. "You said you wouldn't hold it against me."

"I don't," Piper responded. She folded a leg over the other, looking down at her unpolished toes. Sighing, she lifted her head so she and Leona could see every expression on one another. "I shouldn't have said that and I'm sorry. It's a sore subject for me, you *know* that. And now Sebastian is going to be around *forever* and it's just…"

"Is that what this is about then? You're jealous?"

"Of course I'm jealous," Piper scoffed. "How could I not be? You didn't *want me*, Leona. But a human is what brings you to your knees."

"I didn't *not* want you, Piper. I just… I don't think I can love you like that. I don't know if I like women *that* much. I enjoyed the things we did, but I was scared about Gideon coming back for me, I was scared he'd try and hurt you—"

"But risking Sebastian's life is fine? The man you *love*?"

"I'm not going to do this with you if you're going to be like this. Do you want to talk like adults?"

"Spare me," Piper said, rolling her eyes and waving a hand dismissively.

"I've said it before and I'll say it again, you're a hypocrite, Pipe. No, *listen to me*," she hissed when Piper opened her mouth to interrupt her again. "If you're so hung up on me, why did you push Sebastian and me together? Wouldn't you have tried to sabotage that from happening?"

"Do you really think so little of me, Leona? After all this time?" Piper asked, her eyes crinkling slightly. "He made you happy. I would *never* bar you from someone who makes you smile the way you do with him. You laughed for the first time in *decades* when you met him. I didn't trust him then but I do now. I know he loves you the right way."

"Why didn't you leave after that night?" Leona asked. "The night we…"

"Because," Piper sighed, cutting her off, "I couldn't. Part of me wanted to. I was angry and hurt. I've never dealt well with rejection and it reminded me of Margery, using me for another purpose," she said. Leona's face crumpled at those words. "But our relationship goes deeper than us not being compatible sexually. We're best friends. You're my *sister*. I wouldn't leave you unprotected just because you don't like women," she shrugged. "But I was bitter for a long time. It was difficult to be around you. Even now, at times, it still is."

"I hate that I make you feel that way," Leona said, her eyes filled with tears. "I want you to be happy, too."

"I'm happy just being around you, Le. And Whitney. And now those other three," she said, tossing a hand over her shoulder to gesture downstairs. "Too bad Charlotte's married."

Leona snorted a laugh and wiped at her eyes. "Sebastian would definitely beat you to her if she wasn't."

"You think so?"

"Come on," Leona said, lolling her head to the side as she arched one eyebrow. "You think *you're* jealous?"

"Leona, you *cannot* possibly be jealous of Charlotte. Sebastian would *never* betray you."

"I'm glad he has someone who cares for him so fiercely, but I have my moments when I want to claw at her," she laughed softly. "And now they share the sire's bond. I just can't compete."

"Don't think like that," Piper said, reaching over to gently squeeze Leona's knee. "Sebastian loves you and Charlotte loves Victor. Nothing will happen. If it does, I'll kill them all for you."

"You just want me to yourself," Leona teased.

"Not wrong, but… I mean it."

Leona nodded and quickly moved to sit next to Piper on the bed. In a blink, they were hugging each other close, not a fraction of space between them.

After an age of silence, Leona spoke into Piper's hair, "If I could change things, I would have done it long ago, Piper. In another life."

Piper closed her eyes and reveled in the feeling of Leona's touch. "I know. But we're going to be in this life for a little while longer."

"Maybe we could start a vampire dating website," Leona said with a smile.

Piper pulled back and laughed. "We could call it 'Vamp Tramps.'"

Leona burst out laughing and the two dissolved into each other, their earlier tension forgotten. Leona held her best friend close and never wanted to let go. Maybe they'd *all* find happiness someday.

# 13

Days, then weeks had gone by and they hadn't been found by Gideon, so everyone fell into a routine: training, socializing, researching, and soaking up every moment they could get together. They hadn't a clue when or even if Gideon would locate them, but each night could very well be their last.

Sebastian pulled a t-shirt on over his chest, adjusting it to sit right on his body. He glanced over at a naked Leona, who was very lazily figuring out what to wear to cover up. He smiled slightly to himself, drinking in the sight of that beautiful body. He would never tire of her. Ever.

"Take a picture, it'll last longer," Leona teased.

"You always say that," Sebastian laughed, walking over to her. He was in a simple pair of dark jeans, his dark grey t-shirt, and black socks. Enveloping her in his arms, his palms explored her curves. "I'll never have enough pictures of you. Too bad they're all at home."

Leona sighed and gently placed her hand over his, leaning back against his chest. "I told you, we'll go back one day. I'm sorry."

"It's alright," Sebastian murmured into her neck, kissing the cold skin gently. "I understand it's not safe. I wish someone had cleared my browser history before we left, though."

Leona laughed and elbowed him harshly in the ribs, before pulling out of his embrace. She grabbed a light green sundress that just barely reached her knees and a pair of brown sandals that laced up her ankles. She twirled whilst looking at her reflection, then turned to Sebastian. "Ready?"

"I've *been* ready," Sebastian laughed, moving to pull his boots on.

"If you don't have your shoes on, then you're not ready. Typical male," Leona muttered, folding her arms as she watched him.

"You're the one humming and hawing over what outfit to wear to a *bonfire*. It's not like anyone else is going to see us."

"Fashion *never* takes a day off, darling," Leona teased, floating to him as he stood to his proper height. She looked up at him and giggled.

"What?" Sebastian asked.

"You're just so tall. I'm swooning," she laughed, holding onto his arm.

"Gag," Sebastian groaned, pulling her to leave the room.

They went downstairs to join everyone else, who were out there already, enjoying differing drinks — mostly blood. Theodore had something a little *less* creepy.

The coven, Theodore, Jules, and Lucinda gathered around

a small bonfire in the back patio area of the property. It was quite late at night, they were all freshly fed, and they were taking advantage of every moment of peace before the storm inevitably rolled through. The stars shimmered above them and for once in a *long* time, Sebastian felt like things were normal. They were laughing, sharing stories, and just... *existing* together as if the world wasn't ending.

"As long as I've known you girls, you've been very tight-knit," Theodore said, sipping on his bottle of beer. He gulped down a few times, then tilted the bottom of the bottle toward the Labasques. "So what was it about these two beautiful fuckers that made you want to bring them in?"

Victor and Charlotte laughed at the description in unison. Piper sighed and decided to take over telling the story. "Well..."

*"Excuse me?" Charlotte called out, waving her hand at a blonde woman wrapped up in a long, brown coat with a small beret over her curls. "Can you help us out? We're trying to get to... Vic, what is it called again?"*

*"Santaló," Victor answered.*

*"Yeah, that. Do you know where that is?" The woman didn't answer and Charlotte frowned. She glanced at her husband, then back at the woman. "Hello? Do you speak English? Hablas inglés?"*

*The Labasques were parading around the streets of Barcelona but had gotten lost. It was nighttime and the only light came from a nearby streetlamp and the moon and stars above them. They had* gone through a cobblestoned alleyway for a shortcut and hoped for a miracle — thankfully, this woman had come by. They could get help.

"I speak English," the woman responded. She walked up to them and the sight of her nearly took both the Labasques' breath away. She had piercing blue eyes and the prettiest, sharpest facial features either of them had ever seen. She gave a tantalizing smile and pointed up the road. "You're close. Just down there, take a right, then a left. You'll hear the music before you get there."

"Thank you," Victor said, sagging in relief. "Please, let us invite you to dinner for your help."

"I couldn't possibly impose," Piper said, smiling tightly.

"We insist!" Charlotte chimed in, nodding enthusiastically. "Please. We're here to meet new people. See new things. I'm sure we ran into you for a reason. I'm Charlotte. This is my husband Victor."

Piper smirked. "Is that so? Then how could I possibly refuse your kindness, hmm? I'm Piper. Let's go."

They walked down the street, Piper slightly leading, and made small talk.

"Where are you from?" Piper asked, glancing over at them.

"New Orleans," Victor answered, his arm looped with his wife's.

"New Orleans," Piper repeated with a grin. "Small world. I love New Orleans. Been there many times."

"Where are you from?" Charlotte asked.

"Here and there," Piper said, waving her hand dismissively. Her skin was so pale, it was almost translucent. "I like to move around."

"*A nomad's lifestyle, how fun,*" Charlotte giggled. "*I'm so pleased you're letting us treat you to dinner. Are you just passing through the area?*"

"*I was visiting an old flame of mine,*" Piper murmured. "*And yes… I'm looking forward to the meal.*"

*When they were seated in a quaint, intimate restaurant, the dining room covered in small tables and romantic lighting, Victor was the first to speak.* "*Please, order whatever you'd like.*"

"*Mmm,*" *Piper hummed, glancing over the menu.* "*Not sure yet.*"

"*I hear you. I'm having trouble deciding myself,*" *Charlotte said. She was focused more on the wine menu.*

*Victor watched this woman closely, wondering why it was he felt both on edge around her and relaxed. There was something almost ethereal about her, something otherworldly.*

*And her inability to decide on both an entree and a drink piqued his interest.*

"*What are you?*" *Victor suddenly asked.*

"*Victor!*" *Charlotte hissed, widening her eyes at her husband.* "*How rude!*"

*Piper simply smiled and tilted her head.* "*What am I?*"

"*Yes,*" *Victor said, ignoring his wife beside him.* "*There is something different about you. When we met on the street, I felt drawn to you. And I never feel that way.*" *Perhaps before Charlotte, but never after. He only had eyes for her.* "*Did you?*" *Victor asked, turning to Charlotte.*

*The woman hesitated and gave a slow nod.* "*What are you insinuating, Victor? Piper is our guest.*"

"*And you agreed to come to dinner with us, but you're making* no moves to choose something to eat. Or even look interested in any of the food at all," Victor went on, ignoring Charlotte's comments. His gaze was locked on Piper again.

"Hmph," Piper scoffed, raising her eyebrow. "If you think I'm some sort of alien, why invite me in the first place?"

"At first it was out of gratitude and politeness, then it turned into intrigue when I couldn't look away from you. I'm not afraid," he clarified.

"Is that so?" Piper murmured.

"Try me," Victor said confidently. "We are from New Orleans. Nothing surprises us. Our families are rich. I've seen *things* normal people would never believe. We're both spiritual. We both believe there is something more than us out there."

"Oh?" Piper asked in amusement, tilting her head. "Am I safe to assume your original question of 'what am I' isn't pertaining to my race or ethnicity?"

Victor narrowed his eyes and stayed quiet.

"*What do* you *think I am? Do you normally accuse your tour guides of being... what?*"

"I don't know," Victor shrugged. "That's why I asked."

"Victor, enough," Charlotte said pointedly.

"No, I want to know. She can get up and walk away if she's offended."

Piper's eyes swiveled back and forth between the blonde couple across from her. She sighed and leaned back in her chair, folding her hands in her lap. "Asking questions you don't want the answer to in a place you aren't familiar with..."

"What is it then?" Victor asked. "Secret spy? Witch? Succubus?"

"Succubus," Piper laughed, raising her eyebrows. "You seem to have a lot of theories. You have supernatural friends back home then?"

"I'd like to," Victor said. Charlotte glanced at him, then back at Piper, studying her. "You could be the first," he went on.

Piper regarded him carefully, trying to figure him out. She looked at Charlotte, who seemed equally as intrigued yet… perplexed. Piper huffed to herself and sat up, leaning forward across the table. "Friendship wasn't what I had in mind."

Charlotte grabbed Victor's bicep and squeezed. Piper could hear their heart rates elevate, their breathing shift, their blood flow faster.

"What did you have in mind then?" Victor went on, his voice never wavering.

"Dinner," Piper shrugged.

"Dinner… here?" Charlotte asked slowly.

Piper smiled and shook her head.

"Dinner… here," Charlotte repeated, pointing between herself and Victor as she said the last word.

"Brava," Piper drawled.

"You'd make a scene," Victor countered.

"How do you know?" Piper asked. "I could do it without anyone even knowing what happened. By the time they figured it out, you'd be dead and I'd be long gone."

"So why not do it?" Victor asked.

Piper sighed and shrugged. "I'm enjoying myself."

"If you're going to kill us anyway," Charlotte chimed in, her hand still gripping Victor's arm, "then there's no reason not to tell us what you are."

"Vampire," Piper said without another moment of hesitation.

*The word hung in the air between the three of them, but Charlotte broke the silence.*

*"No way," she said with a pearly grin that radiated sunshine. Gone was the look of frustration and fear. "Are you being serious? Do you have fangs?"*

*Piper was surprised and physically leaned back in her chair. "Do I… what?" Usually, the reactions were laughter or uncomfortable excuses for why they had to leave. Not that they ever left, but still.*

*"Do you have fangs?" Charlotte asked again, her grin never leaving her face. "Can you turn into a bat?"*

*"Slow down," Victor laughed, squeezing her knee. "As I told you," he murmured. "I'm not afraid. I knew something was different. Vampires exist?"*

*"Yes," Piper said, unsure of her next move. Killing them would be ideal, but she had never had anyone react like this to her condition before. Like she was… normal. Just another person. She swallowed and shook her head. "You don't seem to be surprised at all." This was no longer amusing for her. It was a bit unnerving.*

*"I told you, we're from New Orleans. Half the people on the streets of the Quarter claim to be something supernatural. They're all on something though," Charlotte said.*

*"How do you know I'm not on something?" Piper responded.*

*"Because you just aren't. It's quite easy to tell. But I've always believed in that stuff," Charlotte shrugged. "You can't live in one of the most haunted cities in the world and not believe at least a little. I've seen ghosts, too, felt them — so why shouldn't vampires be real?"*

*Piper regarded them thoughtfully. This was uncharted territory. "I… have fangs. I cannot turn into a bat. I can read* minds," Piper said slowly, her eyes glued to both of them.

"Wow," Charlotte giggled excitedly. "What am I thinking of right now?"

"My fangs," Piper said, unable to hold in her small laugh.

"Lucky guess," Charlotte teased, narrowing her eyes playfully. "Okay… now what am I thinking?"

"Charlie," Victor said with a chuckle. "Please. She isn't a trick pony."

"You're right, sorry," Charlotte apologized. "We've just never met a vampire before. How exciting!"

Piper tilted her head. "I just told you I planned on killing you and that I'm a vampire. Why aren't you… freaking out?"

"I like to think I can talk my way out of most things, death included," Victor smirked. His father's political side was shining from within. "We're also very prominent people within New Orleans and Louisiana as a whole. Someone would notice if we went missing, and they'd start looking. People have seen us, there are cameras, too. Someone would find you."

"Is that a threat?" Piper asked.

"No," Charlotte said pointedly, slamming her knee into Victor's beside her. "Listen, let's just start over. You said you've visited New Orleans?"

"Yes," Piper said. "With my sisters."

"You have sisters? There are more of you?" Charlotte asked.

"Not sisters by blood, sisters by choice. But yes. There are countless others. But I choose to associate with only my kin."

"You wouldn't ever expand your… family? Is that what you call them?" Charlotte asked.

"We are a coven," Piper corrected. "But… no. I wasn't

*planning on it."*

*"Why not?" Victor asked.*

*"Because we can't trust anybody else. We have been burned by others more times than I'd like and I'm not going to let it happen again by letting outsiders in."*

*"Then why tell us about you?" Charlotte asked.*

*"Because I fully intend to kill you when we leave this place. Your families can send their mercenaries if they'd like. I'll kill them, too."*

*Silence washed over the table again. Charlotte glanced at Victor, then turned her attention back to Piper. Reaching across the table, she folded a hand over the vampire's. "We won't hurt you."*

*Sky-blue eyes flicked down to the manicured hand over her pale one, and Piper eventually dragged her gaze back up to the blonde across from her. "I know you won't. You will never have the chance."*

*"Have you ever made friends with humans before?" Victor asked.*

*"No."*

*"Why not start now?"*

*Piper frowned. "Because I have all the friends I need, as I told you. Humans merely exist as part of our food chain. Lions don't make friends with deer."*

*"We are no deer," Victor said adamantly. "We could give you some of our blood. An offering."*

*Piper laughed, rolling her eyes. "Is this some sort of charity work?"*

*"He's serious," Charlotte chimed in. "We could. In exchange, you could tell us more. This is just... fascinating."*

Piper half-wondered if they were on something. She tilted her head and huffed out a hollow breath. "You don't know what you're asking." And she didn't even know why she was entertaining this. She had been going to visit one of her boyfriends, was she really that bored?

"We want to be a part of this," Victor said. "We have money."

"I don't need money."

"We have power."

"Don't need that either."

Victor frowned and rethought his plan of action. "We have everything a human could want in the world: wealth, influence, a mansion, a good marriage, friends, great careers…"

"Children?" Piper asked. At their sudden silence, she slowly inclined her head. "Ah… You can't have children."

"Is that a problem?" Charlotte asked, unable to hold eye contact. Her shoulders were drawn forward.

"No. Vampires cannot procreate as humans do. We must turn others ourselves. There is no birthing process. Only a transformation," Piper explained. "That's why you want to do all this? Because you can't have kids? That doesn't make sense."

"It's not why," Victor said, speaking for Charlotte. He didn't like talking about their infertility because he knew how upset his wife got. He had assured her more than he even kept track of that it wasn't her fault and it was not a shortcoming on her behalf, but she had never believed him. Maybe now, she would truly see herself as perfect. "But when you have everything in the world, it gets boring. There are limitations to being human. I'm sure you can agree."

"I can," Piper nodded. She regarded them carefully, then scoured *through their brains like filing cabinets to see if she could find any dirt on them that might prove useful. It looked fairly normal. They were from high-up families and seemed to have a normal group of friends. They also seemed to share a best friend. She wondered how long it would be until they drained him — that was, if she decided to go through with this insane idea. "You haven't even given this a moment of thought."*

*"Victor and I are very similar," Charlotte said. "And we seize opportunities when they fall into our laps. Or... give us directions in an alleyway."*

*Piper smirked, her eyes glinting. Maybe she wouldn't kill them today.*

*"Tell you what," Piper said, grabbing her bag from where it was hanging on the back of the chair. "I'll go and speak with my coven and perhaps you can meet them. Or... one of them," she said. Leona definitely wouldn't go for this. Her trust issues were the worst of all of them, for good reason. "If she likes you, then maybe we can discuss things further. If she doesn't, well..." she trailed off, arching an eyebrow. "Now then, if you'll excuse me, I'm off to meet with my caller. I'm sure he's wondering where I've run off to."*

*"Wait!" Charlotte said, standing up as Piper started to leave. "How will you find us?"*

*Piper smirked and rolled her eyes. "I'm the world's deadliest predator. By the time a human notices us, it's too late. Enjoy your holiday," she said, wiggling her fingers in a wave.*

*Charlotte slowly sank back into the chair, watching the space she left with Victor doing the same.*

"So that's it?" Theodore asked, scoffing. "If I knew it was that easy, I could've joined decades ago."

"I didn't go that easy on them," Whitney laughed, shaking her head. "Pipe brought me to Louisiana to see them."

"Sneaky bitches," Leona muttered. She was sitting on a bench with Sebastian, one leg folded over the other, her shoulder tucked safely under Sebastian's arm. The fire flickering on her face matched the auburn waves atop her head.

"Whatever," Whitney laughed. "I got there and I wasn't very nice."

"You? Mean? *No...*" Theodore gasped, smirking behind his bottle.

Whitney stuck her middle finger up at him, causing a few laughs from around the fire. She shook her head, then continued, "But after a bit of discussion, and the reassurance from Piper, I was eventually on board with them. Best decision ever," she smiled, eyeing the blondes next to her. "I came over to their house and they had goblets of blood already warmed up for us. I'm sure Piper gave them some tips."

"Nope," the woman said, sipping her drink.

"Really?" Whitney gawked, raising her eyebrows. She then turned to the Labasques.

Charlotte shrugged and giggled. "We were excited. First impressions were very important to us. *You* were very important to us. Leona, too. We had no idea she was going to latch onto Sebastian like she did."

"Join the club," Sebastian said, the corner of his lips rising as Leona's head snapped up to glare at him. He looked down at her, then pecked her head. "I kid."

"Mhmm," Leona huffed, adjusting in his hold so she was facing her friends again. "I'm glad you and your husband were so quick to end your lives," she laughed in Charlotte's direction. "Was it really that easy of a decision?"

"Yes and no," Charlotte shrugged. "I struggled with infertility and that was difficult for us. There were times when I didn't even want to be alive," she said sadly. Sebastian's heart jerked in his chest. It had been one of the few times he had had to play therapist with Charlotte, despite having no clue what she was really going through. All he could do was be there for her. Apparently, it had worked. For the most part.

"We agreed before that trip, long before, when the doctors had no more answers for us, that we would live our lives to the fullest," Charlotte went on. "We would grasp any interesting or unique opportunities to see more of the world as they came. I think part of me didn't believe Piper was *really* a vampire, but... she drew us in. I doubt she walked those streets intending to meet two humans she would eventually invite to her coven."

"No, I had a dick appointment," Piper scoffed, shaking her head. "It wasn't even *good*."

"At least you got *some* excitement that night, you're welcome," Victor teased, swirling the thick liquid around in his glass.

"We just wanted something different. When you've grown up with money and had everything you could ever want materialistically handed to you your entire life, it gets boring. Children were something I always wanted but could never have, not naturally. We considered adoption… the right time just never came. But traveling the world forever? Getting to see every phase of humanity as it passes? And looking young and beautiful for the rest of time? Vic and I shared one look and it was a no-brainer," Charlotte said.

"It was suicidal," Sebastian muttered.

Charlotte glared at him and shook her head. "You'd be dead if it weren't for me, shut up."

"Apologies, madam," Sebastian snipped back, rolling his eyes.

"In *any* case, I'm glad our coven is complete now," Leona said pointedly, elbowing Sebastian gently in the side.

"To the coven," Theodore said with a warm smile, holding out his near-empty bottle. No need for tension when they had enough of that to go around as it was.

"The coven," came the unified response, and everyone took a hearty sip of their beverages.

"Hey, Mister Anti-Social."

Sebastian turned from his secluded spot in the yard to see a flash of blonde hair. He smiled slightly. He had broken off from the group about an hour after their toast, wanting a moment to himself. Victor was a welcomed distraction from his internal musings, though. "Hey yourself."

"Don't want to be around people still? Some things never change," Victor teased, nudging Sebastian with his shoulder as he came to stand next to him. There was beautiful greenery surrounding them, much of it he assumed Jules and Lucinda planted to conceal their home from prying eyes. It helped they were just outside the Barcelona city limits, too.

"So much has changed," Sebastian countered, shaking his head. "So damn much."

"I know," Victor said, turning to face him completely. "But a lot hasn't. You're still a massive pain in my ass."

"Dick," Sebastian teased, turning to face him as well. "I never knew you and Charlie were so unhappy with your human lives. Hearing you both immediately being willing to give it up broke my heart. You could have talked to me. I would have been there for you."

"You were there for us," Victor reassured. "I promise. Through all of it. We shouldn't have sprung the coven on you like we did without warning."

"No, you were right," Sebastian said, shaking his head, "I wouldn't have believed you. And if you hadn't done any of that, I wouldn't have met Leona. Now I can't imagine life without her."

Victor smiled. "I've waited a long time to hear you say that about someone. You two are good together. She loves you. That's all I've ever wanted. That's all *you've* ever wanted."

Sebastian nodded, swallowing thickly. His chest felt tight again. "Everything just moved so fast. Eight months ago I didn't even know who she was. Now I'm a vampire." He paused and laughed softly, covering his face with one hand. "God, I sound like a fucking lunatic."

"All of this *is* lunacy," Victor said, laughing with him. They both turned their heads to look at everyone surrounding the still-burning bonfire. Leona, Piper, and Whitney were all laughing together and seemingly trying to get Theodore to have another beer. Jules and Lucinda were snuggled up together and sitting on a wide chair near the fire. Charlotte was just standing and observing, but after a few moments, turned her head to meet eyes with Victor and Sebastian. She furrowed her brows in concern and pointed at them, then gave a questioning thumbs-up. Victor and Sebastian both nodded and Charlotte relaxed, then went back to watching everyone else.

Sebastian slowly returned his gaze to Victor and he smiled. "We've come a long way since middle school, huh?"

"Very long," Victor laughed, nodding his head. "Between all the shit we used to get up to as kids, I'm surprised we even survived this long."

"That's the fucking truth," Sebastian agreed. "Remember the party we threw when your parents went on that Mediterranean cruise for two weeks?"

"Oh *God*," Victor groaned, tilting his head back and barking out a laugh. "Charlotte loves that story. How many people do you think we had in the house at one time? Seriously."

"Hmm..." Sebastian pondered, tilting his head to one side. "It had to be over a hundred."

"Had to be," Victor said, rubbing his forehead. "I still have *no* clue how you didn't die from chugging all those beers when the cops showed up. You could've just poured them down the toilet or out the window or something."

"I panicked!" Sebastian exclaimed with a grin. "Hey, we

didn't get arrested, did we? And your parents never found out."

"I guarantee they knew," Victor smirked, shaking his head. "I miss them."

Sebastian sobered and gave his friend a sympathetic look. "I miss them, too, Vic. Maybe when all this is over we can…"

"No, we can't," Victor said. "Piper was very clear that we are to cut all ties with our human families. Charlotte and I had begun discussing arrangements to fake our deaths back when Piper agreed to bring us into the coven, but… a lot's happened since then."

"What was the plan?"

"Plane crash. The small one."

"You were going to kill Tucker for the sake of convincing people you were dead?!"

"No, God no," Victor said, shaking his head impatiently. "I'd never do that to Tucker. Trust me, he's safe to fly another day. I was going to pilot the plane myself."

"But… you don't know how to fly a plane."

"Well, no wonder we crashed then."

Sebastian snorted and shook his head. "What about me?"

"What about you?"

"If I hadn't become immortal, you would've left me behind. At least on paper. Your parents would have come to me. I would've had to take care of everything with them. Your parents and the Baldwins would've been beside themselves with grief. That would have *sucked*."

"I know," Victor said. "It was a subject I wanted to broach with you a while back, but… as I said, a lot's happened since then."

Sebastian nodded. Now they had to think of a way to kill *all* of them, as far as their human counterparts were concerned. "How would you have wanted to die? Seriously."

"Getting turned into a vampire not good enough?"

"Be for real."

Victor sighed and shrugged. "I don't know. Probably in my sleep. It's painless that way. For me, at least. Not for everyone else. What about you?"

"The same," Sebastian nodded. "I'm sure that's how most people want to go."

"Yeah," Victor said. A short silence grew between them, but it wasn't uncomfortable. It was… nice. Victor was the one to break it again. "I'm scared, Bas."

Sebastian looked over at him, the tremor in his friend's voice tugging his heartstrings. He shuffled closer and draped an arm around Victor's shoulders. "Me, too."

"What if we don't win?"

Sebastian sighed. He sounded like Charlotte. He sounded like *everyone*. "We can't think that way."

"But what if we don't?"

"Then… I don't know, we die, I guess. What do you want me to say?"

"I don't know," Victor sighed. "Sometimes I wonder if things would have been easier had I just looked at the map in Spain last year instead of asking some random woman for directions in the street."

"They *definitely* would have been easier," Sebastian teased. "But that's not what happened. And here we are. Back in

Spain with a lot of random women. And a werewolf."

"Lunacy," Victor repeated with a light chuckle.

Sebastian smiled and squeezed his shoulder. "I've never really thanked you, you know."

Victor looked over at him, comfortable in his embrace. "Thanked me for what?"

"For that day you caught me trying to break into your dad's car. For inviting me to dinner instead of calling the cops."

Victor brought his hand up and patted Sebastian's fingers around his shoulder. "You weighed sixty pounds soaking wet. And you were covered in dirt. I was scared you were gonna stab me or something if I called the police," he said with a light lilt to his voice. Sebastian merely muttered a vulgar insult next to him. Victor turned in Sebastian's hold and brought his hand up to hold onto the crook of Sebastian's elbow. "It was the best decision I ever made, Bas. Hands down."

"What about asking Charlie out?"

"*That* was inevitable. Did you *see* the way she looked at me when we first met?" Victor said smugly, tilting his chin up.

"Always so humble," Sebastian said, rolling his eyes. "And always good to ruin a moment."

Victor smiled and playfully nudged Sebastian's chest with his free hand. "Always. But you don't have to thank me, buddy. It was the right thing to do at the time. I gained a brother that day. I've always wanted one," he said, his eyes growing emotional. "You always say we saved you, but... you've saved us, too, you know."

"Really?" Sebastian murmured.

"Of course," Victor said incredulously, a few tears dampening his lower eyelashes. "How could you doubt that?"

Sebastian merely shrugged. He didn't have an answer.

"When this is all over," Victor went on, "we're all going to go somewhere safe. Not New Orleans, not New York, not Spain. Somewhere new, to start fresh. We'll be one big happy family."

Sebastian smiled at the thought. What he would give to simply live a normal, content life with the people he loved. His time in New York and New Orleans had been that for a while with Victor and Charlotte. Their lives had been close to perfect, or at least… that's what it felt like on the outside. He was now beginning to realize all the small cracks and fissures in their facade he'd overlooked throughout the years.

"Maybe we'll live out in the country where nobody can bother us," Sebastian suggested.

"Perfect," Victor grinned. "What else?"

"Um…" Sebastian started, bringing his hand down from Victor's shoulder. "A big garden. We can experiment with food and blood like they do," he said, glancing over to Jules and Lucinda. "Maybe we could start a blood donation nonprofit."

"Isn't that a little on the nose?" Victor said.

"Maybe," Sebastian laughed, nodding. "Honestly, Vic? I don't care what kind of house we live in or where it is. It could be a box on the side of the street for all I care. As long as we're all together, I'll be happy."

"*One* box for all of us?" Victor gawked.

Sebastian laughed and elbowed him. "Well, for you. I'd, of course, get my own penthouse box on top of you."

"You *need* your own box," Victor laughed back, moving on his tiptoes. "I remember when I used to look down at you, Beliveau. Now I can't even reach."

"Short little baby," Sebastian cooed, patting the top of his head.

Victor grumbled and swatted his hand away, then came back down to his usual height. "Asshole."

"So I've been told."

14

reaking sounded as a woman in her sixties rocked back and forth in her white, leather recliner. The television was blaring the news, one of the anchors discussing how the president was trying to get approval to fight a terrorist organization. The woman shook her head and spooned another bite of yogurt into her mouth. She had curlers firmly rolled in her dark hair and a face full of makeup, despite the hour. Her skin sagged a little and she had a less-than-fortunate face — one that would definitely put a service-industry worker on edge should they be unlucky enough to wait on her.

Her watch party was interrupted by a booming noise just outside her apartment door. She jumped and yelped in fright, kicking the footrest of the recliner down. She set her yogurt cup down on the table next to her and quickly grabbed one of her pink, plush robes to wrap around herself. Stuffing her feet into fluffy slippers made of the same material and color, she carefully shuffled toward the door. She grabbed the baseball bat she kept leaning up against the front doorframe, then slowly opened the door and poked her head out.

In the hallway of the building, every other door looked fine except her neighbor's. Dust and rubble scattered the floor just in front of the adjacent apartment and the older woman felt fear strike her.

"Charlotte?" she called out, creeping out of the room. The bat was raised and she cautiously made her way to the blonde woman's apartment. She hadn't seen her in ages and was surprised no other tenants were out investigating like she was. It was the middle of the night — surely someone else heard it?

Charlotte's apartment door hung by its hinges, blasted open by an other-worldly force. The kitchen and living room area were in disarray, the blood bags from the trash strewn on the floor, throw pillows off the couch and in corners of the room, and vases and pictures broken with glass shattered all over the rug and hardwood flooring.

In her bedroom stood Gideon, holding a blouse up to his face. He closed his eyes and inhaled deeply, knowing it hadn't been long since they left. His hair was disheveled and he was still in the same bloody clothing as the night of his brawl with the coven.

He was ravenous for revenge.

He had lost Leona's scent when they all escaped his

castle several days before and he'd been implosive with rage. Immediately, he'd gone back to New Orleans, to that same mansion he had originally relocated Leona in with Sebastian. It was empty, but he'd caught the familiar scent of Leona's friends nearby. He had tracked it across the city to a hospital before losing it again. In that time, he had gone back to the mansion and raided it, looking for any clues as to where they might be. It took him a few days, but eventually, he found mail addressed to a residence in New York City, which was his next stop.

And here he was.

"I'll find you, flower," Gideon murmured to himself, catching her scent in the room. He frowned and continued inhaling, deeper as he went back into the living room. A familiar scent — not vampiric — permeated his senses, causing him to circle the room and sniff each piece of furniture. He dropped to his knees in front of the sofa and pressed his face into the cushions, breathing in. His eyes flashed in recognition and he grunted out a noise of frustration.

"You lying traitor," he growled, before angrily ripping the cushions apart.

"Hello?" a shaky, croaky voice called out, the owner appearing in the destroyed doorway. "Charlotte? Are you okay?"

Gideon looked up and rose from the sofa, moving into the woman's line of sight. She yelped and stared with fear, the bat in her hands clattering to the hard floor. "I— I'm calling the police!"

The vampire lunged at her and grabbed her by the cheeks

with one hand, his sharp nails breaking the skin easily. Charlotte's neighbor cried out in pain, and Gideon harshly yanked her toward him, her feet dangling from the floor. "Where are they?"

The woman was frozen in fear and unable to speak due to Gideon's grip on her face. He was about to roar at her when her body went limp and her eyes closed. He frowned and turned his head so he could listen to her body. No heartbeat. "Useless," he muttered, tossing her to the floor like a ragdoll. He was no stranger to literally scaring people to death, but this time he internally scolded himself for not taking more care with his approach. He looked down at her again, then squatted down. "Ugh," he grimaced, recoiling back from her. "God, you smell like smoke. I did you a favor," he mumbled, rising to his full height. He needed to feed elsewhere.

*After* he visited a certain werewolf.

Gideon stood in an empty, one-bedroom cabin just outside of Buckden, England. The house looked like it had been empty for a while. It was small and minimally decorated. The walls were white and stucco and large, brown beams lined the ceiling. A kitchen and dining area skirted off to the right of the door. In the entryway, there was a small table with a record player and crate of vinyl, in the living room, a brown sofa, and a black, rectangular coffee table. Across the room there stood a television atop a brown entertainment stand decorated with a couple of plants, their long leaves hanging off the edges of the furniture. There was a short hallway with two doors in the back of the house.

Gideon quickly scanned over everything he could see, trying to find any sign of evidence. Inhaling deeply, he closed his eyes and let his tracking instincts take over.

He was at Theodore's home but wasn't surprised not to find him. If he had been inside that city apartment with those *foolish* women, he was probably long gone wherever they were hiding. He didn't know how Damien could be so stupid as to fall in love with such an idiot.

Through Theodore's scent, he caught another, more familiar one. Gritting his teeth, Gideon opened his eyes and immediately slammed his hand through the dining table situated in the middle of Theodore's kitchen. The wood exploded and sent shards in every corner. Gideon stalked forward, stepping on chunks of lumber, and continued breathing deeply to ensure he didn't miss any scents.

It usually didn't take him this long to locate Leona. The first time she had escaped he had been tormented with anguish. He had followed her and that slut of a blonde to the States. Instead of yanking her back home immediately, he'd waited, bided his time. He wanted to *see* why she left. Damien had been the one to distract him and calm him down. He had reassured him that she would come back eventually and to just let her have her fun, let her *think* she has control of the situation. So Gideon took the advice and didn't touch her again for a few decades. She had obviously relaxed and came back to Europe and he brought her back home. He had considered killing that Piper bitch at the time and sorely regretted his mercy now.

When she escaped the second time, he had been less upset and more infuriated. She had Whitney in tow and Theodore had even helped them leave, so Gideon and Damien joined forces in their rage. Gideon, again, had bided his time. He assumed she went back to New Orleans and hadn't bothered to check in on her. To him, a year felt like an hour did to a human. Fifteen years had passed and he'd barely noticed. Only when Damien came whinging to him about Whitney leaving him in a hurry to go off to some party did his interest get piqued and he went to see for himself what his flower had been getting up to across the pond.

Again, he regretted his mercy in not squashing that black-haired bug she called a boyfriend when he'd had the chance.

Gideon slowly walked through Theodore's living room and down the hallway. He investigated the bathroom only to find nothing. He entered his bedroom and sniffed around. Damien's scent was much stronger here. Unsurprisingly. The room had a bed in the center with dark brown sheets and a nightstand on the left side, a bookshelf on the right. If he wasn't so pissed, he'd make a mental note to teach Theodore yet again how to decorate a home.

Walking to the nightstand, Gideon picked up a small, framed picture. It showed Theodore and Damien together, Damien's arm draped over Theodore's shoulder. Damien was kissing Theodore's cheek and Theodore was grinning like a madman in the photo, his eyes squeezed shut in happiness. Gideon remembered this photo. He'd taken it not long ago, during one of Damien's 'breaks' with Whitney. Staring at it only made Gideon more angry. He grunted to himself and crushed the frame with his hands, glass shattering beneath the force of his grip.

He needed to talk to Damien.

Damien flipped some vegetables in a pan as they sizzled and smoked. He tilted the pan back and forth, the oil coating the vegetables. He lived in a cottage in Bainbridge, not far from Gideon and Theodore's homes, and had a small amount of land with a garden, everything he needed to keep himself fed and warm. There was a lot of farming and livestock supply surrounding his village, and no shortage of predators he could get ahead of to sate his appetite. He reached forward to turn the heat off his stove when his front door exploded. The pan fell from the werewolf's hand and clattered to the floor, Damien swearing at both the intrusion and the hot food splattering on his feet and ankles.

"Jesus Christ!" Damien shouted, his chest heaving as Gideon's hulking frame came into view. "What the *fuck* are you doing?!"

"I could ask you the same thing, Hawthorne," Gideon snapped, marching up to him. "I was just at Theodore's house. He wasn't there."

"So?" Damien scoffed, moving to get a dish towel to wipe his lower half off. He winced in pain and wet the towel instead to hopefully ease the blistering. It would heal quickly enough in a few hours.

"So? *So?*" Gideon growled, shoving him back against the fridge. Plates clattered inside the cabinetry around the kitchen and a few magnets fell off the front of the fridge. "Where is he?"

"I don't know, Gideon, get the hell off me," Damien said, shoving him back. He shook his head and walked out of the kitchen, but Gideon grabbed him by the back of the neck and lurched him forward into the doorway of the living room. Damien groaned in pain and turned his head so his face wasn't so crunched against the drywall. The werewolf struggled against his friend's grip and eventually quit fighting it. "Gideon. Get. Off. Me."

Gideon let go of him and walked past him into the living room, pacing back and forth. "I tracked Leona to New York City. All her little friends are with her, including her *tumor.* Imagine my surprise when I smell both of your *mates* there as well."

"I don't have anything to do with that, Gid. Don't come in here and destroy my house blaming me. Go track down Theodore if you're so bothered."

Gideon rounded on Damien and clenched his fists together, his red eyes fiery. "How did he know where they were? HOW?"

"How am I supposed to know?" Damien shrugged, keeping his countenance neutral. "I haven't seen him since before Whitney visited last."

Gideon's patience ran out and he lunged at Damien, grabbing fistfuls of the light brown, buttoned shirt Damien was wearing. He pulled him so close, their noses nearly touched. "I'm not going to ask you again, dog."

"And I'm not going to entertain this," Damien said, his brown eyes flashing yellow for a brief moment. "Tread lightly, Valdis."

"Is that a threat?"

"Did it sound like one?"

A low noise rumbled from Gideon's throat and, unable to curb his temper, he threw a punch at Damien, his fist connecting harshly with the wolf's right jaw. Damien stumbled back, but Gideon pulled him forward again and punched him a second time. "Where are they?!" he roared.

"I don't know," Damien said, his voice garbled.

"Answer me!"

Damien coughed up blood as Gideon punched him again. This time he went down to the ground. "I already told you," he spluttered. "I haven't seen Theo in months."

Gideon huffed and backed up one step. "Why is he with *them* then?" he asked again in frustration. "You were the only one who came to *rescue* them that night. He would only know from you."

"What if one of them called him?" Damien grunted, flexing his jaw.

"And why the hell would they do that?"

"Do I look like a fucking fortune-teller to you, Gideon?! I don't *fucking know*," Damien snapped.

"You're protecting him. You're protecting *her*."

Damien opened his mouth again to try and get his jaw right, then glared up at Gideon as he stepped closer. "Touch me again and I will shift," he warned, sitting up. "I know you're pissed, but if you *ever* treat me like this again, I won't be the only one with a broken jaw," he said stiffly. "I *told* you. I don't fucking know where Theodore is or why he was in New York."

"You expect me to believe he just happened to find them on *accident*? What sort of fool do you take me for?"

"I don't take you for a fool at all," Damien said, holding his gaze. "I'm telling you what I know. Which is nothing."

Damien had returned to his home after the fight and the coven escaped. He had shown up at the end and had ultimately wrenched Gideon off Piper, Whitney, and some man he had never met before. Truthfully, he had only been trying to protect Whitney. The other two were happy accidents. The vampires had wasted no time evanescing away and Damien had kept his strong grip on Gideon as long as he could to buy them some time. Gideon had been furious then, but it didn't compare to now. Damien had escaped with his life and healed back at home. He had hoped the next time he saw Gideon, he'd be calmer, but he had been wrong.

The werewolf kept himself guarded physically and mentally. Gideon was crazed in a way even Damien had never seen before, which, on this occasion, proved useful for him. He wasn't focusing like he normally did, and Damien was hiding his thoughts with far more success than if Gideon had been in a *good* mood. There were some abilities he couldn't work around, but after knowing this immortal for as long as he had, he had learned a few tricks to keep him in the dark.

"I have to find her," Gideon said, his voice hoarse. Unrecognizable. "And him. All of them. I'll choke them with their own intestines."

Damien stayed quiet, watching his friend. He wasn't even sure he could call him that anymore. This obsession with Leona had hollowed him to the worst parts of himself, and now that Theodore was on his radar, he was terrified. He truly had no clue where Theodore was, and when he'd informed him of the fight, he hadn't expected things to get this out of hand. Even Damien hadn't known they would go to New York. Whitney hadn't trusted him *that* much, especially after what happened when she left him to go back to the ball. Despite his history with Theodore, he hadn't thought the man would be stupid enough to paint a target on his back *again* and go find them.

And Whitney…

"I'll see if I can get in touch with him. Or Whitney," Damien said, hoping it would end this psychotic episode and get this immortal the hell out of his house. He slowly stood up. "I'll find you if I hear anything."

Gideon looked at him and stared into his eyes, his own frantic. "I don't believe you."

Hurt flashed against Damien's face. "You don't trust me? After all these years?"

"You're *fucking* both of them. You're protecting them. I can see it," he said, closing in on him.

"I can't make you believe anything," Damien said, his voice even. "And I'm not going to fall over myself to try. You can get the fuck out of my house if you're going to continue throwing wild accusations at me."

Gideon laughed, but there was no mirth behind it.

Shaking his head, he grabbed him by the collar. "Or what?"

"You'd kill me?" Damien asked softly.

Gideon gritted his teeth and stared at him for what felt like eons, before shoving him back. Damien loosed a breath and straightened his clothing. Before he could say another word to Gideon, the vampire was gone. He stared at the space he'd been standing in, then ran a hand through his hair.

They were all fucked. *Royally.*

# 15

"Oh no."

Sebastian's head snapped up to look at Charlotte, whose expression was even paler than usual. "What?" he asked, his voice laced with panic. "What is it?!"

She was looking down at a tablet that belonged to one of the Spanish vampires. They had either forgotten or lost their phones in the time leading up to and during the battle with Gideon. Sebastian stared at her, but she wasn't moving an inch, other than her trembling hands. Her eyes were wide, and in a moment, Sebastian was by her side, looking down at the screen.

It was a news article.

### *HOME INVASION LEAVES WOMAN DEAD*

*A woman is dead after an apparent home invasion in an apartment building on the Upper East Side.*

*Georgia Whittaker, 62, was found dead inside her neighbor's apartment. Police have not released a cause of death, but have told us there were no physical wounds on her body other than a few bruises.*

*The apartment belongs to Charlotte and Victor Labasque, a prominent couple whose primary residence is in New Orleans, Louisiana.*

*They were reported missing a week ago.*

*The apartment's door was broken open and the interior was in disarray. Police are still combing the flat for evidence.*

*We will continue to keep you updated as we learn more.*

"Shit," Sebastian agreed, taking the phone from her. There were pictures of the apartment inside from the doorway. It looked like a tornado ripped through it. "Do you think…?"

"What's going on?" Leona asked as she came into the living room where the two were sitting. "Seb?"

He merely handed her the tablet, the article still pulled up. Leona's face fell as she read it a few times over. She looked up at Sebastian, her body language rigid. She knew it was him. She *knew* he had tracked them. How long would it be before he found them here? They were an ocean away from New York, and countries away from England, but… Gideon wasn't the type to give up. He had scoured the world for her multiple times.

And he had always found her.

"I won't let him touch you," Sebastian said, standing and going to Leona's side. He clicked the device dark and set it down on a nearby end table. Pulling her into his arms, he stroked her hair to try and calm her nerves. "I promise. He won't even come near you. We're safe here. There's so many of us and only one of him. And we have Theodore."

Leona's shoulders shook and her grip tightened on her lover. Squeezing her eyes shut, she buried her head into his chest, a few weeps escaping her. Sebastian's hold merely hooked further around her, keeping her in a fortress.

"I'm sorry," Leona whispered against his chest.

Sebastian moved back so she could look at him. He held her cheeks with his hands and wiped her tears. "Listen to me," he said firmly, but softly. "You have nothing to be sorry for. His actions are not your fault. He is *deranged*. He's pissed because he's never not gotten his way, and now he can't control you anymore. He is an abuser. When they lose their power, their mind goes with it."

"But he *hasn't* lost his power, Seb. He has all the power."

"No he doesn't," he said, unsure of where this confidence came from. Perhaps it was his immortality. Perhaps it was just his devotion to this woman he was destined to protect. "He holds no power over you. Not anymore. Do you hear me? *You* hold power over you."

Leona sniffed and stared up into his eyes. For a moment, those red eyes took her right back to when she was bending over backward for Gideon. But there was a softness within Sebastian's gaze that Gideon never possessed. He was good. He was kind. He was gentle. She smiled sadly and finally nodded, hearing what he'd said. "Okay."

The bubble they'd existed in the last few weeks had been a much-needed distraction, but reality had come crashing into this house in Spain. Suddenly, the world that had expanded beyond comprehension for Sebastian had shrunk right back down. For the first time, he truly understood the fear Leona felt when it came to Gideon. He was a *monster.* He had only gotten a glimpse of the havoc he could wreak — what else was he capable of?

"What is going on?" Piper asked as she, Whitney, Victor, Jules, and Lucinda walked in to join them.

"Gideon broke into Charlie's apartment," Sebastian explained, Leona still curled into his chest. "He killed her neighbor. It's all over the news. They're looking for Charlie and Vic," he said, eyeing his other best friend across the room. "Looks like we can't go back to the States at all for a while."

"Shit," Victor breathed, sitting down heavily in an armchair. "So on top of all this, we're wanted fugitives?"

"Happens to the best of us," Whitney sighed, joining Charlotte on the sofa. "Were you close to your neighbor?"

"No," Charlotte said as she shook her head. "But... she didn't deserve to die."

"The article said there were no physical wounds except bruising. They would know if she was strangled," Sebastian added.

"Gideon doesn't strangle people," Piper said, Leona making a small noise in agreement. "She probably got scared to death. Literally. I'm sure the bruises were from him grabbing her. Was she young?"

"No," Charlotte repeated, closing her eyes. "Older. Sixty-two."

"Well..." Piper said, knowing Charlotte was upset. "I'm

sorry for your loss."

"How did Gideon know you were there? You told me he didn't know about the New York residence. Only New Orleans," Jules said, looking at them.

"He's very good at tracking me," Leona said, finally pulling away from Sebastian. She started to pace, her fingers fiddling with themselves. "It's partly our bond, partly his power. Tracking is one of his enhanced abilities. His sense of smell is stronger than mine."

"Lovely," Sebastian muttered. "Can he turn invisible too? Shoot lasers from his eyes?"

"Not funny," Leona said flatly. "It's only a matter of time before he comes here. We need to leave."

"Leave?" Lucinda scoffed, shaking her head. "You're not going anywhere."

"We can't put you in that sort of danger," Leona pressed.

"That's not up to you. We protect our own. If he wants a fight, he'll get it. But you aren't going to do it alone. You came here to train. So let's train."

Sebastian smiled slightly. *Finally*, someone who fucking wanted to contribute as much as he did. Someone who wasn't *scared* of this menace. Or at least… scared as much as everyone else.

"We shouldn't waste time," Sebastian said, his voice strong. "I could have other abilities, too. We need to see if we can find them. He could be here tomorrow for all we know."

"Sebastian's right," Charlotte finally said, standing. She clenched her jaw together and looked at Leona. "We are your family now. And families protect each other."

Leona looked around, all of her closest people nodding. She felt a balloon grow in her throat and with great effort, she swallowed it back down. She had always had Whitney and Piper in her corner, but seeing everyone rallying for her, for a mess that wasn't even hers to clean...

It meant the world to her.

And for the first time in centuries, the fear that had consumed her was fading.

"Alright," she said, a slow smile spreading across her lips. "Let's get to work."

# 16

It had been a week since the news article and Gideon had not shown up.

The coven had been working tirelessly to train, only stopping to feed. They had all agreed not to hunt out in the open to keep their scents in the house. Only Jules and Lucinda were allowed out of the house, and even then, it was limited. They replenished their supply of blood from various hospitals within the country, willing donors, and animals. Lucinda was in charge of hunting for Theodore. It took a lot to feed eight vampires and a werewolf and not make anyone suspicious.

During their training, no new abilities had been revealed to anybody, but they were all getting better with their fighting patterns. Sebastian had gotten to the point where he could beat everybody in full combat except Theodore, but even then, the werewolf had to shift to overpower Sebastian. It was good practice for all of them, purely because they didn't know what Gideon would have under his sleeve. Whitney had assured them that Damien wouldn't fight against them with the vampire, but they had to operate on the side of caution. Anything went now.

"Let's go again," Sebastian said as he stood up, the claw marks on his chest closing up rapidly. He had blood on his clothing, but he didn't care.

Theodore, who was now a large wolf with light brown fur and golden eyes, bared his teeth and growled.

*I'll kick your ass all day.*

Sebastian smirked as he heard the thoughts from the dog, then lunged for him. Theodore mirrored him and snarled as he pounced on Sebastian, chomping at whatever he could reach. Sebastian struggled and tried a new strategy. Prying him or punching him off hadn't worked the last five times they'd sparred, so he would have to resort to his other ability. Sebastian dug his hands into Theodore's fur, his fingertips finally meeting velvet skin. He grunted as Theodore bit into his shoulder, and the pain was enough to spark his hands to life. Volts went through the werewolf, his fur sticking out with the electricity. Theodore yelped and immediately fell off Sebastian, seizing slightly.

Whitney rushed over and knelt beside Theodore as he turned back into his human form. "You okay?" she asked softly.

"Yeah," Theodore sighed, wincing as he sat up. "I'd say that was cheating but… cheating may be the only way to win."

Sebastian sighed and shook his hands out to rid the buzzing feeling in his palms and wrists. "I don't think that was full power," he said, looking at Jules. "I was able to control it enough to not kill him."

"As much as I want to let you test these abilities, I don't want any of us to be on the receiving end of your full power with that lightning," Jules responded. "Try full power on that dummy there."

Sebastian looked to where she nodded, one of the training dummies propped up on a wheeled pole on the ground. Walking closer to it, about a yard away, the vampire focused. He thought about how angry he'd been at the world when he was turned, how angry he was at all the heartache and pain Gideon had put Leona through…

A bright light exploded from Sebastian's hands and shot into the dummy, catapulting it back against the wall. Black smoke billowed from the now charred heap of ash on the floor. There were still small currents glowing through the rubble and Sebastian's body. He shook his hands out again, wondering if he'd ever get used to that.

"Hell yeah," Victor laughed, going to give him a high-five. When their palms slapped together, a pop sounded, making Victor wince and yank his arm back. "Ouch."

"Sorry," Sebastian said sheepishly.

"It's alright," Victor said. "If that doesn't kill him, it'll stun him enough where we can rip that fucker to shreds. Right?" he asked, turning to look at Jules.

The woman nodded. "It gives us a fighting chance. One we haven't had before."

Victor smiled and looked over at his best friend, then frowned. "Whoa…"

"What?" Sebastian asked, his face falling. "What?!"

"Your eyes…"

Sebastian blinked at those two words. "What about them?"

"They're… not red. Kind of," Victor said, leaning closer to him. "They're sort of flickering. The irises."

Lucinda and Jules approached him, the rest of the group not far behind. Lucinda took Sebastian's chin in her hand and examined his eyes, which were fading from the lively description Victor had given back to their usual crimson hue. She hummed in thought, then looked down at his hands. "Use it again," she said, pointing to his wrists. "On anything."

"Alright…" Sebastian said slowly, holding his hand out to the ash in front of him. He zapped it again, the dust exploding around them.

Lucinda took hold of him again, waving the air clear with her free hand. Sebastian's eyes were glowing red, pulsating and flickering with bright orange hues. She smiled slightly. "Asombroso…" she whispered in a bewildered tone.

"What?" Sebastian asked again.

"Read my mind," Lucinda said, letting go of him, but staying close.

Sebastian frowned, wishing someone could give him answers. He focused on Lucinda.

*Do they change with every ability? I have never seen this before…*

"Do what change?" Sebastian asked. "My eyes?"

"Yes," she answered. "When you use your electromagnetism, your eyes glow, as if there is a storm inside," she explained. "And when you read minds, they stay the same. I've never seen…"

"Why does he have red eyes in the first place?" Leona asked, stepping forward. "They were brown as a human. Gideon is the only immortal I have known with red eyes. All of ours stayed the same after the transformation."

"Bodies change with the venom. It affects everyone differently," Jules commented. "You think my eyes were purple as a human? I woke up this way. Lucinda's hair changed with her transformation," she said, nodding to her partner. "None of you changed physically?"

"I got taller," Victor said. "A bit. I had a tattoo that disappeared as well."

"Me, too," Charlotte agreed. "My eyes get brighter when I feed. Duller when I'm hungry. I've noticed that."

"We should still do more research," Leona said. "We need to learn more about Sebastian's heritage, too."

Jules nodded. "I have many texts, but… I can contact some friends. Get more. Soon."

17

Jules had left the house and went traveling to find her mystery friends she'd mentioned, leaving the coven, Lucinda, and Theodore at the safe house.

Sebastian stayed up all day and night reading every book he could find in their house about their kind, about history, about the past. Surely there had to be *something* hidden away somewhere that would start giving them some answers. He hoped Jules made it back in one piece, both with explanations and before Gideon found them. As time ticked on, he wondered if they really could stay hidden forever. But given Gideon's history, Sebastian had every reason to believe their time would run out eventually.

Staying in one place forever was no life for anyone, let alone an immortal.

"When's the last time you fed?"

Sebastian looked up to find Leona in the doorway, holding a mug of what he smelled to be blood. He relaxed and gave her a small smile. "Thank you," he murmured, taking the mug from her when she walked over to him. Gratefully, he downed the entire mug. "What was that one? I liked it."

Leona's eyebrows raised. "AB-negative mixed with A-positive. You're a mixed drink man, I see," she laughed, perching down on the arm of the chair he was in. She placed her hand on his cheek and sighed. "What have I done to deserve you, my love?"

Sebastian leaned his head into her touch and brought his hand up to envelop her fingers. "You deserve everything you want in the world. And if that's *me*, then… I'm the one who's undeserving," he said quietly.

"I'm scared, Seb," she said, her voice small and wavering. "I thought I wasn't, but… I am. Every answer we get raises three more questions."

"I know," he said, setting the empty mug down on the table next to him. His book joined the crockery, then he pulled her sideways into his lap. "I told you I won't let him touch you again."

"You and I both know he's too strong," Leona whispered. "He's never going to give up until I'm with him again. He'll kill you. I'll *die* before I become his slave again."

As Sebastian cradled her, he considered what she was saying. It wasn't anything that hadn't crossed his mind a million times, and yet… he stayed. He knew dying at the hands of Gideon was an extremely likely possibility when he was a human and traveled across the world to save her. He *had* died at the hands of that psychopath. But he was resurrected and was still willing to die again. Charlotte had been right:

they were *family*. There would be no second thoughts when it came to jumping in front of whatever fatal force hurtled their way.

"If we die then we die," Sebastian said simply, causing Leona to look up at him. "We don't know when we'll die. Gideon could come through that door *right now* and rip us apart before we even had time to get up. He may be here tomorrow and we might lose. All that matters is right now. If eight months ago up until this second is all the time I get with you, it was already better than the other three decades I was a human. I've never felt anything remotely comparable to what we have. It's chemical. I was *meant* for this. It feels like destiny," he said, searching her eyes. "This whole… song and dance. Meeting you, warring with Gideon, becoming a vampire, and now training for the end. It feels poetic, in a way. I can't explain it. It's here," he said, bringing his hand to his chest. "Like it was always going to end this way."

Leona sat up in his lap and laid her hands on either side of his neck, her thumbs gently trailing along his jawline. "I've loved you for three hundred years, Sebastian Beliveau. I just didn't know it until we met in *this* life. But everything I've been through led me to that party in New Orleans, to a brooding, grumpy man that didn't like the drinks the bartenders made," she laughed emotionally, tears pooling in her eyes. "And I'll love you until Death rips us from each other's arms."

"Death can try," Sebastian scoffed, shaking his head. "Death will take one look at us and weep at the thought of separating us."

Tears finally spilled from Leona's eyes and she coughed

out a cry, before leaning forward to kiss him with everything she had in her. Her fingers tangled in his hair to pull him closer, closer, closer. Sebastian's hands roamed up her back, caressing her in a way that made her bones yearn for him.

They remained that way for a while, kissing, their tears mixing together, the only sounds in the room being their unified moaning and the hissing of clothes rustling against each other. Eventually, their kiss grew more insistent, and touches over clothes weren't enough.

Sebastian closed his eyes as Leona rested against his chest, their clothes disheveled but at least back in place to cover their lower halves. He absently stroked her back and played with the ends of her hair.

"I love you," he murmured. "I love you forever."

"I love you, too," Leona purred, nuzzling into his neck. She pressed a few kisses there, then bit down, eliciting a small grunt of pleasure from Sebastian. Blood stained her lips when she pulled away from the deep kiss, and Sebastian helped her lick them clean. The puncture wounds on his neck disappeared, and Sebastian returned the favor on his lover's jugular.

Though he had never fed on a human, doing this with Leona felt natural. It brought them closer. He could feel her emotions and she his.

"Do you think if I had been alive in your time, you would have wanted me?" Sebastian asked, pulling back from his bite.

Leona smiled and swiped her thumb along his lower lip, then licked the crimson liquid off. "I think so. I have a thing for tall, dark, and handsome," she giggled.

"Yeah, we know," Sebastian deadpanned, rolling his eyes. "I wouldn't have been able to impress your family with riches or fancy horses. In fact, I'd have probably been some stableboy sold away by my family."

"I *wish* I had a stableboy like you," Leona said, gently trailing her nails down his cheek. "Would've saved me a lot of trouble. Would've saved a lot of people a lot of trouble."

"Your father definitely wouldn't have approved."

"Isn't that the point of a bad boy?" Leona giggled, pecking his lips. "Once upon a time, things like a wardrobe full of frilly dresses and all the jewels I could hope for were the most important things in the world to me. I thought money and fame and power were the keys to a happy life. My father was so obsessed with his children marrying into prominent families. I know he just wanted the best for us, but... why did it *matter*?"

She rested her head against Sebastian's and closed her eyes. "I found out later that not even immortality can provide happiness. I had all the money I wanted. I had the body I wanted. I never had to worry about disease or dying in childbirth. I thought I was condemned to a purgatory of damnation all these years. Until I met you," she said, kissing his lips again. "You brought me back to life."

It was Sebastian's turn to grow emotional. He kissed her again, and again, and again. A faint preview of what was to come.

"Do vampires get married?" Sebastian asked after an age of kissing.

Leona opened her eyes to meet his, then she gave a cheeky smile, her head tilted slightly. "My, my, Mr. Beliveau… Are you asking for my hand?" she teased, pressing her hand against her chest.

"I'm serious," Sebastian laughed, moving his leg to nudge underneath her. "Jules and Lucinda aren't married… are they?"

"They are. I'm pretty sure," Leona shrugged, leaning back in his embrace, her arms now draped over his shoulders. "I guess you… *can* get married. The normal human way. There isn't some special vampire ceremony or anything. It's more primal than that. But we live forever so it's not like you *need* it."

Sebastian stayed quiet, willing her to continue.

"I just mean it's more instinctual. Kind of like how animals choose a mate. It's like that. There are many sires and fledglings that live long and happy lives together, all because of that bond. But you don't have to have that bond to be *bonded*. Does that make sense?"

Sebastian nodded slowly. "Are we mates?"

Leona smiled. "I definitely chose you. And I'm *fairly* certain you chose me. So yes. These feelings we share don't happen all the time. I've been with hundreds of men and it's never felt like this. Women, either."

"But my dick's the biggest, right?"

"You are a *pig*," Leona groaned, shoving at his chest. She stood up and adjusted her clothing, then ran her hands through her hair. "Why did you ask me about marriage?"

Sebastian stayed sitting in the chair, looking up at her. "I have never considered marriage. There has never been anyone in my life even remotely close to triggering those thoughts. Commitment has never come easy for me, except when dealing with Victor and Charlie. I… guess I never wanted to end up like my parents. They *had* to have liked each other at some point. Even just a little bit. It couldn't have been all bad all the time."

"Some people just aren't meant to be together," Leona said gently.

"I guess," Sebastian said with a weak shrug. "I never wanted to end up like Dad. It was hard for me to grow close to anyone because I was scared," he admitted. "What if there's something in my genes that I got from him that makes me want to hurt people someday? I *know* my mother wouldn't have fallen in love with him if she had known what he was capable of. And I can't imagine anything that poor, sweet woman would have done to him to make him like that. So why did the switch flip? What changed in him that made him a monster?"

"You are not like him, Sebastian," Leona said, moving down to her knees in front of him. She grasped his hands and squeezed, then pressed a few kisses to his fingertips. "You're not."

"You don't know that."

"I *do*. You're the kind of man that, when faced with *literal* vampires, was more worried about the fact that we were going to hurt your best friends rather than us potentially eating you.

You're the kind of man who opened your mind and heart to a three-hundred-year-old vampire with a crazy ex-boyfriend. *You* are the man who stood between me and Gideon multiple times to protect me. You are the man who planned an elaborate ball in my honor just to make me smile again. You really think a bad person could do all that?"

Sebastian sighed gently and cut his eyes down. "What if I *was* asking for your hand, Leona? What if it was the seventeen-hundreds and I was a stableboy who fell in love with the princess of the castle? What if I asked you to run away with me? What would you do?"

Leona smiled tearfully and made him look up at her. He could see it all in those beautiful sage eyes of hers. "I would wrap my arms around you," she said, her hands sliding from his face to his neck, "and I would tell you you don't even have to ask me. I'm yours."

She pulled him to her and crushed their lips together. Sebastian snaked his arms around her and stood up, taking her off the ground with him. They span around, their laughter melding into sweet kisses with the promise of eternity.

# 18

Jules walked through the front door of her home, shaking her hair from the light drizzle that had started outside. Lucinda was the first one to launch out of her chair, wrapping herself in her partner's arms in a matter of seconds. The other vampires were gathered around, sitting in chairs and sofas.

"I was worried," Lucinda whispered into her hair, squeezing her tight. It had been about a month since Jules went off on her journey for answers, and though they were all thankful Gideon hadn't shown up, they had all been concerned about the radio silence from Jules.

"I'm alright. Just took some digging is all," Jules reassured, shedding her coat. "I'm glad to see everyone is still in one piece and the house is standing. I take it we didn't have any unwanted visitors?"

"No," Theodore said from the corner of the room. He was leaning up against the wall, his arms folded. He tended to keep to himself among the group. There wasn't *much* love lost between him and these vampires.

"Good," Jules said. "I need to feed first and then I'll debrief everyone."

Lucinda followed Jules into the kitchen, and the room was quiet again. Sebastian felt nervous. What if she hadn't found anything useful? Did she know the true history of his lineage? He had read every book in the house and hadn't found out much more than they already knew. They had some interesting texts in their library. There were so many things that went into the lore of vampires he hadn't realized. There were dozens of translations from varying areas of the world detailing legends about creatures of the night and humans with the properties of leeches. It fascinated him to no end to see all the different variations of what most humans believed to be a mythical beast.

He had been one of those humans. He felt so naive, even now.

"How do you survive in that head of yours? You're stressing *me* out," Charlotte laughed as she looked across at Sebastian. She was sitting on one of the small sofas, Victor at her side, their hands laced together. Sebastian and Leona mirrored them across the coffee table.

"Don't you think it's rude to listen in on other people's thoughts without permission?" Sebastian asked pointedly, a frown etched on his face.

"Crybaby," Charlotte teased. "You know worrying about things won't make a difference. Whatever's gonna happen is gonna happen. No use making yourself miserable before—"

"Before it even happens, yeah, I know," Sebastian interrupted, waving a hand dismissively. She'd been telling him that for years and it never helped. He couldn't help it.

"It's alright," Leona murmured, squeezing his hand. "Whatever it is, we'll fight our way through it together."

Sebastian relaxed marginally at her soothing words. There wasn't anything anyone could say that would make him feel less on edge. Unless Jules walked back in and gave them some sort of holy grail and guide to kill Gideon with. That would be helpful.

Jules walked back in with Lucinda and stood near everyone else, looking around at them. "Alright… Here's what I know. Xavier was apparently involved in multiple supernatural communities during his time. Not just vampires. Though he was human, there are records and past accounts of him interacting with witches."

"Witches exist too?" Sebastian asked. Only he, Charlotte, and Victor seemed to be surprised. What else didn't they know about the world?

"They do," Jules continued. "They blend in pretty well with the rest of the world, considering they can be out in the sunlight and eat food. And it seems spell-casting, voodoo, tarot cards, spirituality… whatever you want to call it, is growing in popularity among the mortals. They see it as a trend, but it gives the witches a chance to stop hiding."

He wondered how many real witches he'd passed on his countless treks throughout the French Quarter. He had never bought into anything like that and always lumped it in with religion. He felt *ignorant*.

"There are different kinds of witches. Some can cast minor spells, some are unassuming and can't do much more than turn a light off without getting up, some create potions and distribute them among other supernatural beings, and some... deal with more nefarious ideas. Blood magic."

Momentarily, Sebastian did a quick survey of the room with just his eyes. Everyone seemed to be entranced by what she was saying and not questioning it at all. Their thoughts were jumbled in his head. He couldn't decipher them *and* listen to Jules at the same time. It was all just so unbelievable, which he felt silly for thinking, given what he was now.

"What is blood magic?" Charlotte asked. "Like... a curse? Necromancy?"

"Not exactly," Jules answered. "Blood magic comes in many forms. It can be used as a bonding mechanism, tying two people together forever. It can also be used as a curse, a sort of... protection, for the person who casts the spell or requests the spell."

"I'm guessing Xavier went for the latter?" Sebastian said.

"Correct," Jules nodded.

"How is it a curse if it protected him?" Leona asked.

"I'm getting there. I spoke with the daughter of the witch who worked with him. Witches are not immortal like us, but they do have extended lifespans beyond a regular human. This witch was still *very* old," Jules said. "She told me Xavier sought her out personally. She believes a vampire told him where she was before he killed them. Xavier asked many questions and was searching for a better way to kill vampires. A poison. A bomb. Anything. When she couldn't provide that, he threatened to kill her."

Sebastian squeezed Leona's hand. Not that he thought Xavier was a saint, and perhaps he should have expected this, given he slayed vampires, but he hadn't expected him to be an outright killer.

"She offered him a curse against vampires. One that would doom any immortal who aimed to harm him or his loved ones. He accepted and they started the ritual," Jules said. "Using his blood, she put a shielding hex on him. Xavier misunderstood the spell. He thought it was an all-encompassing protection spell. That he couldn't be killed by vampires. That was not the case."

"No it wasn't," Leona muttered under her breath.

"This misunderstanding made Xavier arrogant. He was negligent and stopped being cautious with his hunting."

"Probably why it was so easy to find him," Leona said. "He didn't even act scared."

"Exactly. But as we all know, his hubris was part of his downfall. Though the blood magic did not make Xavier impervious to mortal wounds caused by vampires or otherwise, it *would* curse whomever did eventually kill him. Blood curses are vengeful. They activate and don't usually disappear until a debt has been repaid," Jules continued. "In this case, the debt being Xavier's death. The curse will not break until the favor has been returned."

"My head hurts," Victor mumbled, putting a hand up to his temple.

"So..." Sebastian started, "Because Gideon murdered Xavier, he triggered the blood spell and is now... cursed?"

"Yes. He bound himself to Xavier the moment he spilled his blood, unknowingly. That's why you have red eyes and we don't," she said. "You are connected to Gideon through Xavier's ancestry. *You* are Gideon's curse. Your blood line, at least."

Sebastian blinked and let those last words sink in. Everything inside his body felt like it had been ignited.

This *was* his destiny. Leona was. All of it. He was born for this.

"What happens if he kills me?" Sebastian asked. He supposed Gideon already had killed him, if they were being technical, but… he made it out still.

"Then the curse will remain, just like it did for Xavier. Then… should another person of your descent come along, the duty will fall to them."

"The duty?"

Jules nodded, understanding the confusion. "The duty of breaking the curse. Of killing Gideon. It must be done by the one whose blood started the curse — that being Xavier. As I said, he died, and you are merely next in line in the succession to carry out the sentence. You carry his blood in your veins, no matter how diluted."

"But my parents…" Sebastian trailed off, his mind whirring. His parents certainly had no connections to anything other than the liquor store and the hospital. Surely they couldn't have been destined to kill some ancient vampire to fulfill a prophecy from centuries ago?

"The way blood curses were explained to me is… the aura of the hex will always lie dormant in those cells. Until it's fulfilled and broken, it'll keep passing along to the next person of descent after the affected die. Xavier was the one originally affected, then he died. I assume it passed along to one of his descendants, and again, and again until it got to you. Just because none of your family triggered the curse doesn't mean they *couldn't* have. Had Leona bumped into one of your ancestors a hundred years ago and they both caught the attention of Gideon, then perhaps that person would have been the one to break the curse. But that's not what happened. Leona chose *you*," Jules said, holding eye contact with Sebastian. "If you die, then it could be another three hundred years before a curse breaker is revealed. When you became immortal, the hex within your cells activated and made the link known. As I said, the spell originally meant to protect the bloodline from all those who threaten it. To doom them. Gideon is a direct threat to your bloodline.

"But why *me*?" Sebastian asked, feeling overwhelmed. "I know I'm connected to Leona, but... surely someone else somewhere in history could have had that connection? Other members of my family died and were nowhere near Gideon, I'm sure they weren't some vampire slayer in disguise."

"He killed you, technically, just as he killed Xavier," Jules explained, "I can only assume that it what ultimately triggered the curse within your veins, along with your transition to immortality. The fact that *Gideon* was the one to stop your mortal life. If you had died from natural causes with no connection to this life, I can only presume the curse would have remained just as it has for all your other ancestors who died and didn't trigger it."

"So basically… it's Gideon's fault that I'm the one destined to kill him? Because he killed Xavier and then… killed me? At least, human me?" Sebastian asked.

"That is how I understand it, yes," Jules nodded.

Sebastian was drowning in the irony. It truly was poetic for Gideon, and a fitting end.

"What happens after the curse is broken?" Piper asked, folding her arms. "Let's say Sebastian somehow kills Gideon. What then? Is it just… over? No more?"

"No more," Jules agreed. "Like I said, it's a long-form protection spell. Intent to protect the *bloodline*, not the individual. It aims to preserve lineage. That's why blood is needed. It works with the properties of the cells. Not the entire entity or body."

"What if someone else kills Gideon?" Leona asked. "Will the curse still remain?"

"I do not know," she said. "But we have to consider that there is a reason nobody has been able to slay him thus far. It must be the curse at work. I believe that it is impossible for someone else to kill him, that Gideon's demise is destined to be brought on by Sebastian only. By Xavier. You're still connected to all of that. You brought Gideon to Xavier," Jules said to Leona. "Now you're bringing Sebastian to Gideon. It's all meant to happen. Sebastian was always going to die and resurrect. It's his fate. This is why nobody has been able to kill Gideon all this time, why Xavier was the only one who came close. Someone, say Leona, can kill Gideon with her own hands, but that doesn't mean Sebastian didn't lead her into that situation and cause it."

"So," Sebastian said, trying to wrap his mind around this confusing revelation, "because Leona found me, and I'm the reason she was stolen and brought back to Gideon's castle this last time, and why he's hunting us now, even if she kills him — or someone else other than me kills him — it would still break the curse because ultimately it's *my* fault he is running around acting crazy?"

"More or less," Jules said with a nod. "You're the reason you're all here. You came here to train. You protect Leona. You are a direct threat to Gideon's power over her. Therefore whatever happens next has to do with you to some degree. Leona — or any of us — have never had the chance to kill him until you showed up. That ultimately fulfills the curse's terms in that a member of Xavier's bloodline must be responsible for the death, no matter who physically delivers the final blow."

"There is one *slight* snag in this plan," Victor said, shaking his head. "We don't know how to kill the fucker."

"None of us are truly immortal. Gideon dies the same way any of us do. It's just harder to make him so vulnerable," Jules said.

"It's *impossible* to make him vulnerable," Charlotte corrected, her eyes wide. "We all almost died trying, and I'm pretty sure he was only *playing* with us then."

"You do not have to tell me how powerful he is," Jules said firmly. "He has killed many vampires I care about."

A short silence settled in the room at that confession. Sebastian regarded the Spanish woman thoughtfully. Leona hadn't been the only one scarred by Gideon's eternal rampage.

"Can we make weapons?" Sebastian then asked. "Isn't

holy water harmful to y'all? To… *us*," he corrected.

"It is. Not fatally, but it's enough to distract someone," Leona said, thinking about that damned glass of water Xavier had when she approached him.

"Well, we can't just get a spray bottle and treat him like a cat on the counter," Charlotte huffed, throwing her hands up. "What do you suggest? A water gun? A hose?"

Sebastian understood her exasperation, but it still annoyed him. "We're just throwing out ideas, Charlie," he snapped.

"Why don't you tap into that inner vampire slayer and come up with something then?" Charlotte snapped back. All this talk of Gideon and blood curses and impending dooms put everyone on edge. Sebastian couldn't blame her or anyone else.

"What are your — *our* — other weaknesses?" Sebastian asked. "Sunlight," he started, counting on his fingers. "Holy water. Stake to the heart. Being burned. What else?"

"We can be drained," Leona said, folding her arms. When everyone looked at her, she shrugged, her body tense. "Similar to blood loss in a human. We lose all our blood, sometimes there's no coming back from that. We just usually heal too quickly from a wound for that to be the case. But if you were weakened, starving, or otherwise affected by sunlight, holy water… The wounds would be very slow to heal and bleeding out is more likely."

"I have read about some poisons affecting our abilities," Lucinda said. "Drinking from a person with AIDS, for example. With cancer. I am sure the potioneering witches could come up with something as well."

"Okay…" Sebastian said slowly, the cogs in his mind turning. "How fast do you regrow limbs?"

They all looked at each other, waiting for someone to answer.

"It takes a while," Theodore finally said from the other side of the room. "I've ripped apart plenty of nightwalkers in fights for my life. None of them died, but I have encountered a couple on multiple occasions. Each years apart. They looked good as new the next time I saw them."

"Alright, so not instantly," Sebastian said. "Ripping Gideon's limbs off would be ideal. Can't fight us if he's just a torso and head on the ground." Everyone nodded and hummed in agreement. "What about taking off his head?"

"That will also kill us," Jules agreed. "Though, not an easy feat. Most of the time, it's very difficult to get a good enough edge over any vampire to rip their entire head off."

"I doubt we'll be able to get our arms around him to even get *close* to doing that," Charlotte sighed, shaking her head. "This feels hopeless."

"It's not hopeless," Sebastian said with a frown. "We'll use everything in our arsenal."

"Well, we can't just invite him out into the sunlight to fight. None of us, other than Theodore, would even survive," Charlotte responded.

"They sell UV light bulbs," Sebastian countered. "Maybe we could get a powerful flashlight and shine it on him? I know it might not *kill* him, but it should stun him. Weaken him at the very least."

"That could work," Leona agreed. "Where do we get

these lights?"

"Pet stores. Online," Sebastian shrugged. "They aren't hard to find. And they make flashlights that can blind people because they're so bright. We can get some and try it."

"Who's gonna volunteer for *that* job?" Piper scoffed, shaking her head. "I want to kill Gideon as much as anyone else, but I don't want to get blasted in the face with the sun just for the sake of an experiment."

"I'll do it," Sebastian said tightly. "If we all work together and… make a *real* plan, I think we have a shot. And we have another weapon we didn't have last time," he said, turning to look at Theodore. "You will fight with us?"

Theodore's eyes moved to Whitney, his throat tight. If Damien chose to fight by Gideon's side… Would he choose to fight them back? Would Whitney? *Could* they?

"I will fight Gideon," Theodore finally answered.

Sebastian nodded and looked at Jules, then to every other vampire in the room. They were a strong group, and Gideon was just *one* immortal. They had a *chance*. Leona could finally be unchained and rest with both eyes closed during the day. She could travel without worries. She could *love* freely.

They didn't have another choice but to win.

Later that night, Sebastian flipped through pages of one of the books Jules had brought with her from her travels. He was trying to make sense of this whole curse thing, but it was making his head spin.

It was almost overwhelming. No, it was *really* overwhelming.

"Hey, you," Leona said as she walked into the library. "I was wondering where you were."

"Sorry," Sebastian said, closing the book. "I was hiding from everyone else. Not that I don't love talking about blood and immortality and how to kill your ex-boyfriend, I just…"

"Needed some time to yourself?"

Sebastian sighed and nodded. He was so glad she understood him. "Are you okay? What did you need?"

"Just you. I'm fine, sweet man," Leona smiled, coming to sit sideways on his lap. Her favorite position. Looping her arms around his neck, she pecked a gentle kiss to his cheek. "What are you thinking about? Aside from the obvious."

Sebastian rubbed her sides gently as he held her, his book forgotten. "I was thinking about Xavier. Wondering where he is exactly in my family tree. Jules gave me some familial texts that explain lineages, but… most of it is in French. Like, *old* French. It's hard to make out."

"Let me see," Leona said, picking up the book he'd been reading. Sebastian guided her with his finger along the page to the parts that interested him. "Hmm… père means father, so… let's follow this," she murmured, tracing her finger along the faded words scattered around a lined chart. "Here's Xavier, there's his father's name." She pointed. "There are no marriage records here for Xavier. What else did Jules give you?"

"This one," he said, jerking his chin to another book on the desk in front of him. "It's more of a Louisiana history. I found one with almost the same surname. Bellevau. But if there are no marriage records…"

"That doesn't mean the woman who mothered his child didn't take his name. There *could* have been a marriage, it just wasn't documented or lost. Or perhaps we haven't obtained the documentation yet," Leona explained. "Show me."

Sebastian kept one arm around her as he leaned forward and slid the book from the desk and into their laps. He flipped to a page he'd earmarked for later. "Here," he said. "That's the same, right? Again, it's in French. I know a little more of this because it's Creole-French, but… still. I'm rusty from my whole *two years* of it in *middle school*."

"I can help," Leona chuckled, shaking her head. "Yes, Maria Bellevue," she continued, tapping the name on the page. "Medical record from Natchitoches in… this number looks like eighteen-ninety-three."

"But… that's more than a hundred years after you — or Gideon — killed Xavier."

"It was the seventeen-hundreds, Seb. Record-keeping was sparse among anyone but royalty. There were many expeditions at the time. The logical answer is that Xavier wed, or at least impregnated a woman from his time and she sailed with a crew to the New World. She probably went to Fort Maurepas."

"Fort Maurepas is in Mississippi," Sebastian said, "or… it was."

"It wasn't Mississippi then. It's not far from New Orleans. Or any of the old settlements in what Louisiana was back then. French explorations were very common at the time. Europe was *very* interested in the South and what expeditions were uncovering. Given the strife in France at the time, it's no wonder townspeople wanted to start fresh."

"So what about this Maria person? What are these records?"

"She was giving birth. A boy, according to this," Leona said, looking down at the page again. "Same surname, so... I want to guess that she is a direct descendant of Xavier's wife. Or... whatever."

"Okay, so that's a little over a hundred years ago. Does it say what the baby's name is?"

"Hmm..." Leona hummed, her eyes quickly scanning the page. "I can't see, but look here," she said, pointing down at another name on the list. "This one is Beliveau. Looks like... Henry Beliveau. Born in... eighteen-ninety-three!"

"That must be Maria's kid," Sebastian exclaimed, blinking a few times. "I don't know how I missed that."

"You've been reading nonstop for hours... days, really. It's alright," Leona reassured.

"Wait," Sebastian muttered, closing his eyes.

"What is it?"

"Henry... I think that's my grandpa's name."

"Seriously?"

"Yeah. We weren't close or anything. He died before I ever really got to know him and my parents never spoke much about him. I don't think he was a very nice dude," Sebastian said. "I should have asked more..."

"It's alright. So... Henry, then... your father. What was his name?"

"Tobias."

"Alright, is there a more recent book of Louisiana family histories you have? This one only goes up to the nineteen-hundreds."

"Um… yeah," Sebastian said, pointing to one stacked on the far side of the desk. Leona was up to grab it and back on his lap in an instant. She cracked it open and began flipping through, before Sebastian's hand shot out to stop her. "There. Look."

"Tobias Beliveau, right there. Married to Eileen…"

Sebastian's throat tightened and he blinked back some threatening drops of remorse. He gathered himself. "Yeah, that's Mom. And… look," he said, pointing to his name.

"I didn't know your middle name was Tobias," Leona mused, glancing at him.

"It's not a name I like to associate with," Sebastian muttered. Leona dropped the subject. He continued. "So Xavier is… one, two…" he mumbled, counting on his fingers. "We don't know for sure, but… maybe my great-great-great grandpa? One more great?"

"Yeah," Leona nodded. "Probably one more. People didn't live very long back then."

"Okay, so great-great-great-great grandpa," Sebastian nodded. "Bet he would've lived longer if he hadn't started fucking around with spooky shit."

"Maybe. He could have died of plague or famine, too. Which way would you prefer?"

"Starving, dying on the side of the street from disease, or getting my heart ripped out of my chest… hmm, this is a tough one," Sebastian muttered, tapping his chin thoughtfully with his finger. "Considering I *have* been starving before… *and* I've had Gideon's lovely talons through my chest, I think I'm going to have to go plague. Final answer."

Leona laughed softly and shook her head. "Do you feel any better now that you've gotten some answers?"

"Sort of," Sebastian shrugged. "How on earth did a *human* come so close to killing Gideon? I know he had the hexes and curses, but…"

"Unfortunately, they weren't enough. We would have saved ourselves a *lot* of trouble had they worked."

Sebastian snorted. "Yeah. What *did* happen between him and Gideon? The first time."

Leona exhaled in thought and rested her head on Sebastian's shoulder. "He only told me the stories afterward. Obviously, beforehand I didn't really *know*. I had no clue what Xavier was capable of."

"Can you show me what Gideon told you?" Sebastian asked. "With your mind thing. By the way, when do I get to do that?"

Leona laughed softly. "Practice makes perfect, my sweet. Look at me," she said, sitting up. Gently, she pressed her hand against his cheek and his eyes glazed over once more.

*Gideon stalked through the streets of Coventry. It had just rained and he could smell the water lingering in the air and animals nearby scurrying behind bushes or into sewers. It was the early 18th century and he was taking a break from courting his delicious*

*new bird to track down a meddlesome human who had murdered one of his friends.*

*Pierre, a French vampire whom Gideon had known for about a century, was nothing more than a pile of ash now. There had been whispers of a vampire slayer lurking around England, trying to eradicate their kind one by one. Gideon had never laid eyes on this supposed killer, but given Pierre was nearly as old as he was, he was on edge. This needed to be taken care of.*

*Damien had come with him for backup and was helping him track. They hadn't been able to catch his scent from Pierre's crime scene, but Gideon assumed he had to have some weapons on him: stakes, holy water, maybe even some matches to help with the flames. Gideon had tracked down more menacing creatures with less, he wasn't overly concerned about finding this piece of dirt.*

*Gideon was in a long, black coat and his usual dark suit. His dress boots clicked against the wet, cobblestoned pavement, his hands stuffed in his overcoat pockets. His collar was popped up and some of his hair curled around his temple and ears with the dampness soaking the air around him. He was focused on the dark road in front of him as he walked, but his pointed ears were tuned in to everything happening around him.*

*He could barely make out Damien's scent, but he hoped he was just scouring the area and had made a big perimeter. Not that he was worried about him taking care of himself, but it would be one less thing for him to think about. Damien had almost killed him once upon a time — or rather, they had nearly killed each other — so surely this human wouldn't come close to harming either one of them.*

*Gideon continued prowling the streets until an unfamiliar*

scent caught in his nostrils. He stopped and inhaled deeply, looking around. His pupils dilated. It wasn't Damien, but it wasn't a regular human either. He could smell the remnants of magic lurking nearby. A witch, perhaps?

Cautiously, Gideon followed the scent, his senses on high alert. It was nearly pitch black outside, but that gave him an edge.

He rounded a corner and spotted some specks of liquid on the ground. It was not water. Closing in on the observation, he kneeled and ran his finger over the mystery fluid. Gideon rubbed it between his fingers and crimson spread across the skin. He smelled it, then rose to his full, intimidating height.

Blood.

Suddenly, his entire body was wracked with warning bells.

This was a trap.

Gideon barely managed to sidestep a fatal attack with a spear, the wooden weapon grazing his side. He groaned in pain and looked down at his skin, which was burned, bloody, and bubbling. The faint scent of holy water whiffed by him and his eyes followed the spear that had now clattered against the wall of one of the buildings surrounding him and down onto the stone ground.

A noise registered in his head before he looked away from the weapon, and the hiss of clothing nearby alerted him to his perpetrator's presence. Moving quicker than light, he was in front of the suspect: a man with long, black hair in dark clothing with all sorts of weapons and other artifacts strapped to him and in the bag slung around him. Gideon bared his fangs with a growl and grabbed the man by the throat, lifting him. "You die tonight, human."

"Only one will die tonight," the man said as menacingly as he could with Gideon's vice around his neck. As Gideon moved in to drain his blood, the man smashed a bottle of amber liquid against the vampire's head, causing Gideon to immediately drop him.

Gideon cowered and brought his hands up to his face and neck, and any other part of his exposed skin that had been doused with… What was this?

"What's happening?" Gideon barked in a strangled voice. This was not holy water.

"You're dying," the man said.

"What have you put on me, flea?"

"Essence of sunstone," the man said, pulling out another stake. "You can't move. You can't do anything. You're immobilized."

"Who are you?" Gideon asked, looking up at him. His face was marred red and sizzling, smoke seeping out of his pores. He was nearly unrecognizable.

"Death," the man purred. He drove a stake down into Gideon's shoulder, but it didn't quite reach his heart. While he pulled out another one to finish the job, a roar that could have shaken the earth sounded behind him. Before he could turn to see what monster had come for them, the man was tackled to the ground by a giant, hairy beast.

Gideon grunted in pain and pulled the stake from his shoulder, then limped up to a standing position. He looked over and expected Damien to have ripped the human to shreds, but when he heard whimpering, he snapped his head over. His vision was blurred from the attack, but it looked like the man had managed to put silver on Damien's body. He could hear the familiar sizzling sound of the metal burning the fur and skin.

"Get him!" Gideon barked. He was too weak to move. Damien

shifted back to his human form and shoved the silver chains off him, his skin welted with burns. The human man took the chance and hobbled away from them, leaving a trail of blood as he went. Damien must have gotten one good bite in.

"Help me," Gideon groaned. Damien, compelled to do so, worked through the stinging pain of his wounds and went to support his friend to get them home.

"Who the fuck was that?" Damien breathed, wrapping Gideon's arm around his shoulder so he could hold him up.

"That..." Gideon breathed, shaking his head, his vision still spotty, "was the end."

"The end?" Sebastian questioned as Leona pulled out of his mind. "What did he mean?"

"The end of us. Our kind. He was scared," Leona explained, still on his lap. "I've never heard him sound so frantic than when he spoke about Xavier. He had gone thousands of years with no threat, and all of a sudden, this human comes and puts him on his back. Had Damien not been there, he would have succeeded in killing him. Gideon was so arrogant, he fell right into his trap. It did not happen again. He returned the favor when I came around and distracted Xavier in that pub."

"But..." Sebastian started, frowning. "Why don't we get some of that sunstone shit he had? If that's his weakness."

"It's every vampire's weakness," Leona explained. "We did heavy research on it together before things went bad.

Before he killed Xavier. It is *not* easy to obtain. It takes a lot of mining to even get the sunstone, and you can't find it everywhere. We found some in Norway after scouring the globe for it. I've heard rumors there is some in Sweden. But we can't just *go* there and get it. It is mixed with holy water and liquid silver. I thought we were just learning together, I was young and stupid. I didn't even think about the fact that this human obtained our weakness and that's why Gideon was so crazed."

"How do you know the sunstone works? How did you figure it out?"

Leona tensed and stood from his lap, folding her arms. She sighed and leaned against the desk near Sebastian's chair. "He used it on me. Once before Xavier's demise and… many times afterward. He experimented on me until the results mimicked what happened to him in Coventry."

Sebastian should have known. His expression sobered and he stood up to be closer to her. Gently, he rubbed his hands up and down her bare arms. "I'm sorry."

"Not your fault," Leona mumbled. "I would love to go abroad and mine for this gem and use it to kill Gideon, but… I do not think that's an option. When we did it, it took years. We don't have that sort of time. Jules and Lucinda wouldn't know where to look, even with my instruction. And even *if* we were able to obtain everything we needed, we don't know if we'd be able to even get it on him. Ingesting it will kill you."

"How do you know?" Sebastian asked again.

"Gideon used it on some vampires he deemed 'lesser.' They were also experiments for his theories. He tried to do it to me when you rescued me. I was able to break the vial. It spilled on us, but… I don't even remember it hurting. I'm sure it did," she mumbled. "My adrenaline or… whatever you want to call it, was just in survival mode. I had to get out of there. I had to force myself to move. But between that and being starved, I was severely weakened. Charlotte had to help me escape and get you to her apartment when we arrived in New York. I was pretty useless."

"You could never be useless," Sebastian reassured softly. "Maybe Jules and Lucinda have some sunstone lying around."

Leona laughed softly and leaned in for a hug, pressing her head against his chest. "I love you."

"I love you," he repeated, kissing the top of her head. At least now he knew Gideon *could* get scared.

When Sebastian finally got his hands on him, he wanted to *terrify* him.

# 19

Sebastian eyed Leona as she lay on the bed, her bare back partially visible under the covers. He smiled slightly to himself, admiring her beauty. They had been trying to keep their strength up with feeding, but it seemed their naps between working became longer and longer. He was glad she was getting the rest.

He walked downstairs, the house eerily quiet. He supposed everyone else was recuperating or downstairs training — as they spent most of their time now.

A familiar scent permeated his senses and Sebastian turned toward the back portion of the house. He waded through the rooms and saw Theodore standing on the porch, a cigarette dangling between his fingers. Sebastian considered going back upstairs, but something in him propelled his feet to walk toward the werewolf.

Theodore quirked his head slightly as he heard the sliding door open and close. Having nothing to say, the scarred man breathed out some smoke and turned his gaze back toward the countryside. Sebastian walked up to stand next to him, his hands curling around the railing. The smell of smoke caught him off guard when he got close; he used to be an avid smoker, but now it just disgusted him. He huffed in amusement under his breath, which caught Theodore's attention.

"Something funny?"

Sebastian shook his head and smirked. "No, just… not long ago cigarettes were some of the most intoxicating things to me, and now I can't stand the smell of them. You'd think immortality would drive me to want to try *more* dangerous things."

Theodore glanced down at the cigarette and held his hand further away from Sebastian. Blowing another drag out away from him, he leaned against the railing. "Maybe that's why you're immortal. You aren't drawn to the things that kill you."

"I wouldn't go that far," Sebastian said, his gaze forward to eye all the structures barely visible beyond the foliage. "I was drawn to Leona, and that ultimately killed me. Brought me back to life, too, but… I suppose I can give smoking up for all the other abilities I was granted."

"You're taking this entire situation with remarkable grace," Theodore said, arching an eyebrow. "You aren't resentful at all?"

"Of course I am," Sebastian muttered, glancing at him. "I was very resentful at the beginning. I didn't want this. Leona was going to let me die. Charlotte is the one who turned me, against my wishes. In some ways I'm thankful she was so selfish, but…" he trailed off, sighing. "It's complicated."

"I get it," Theodore said, tapping some ash off the porch. "It's a noble thing you're doing, fighting for her. Vampires older and stronger than you have cowered in the face of that monster."

"Someone has to do it," Sebastian said simply. "Why are you doing this? *Really*."

"Helping you?"

"Yeah."

Theodore took another drag and slowly blew smoke from his nose. "Well," he started, tilting his head, "I just need to move on."

"From Damien?"

The werewolf looked over at Sebastian. "You know about me and Damien?"

"I heard you thinking about him when you first came to New York. And Leona was worried you'd betray us over your loyalty to him. And… Whitney isn't overly *friendly* with you. It wasn't difficult to connect the dots. And your feelings toward Whitney are written all over your face any time she's in the same room as you."

Theodore pressed his lips together in a firm line and cut his eyes away. "Yes, I need to move on from Damien. From all of it. He chose Whitney and it has taken multiple centuries for me to come to terms with that."

Sebastian nodded, sympathy flowing through him. "How do we know you aren't just going to kill Whitney as revenge?"

"I'm not some crazy scorned lover," Theodore snapped.

"Crazy scorned lovers seeking revenge is *kind of* the theme of this whole shitshow. It's a fair question," Sebastian shrugged. "Whitney doesn't even seem to be on speaking terms with Damien anyway. He was the whole reason Gideon found Leona and me in the first place. We've been running from him ever since. She feels like it's her fault."

"It's nobody's fault," Theodore muttered. "Gideon is just fucking insane."

Sebastian snorted and ran a hand through his hair. "Something we can agree on."

"You really don't like me, do you?" Theodore asked, watching him closely, bringing the cigarette back up to his lips.

"I don't trust you," Sebastian clarified. "And… you're not my favorite person in the world, no. You stink," he said, smirking as Theodore rolled his eyes and gave him a crude, one-fingered gesture with his free hand. "I'll like you much more if you actually do help us kill Gideon and we all make it out of this mess alive." He paused, then continued, "Do you think Damien will fight?"

"Against Whitney? No," the other man said almost instantly. "Despite my… *misgivings* about their relationship, he cares for her, and he cares for me. He won't fight us. But I doubt he'll fight Gideon either."

Sebastian wasn't convinced. He could only imagine what forces of persuasion Gideon was capable of.

"How did you meet Damien?" Sebastian asked.

Theodore smiled slightly to himself and stubbed the cigarette out in an ashtray. "He turned me into a werewolf."

Sebastian's eyebrows shot up into his hairline. Theodore noticed and laughed under his breath. "I met him as a human, not by choice though. I was supposed to be his dinner. He was a bit *too* loud with his attack though and drew the attention of nearby villagers. The commotion caused people to come out and investigate. He fled, leaving me bloodied and scarred on the ground. I still don't know how I didn't die," he said. "The scratches infected me and I contracted lycanthropy," he said, then glanced at the vampire. "The disease werewolves carry that make them what they are. I navigated the first several months, years even, alone. I was not discreet about my hunting, and I eventually wandered into Damien's territory, making rather a mess of things. We lived near each other, still do. He came to take me out — again — but when he recognized me, he took me in. We grew close after that. Very close."

"But... what happened?" Sebastian asked, shaking his head. "What about Whitney?"

Theodore's eyes were glossy and he plucked another cigarette out of his pack, his fingers trembling just enough for Sebastian to notice. "Whitney didn't come along for a while. I ran with Gideon and Damien. He and Gideon were already friends by the time I met him. Damien and I... fought. A lot. He's hotheaded," he explained, shaking his head. "And he's a flirt. I got jealous a lot. Monogamy is not suited for immortality."

Sebastian frowned. Would that end up happening to him and Leona?

"I thought we were happy. I thought everything was fine. I realize now how blind I was to everything. I was too afraid to admit the truth, that I was losing him. Then

Gideon turned Leona, she met Piper and Whitney not long later. Everything just… changed when Whitney came into the picture. Damien didn't have time for me anymore. He just wanted this shiny new vampire with a pretty face and good tits," he grumbled. Sebastian internally winced at the vulgar description. "Damien kept me on a leash *just* enough, giving me attention when he fought with Whitney, using me to scratch an itch when Leona left the first time… My heart could only take so much."

"What made you leave?" Sebastian asked softly, his eyes solemn.

"Leona," he admitted, then waved his hand dismissively as Sebastian tensed. "Not like that. Gideon's treatment of her disgusted me. Damien just sat back and… turned the other cheek. I don't know *how* Whitney stays with him. I don't know *why* I still love him. He's almost as bad as Gideon when his temper gets out of control. But I cared about Leona. I cared about all the girls. I have *always* cared for them, protected them. I left when I couldn't any longer. Gideon wouldn't have me back anyway."

Sebastian felt a *little* more at ease around him. "Do you think you would be able to kill Damien if he turns against us and fights?"

Theodore's eyes stung and he dipped his head. Sebastian heard him sniffle. After a few moments of silence, Theodore looked back up, his eyes now red-rimmed and moist. "I don't know," he croaked. "How can you love and loathe someone at the same time?"

"Trauma," Sebastian said, his eyes locked on Theodore.

"I hate the choices I made centuries ago when I didn't know better. I hate being this *thing*. I hate spending eternity trapped in a cage of unrequited love."

"There hasn't been *anyone* else who turns your head?"

"Not once," the werewolf sighed. "It's maddening."

Sebastian wasn't sure what else he could say. Comforting a gay, heartbroken werewolf was not something he was experienced in. Especially when his ex was *also* insane.

"Well," Theodore sighed, breaking the silence for him. "Unlike you leeches, I actually need my beauty sleep," he teased with a slight smile, stubbing his second cigarette out. "Goodnight."

Sebastian watched him walk back inside, then he turned back to look up at the dark sky littered with white dots. Sighing deeply to himself, he stood there until he couldn't see the moon anymore.

# 20

Charlotte walked down the hall, her hair damp from the shower she'd just taken. She was in a pair of champagne-colored satin pajamas. As she passed Whitney's door, she could hear the faint sound of… crying? Backtracking, the blonde stopped at the door and gently knocked. "Whitney?"

The sniffling suddenly stopped and a shaky voice answered, "Not a good time."

Charlotte frowned and reached down, turning the knob. Slowly, she opened the door and peered inside. Whitney's eyes were red as she looked at her from the edge of the windowsill. "Can we talk?" Charlotte asked softly.

Whitney sighed and dabbed at her eyes, then nodded. Charlotte entered the room and shut the door behind her, then crossed the space. She perched on the deep windowsill with the brunette and placed her hands on the woman's knees. "Why are you crying?"

"I'm fine, it's nothing," Whitney said, shaking her head.

"Come on… you said we could talk," Charlotte tutted, squeezing her knees.

Whitney looked at Charlotte and couldn't help but feel… better. Somewhat. She arched an eyebrow and leaned back against the wall by the window. "You sure you didn't get mood influencing as an ability?"

"Beats me," Charlotte laughed, shrugging. "Sebby always says I can turn his mood around. For better or worse. Makes sense that I'd be able to do that with other people. Maybe it's just my charming personality and soothing nature," she teased, fluffing her wet hair.

Whitney laughed quietly and eyed her as she shifted to rest her temple against the pane of the glass. The moon lit up her pale features, her brown hair shimmering. "I was just thinking about Damien. Wondering if he's okay. Where he is."

Charlotte frowned sympathetically, then moved one hand from her knee to her fingers. Giving them a comforting squeeze, she raised her eyebrows. "Tell me about him."

"He's… tall," Whitney laughed, shaking her head. "And so damn stubborn. He is a force when he wants to be, but he's sweet with me. Most of the time. I know nobody understands why I love him, but I can't help it. He's charismatic, intelligent, witty, loyal… I would die for him if it came down to it."

"Would he do the same for you?" Charlotte asked.

Whitney tensed, then turned her head more to fully look out the window at the scenery below. "I like to think so. I hope neither of us are ever in that position."

Charlotte nodded and joined her in looking out the window at the dark ground below. "Okay, so tall, handsome, loyal... bad boy?"

"Definitely," Whitney gushed, a huge smile on her face. "He stole my heart the second I laid eyes on him."

"What does he look like? Other than tall and handsome," Charlotte giggled.

"Oh," Whitney said, sighing dreamily as she looked up toward the ceiling. "He's broad-shouldered and has this long, wild, black hair. He looks like a madman sometimes. He wears it back in a bun for me when I'm around, it's sexy as hell," Whitney continued, shaking her head. A small smile spread across her lips. "He usually has a beard. It's black, like his hair, but not bushy. His voice isn't quite as deep as Sebastian's, but it's sort of... gravelly? If that makes sense. He definitely *looks* like a werewolf. He's not as scarred as Theodore, I think he'd *die* if anything messed up his pretty face. When he's not shifting, he's always in a pair of worn jeans and some old shirt. He said he rips through his clothes too much to worry about updating his wardrobe. He's a big bloody bloke," she said. "Words don't even do him justice."

Charlotte smiled. "How did you two meet?"

"Through Gideon. Technically," she said. "I had no part in Gideon's nonsense, but I knew of him. This was just before Leona was turned. Gideon was... courting her, at the time, if I recall correctly. I was wandering around the forest one night after feeding on a few bears. I tried to do my best in not hunting humans when I could spare it. On my walk back, I smelled more blood, but knew it wasn't an animal's. It was similar, though I knew it wasn't a human's either. It intrigued me," she said.

"I came across Damien who was hurt from… some sort of fight. He claims it was just someone he didn't like who he overpowered, and even though he never actually told me who it was, I feel like it was either Gideon or Theodore. Not many people are able to beat Dame like that, except those two."

"What about you?"

Whitney scoffed. "I could kick his ass all day long."

The women laughed together and a comfortable silence settled over them for a moment, then Whitney went on. "I helped him with his wounds. Damn thing was naked from shifting back into his human form, I never stood a chance," she said, exhaling sharply. "I remember kneeling next to him, helping clean his wounds as best I could, and just… melting. I'd never felt anything like it. Like puzzle pieces moved into place, as cliche as that sounds. I couldn't even hear the forest around me anymore. At that moment, it was me and Damien. We actually shagged right there on the ground."

"No!" Charlotte gasped with a laugh, her hand flying up to cup over her mouth.

"I know," Whitney laughed again, covering her face as her shoulders shook with humor. "I told you, I never stood a chance! This big, hairy bloke is naked on the forest floor, bloodied up and looking at you like you're the only woman in the world. What would *you* do?"

"Hey, I'm not judging, I was covered in food the first time I met Victor," Charlotte said, giggling again. She put her hands up defensively, then dropped them when Whitney gave her a confused look. "Sebastian slammed into me and spilled my lunch on me. We were in college. Idiot," she grinned, shaking her head. "But they both still loved me the same."

"Did you and Sebastian ever…?"

"No," Charlotte said, shaking her head. "I always had eyes for Victor, and Sebastian knew and respected that. He's never made a pass at me. With how close we all are, there have been… strong feelings that float between us, but nothing was ever acted on."

"What about now that you've sired him?"

Charlotte tilted her head back and forth, then shrugged. "Maybe a little. But I'd never betray Victor, and neither would Sebastian. He also wouldn't betray Leona like that, nor would I. But I definitely understand more what Leona is talking about when she tells us about the bond she shares with Gideon. It's intrinsic. I feel everything Sebastian feels."

"Yeah," Whitney nodded. "Piper feels that way with you. And I with Victor."

"Have you two ever sired fledglings before us?"

"No," Whitney admitted, shaking her head. "First times."

"Wow, lucky us," the blonde laughed. "I'm sure Damien is fine. But…"

"What?" Whitney asked, her eyebrows furrowed. "You can say anything."

"How could you be with someone who's so close to the monster who has tortured your best friend her entire life? Who tried to kill her, kill *you*, and Sebastian? All of us?"

Whitney sighed deeply and moved her head back against the wall behind her again. "I don't know. I try to fight it, but

I keep coming back. There's something about him that just makes me want to stay. He is nice to me most of the time, but there are a lot of times he can't be bothered to give me the time of day. He treats me like I'm an obligation sometimes and I... I do get tired of it, but... he's mine. I'm his. It's complicated."

"What about Theodore?" Charlotte asked. "Is it ever awkward?"

"Oh yeah," Whitney said, rolling her eyes. "Listen, I don't have anything against Theo. It's Damien's decision when he cheats on me with him. Theodore, poor thing, just wants to be loved. I didn't know I was taking Damien from him when we met and got together. They were broken up at the time. It was a mess when I found out," she sighed. "There was this huge blow-up, threats were thrown around, blood was shed, and I was half-convinced Theodore and Damien were going to kill each other, or that I'd kill both of them. Gideon was actually the one who smoothed it over," she said, shaking her head. "Then he imprisoned Leona and... it was this whole thing."

"Sounds like it," Charlotte said, raising her eyebrows. "I'm thankful he showed up during the fight so you and Vic could escape. And Piper."

"Yeah... Me, too. I didn't expect him to, not after the other times. I wouldn't have blamed him though if he hadn't come. I wouldn't want to be there either, not when Gideon is on one like that. He was also probably keeping his distance from me. I hold grudges," she said. Now she wished she had at least talked to him a little bit more. She had briefly gotten in touch with him before the fight, but... she just missed him now. "I also worried that if I was around him again too much that it would cause problems. I felt guilty enough about the ball."

"That wasn't your fault," Charlotte said. "You couldn't have known."

"I know, but… again, I let my feelings for him cloud my judgment and it put my loved ones in danger."

"We're all here," Charlotte reassured, reaching to squeeze her hand again. "Damien is there somewhere. Everything is going to be okay. We'll get the happily ever afters we deserve."

"You are *such* an optimistic person," Whitney laughed. "It's nauseating sometimes."

"So I've been told. You've been spending too much time around Sebastian," Charlotte teased, nudging her leg with hers. "I'm serious though. I want nothing but the best for you. For all of us. Even Theodore and Damien. I want *happiness*."

"Me, too," Whitney admitted. She looked across at Charlotte, then leaned forward so they could embrace. "Thank you, Charlotte. I feel much better than I did before. I'm glad you stopped by to talk to me."

"Thank you for opening up," Charlotte murmured in response, squeezing her close. "Everything is going to be okay."

# 21

Night had fallen across England and Damien was in his living room, watching a sports game on the television. A ringing sound broke out in the small cottage, interrupting his relaxation time, and Damien looked over. He grabbed the cell phone from the small end table next to his sofa and checked the name. Rolling his eyes, he answered the call and put the phone up to his ear. "In a better mood?"

Gideon's voice all but exploded from the other line. "Excuse me?"

Damien winced and folded a leg over the other. "I guess not. What do you want?"

Silence came from Gideon and it immediately unnerved Damien. The werewolf shifted in his seat and checked the phone to make sure the call hadn't dropped. He put it back up to his ear. "Hello?"

"I want you here."

The hair on Damien's body rose. "What do you mean? Where are you?"

"I'm at home. I need to speak to you."

Damien frowned. Gideon's tone had gone from ravenous to calm in a matter of seconds, with not a whole lot being said between them. "Why don't you come here?" Damien asked carefully.

"No. You come here. Now."

The line died with a series of beeps.

Damien looked back down at the phone screen and stared at it for a few seconds. He knew it would likely be in his best interest to ignore Gideon and let him finish his tantrum, but… this was unlike other times when the vampire had been scorned or pissed. The only other times that came remotely close were when Leona escaped each time and when they encountered Xavier. Even then, *this* behavior was different. It scared him.

There had been many years when he worshiped the ground Gideon walked on, despite their first meeting nearly killing them both. Gideon had been the family he'd always wanted but never had. They looked out for each other. When somebody bothered either of them, the other was *always* there to teach them a lesson. Gideon had *understood* Damien in a way nobody else had, and each time Whitney left, Gideon was there to validate his feelings. He was there to console him over Theodore. He was always *there*.

And now… he felt like he was losing his brother, his best friend. Gideon was a violent, sadistic demon now, a version of himself Damien could barely stomach to be around. He had gotten beaten to a pulp the last time he managed it. Was that what would happen this time? Perhaps Gideon truly had gone insane, once and for all.

Against his better judgment, Damien put his phone back on the table and got up. He walked out to his back garden and stripped naked, shifted into wolf form, picked up his clothes with his mouth, and trotted away.

Gideon sat at the base of the grand staircase centered in the foyer of his castle, staring at the bloodstains marring the floor. He clenched his jaw, then unclenched, then clenched, then unclenched. His hair was unkempt and he was still in the same clothes as when Leona was stolen, as when he found the apartment and killed that nosy woman. There were spatters of dried blood on his cheeks, down his neck, even on his hands. His eyes were dark from not having fed, and he felt himself slowly losing grip on the world around him.

Quirking his head, his ears zeroed in on the sound of movement. Gideon inhaled and caught the familiar scent of Damien, then cut his eyes back down to the red splotches on the floor.

"You know we could have just kept talking on the phone, you don't have to make me come here every time you need something," Damien said as he pushed open the large, iron front doors, then stopped at the threshold. Everything still looked the same as it had weeks ago.

"What took you so long?" Gideon asked, his eyes still

on the floor. They were wide, but there was nothing behind them. His voice was calm, which made Damien tense as he slowly shut the doors behind him.

"You called me half an hour ago. It takes a while to get here even on four legs. And I didn't want to show up naked, so I had to carry my clothes in my mouth and try not to get dirt on them. What is so important?"

"Why do you lie to me, Damien?"

The werewolf frowned and his body went rigid, but he tried to keep his face relaxed. Normal. "What are you talking about?"

"YOU KNOW—" Gideon boomed, then lowered his voice, "… what I'm talking about."

Damien jumped as the furniture, artwork, and lighting fixtures around them rumbled with the force of his voice. He turned his attention back to Gideon, who was still sitting on the second to last step. "Gideon, I haven't seen Theodore, if that's what this is about. I *don't* know where he is. I didn't know he was in New York. I don't know where he or the others are now. You haven't been able to track them down?"

Gideon spared a small laugh and shook his head, his eyes still downward. "You lie to me again? Do you have no value for your life, Hawthorne?"

"What do you want me to say to you? I'm not going to go find them. I told you I would not fight with you if it was against Whitney or Theodore. Years ago, you said it would never come to that."

"Years ago we didn't have the *flea* that is Sebastian Beliveau," Gideon hissed.

"You can't handle a fragile little human?"

At this, Gideon finally snapped his head up and glided over to Damien in an instant. A cold hand wrapped around the werewolf's throat and Gideon slammed him down so hard against the flooring, the stone cracked. "He is not *just* a human. Killing him would be too easy. I want him to *suffer*. I want Leona to watch him *choke* on his blood as he begs for mercy. I want him to watch me rape her corpse until he's *wishing* I killed him the first time I ever laid eyes on him. I will kill all of his friends, all of *her* friends, and feed him their entrails before I let him know the peace of death."

Damien coughed and pulled at Gideon's fingers. His nails were digging so deep into his neck, blood was drawn. The vampire's eyes dilated and he inhaled deeply, leaning closer to Damien. "So I ask you again," Gideon growled, "where — is — *he*?"

"I told you," Damien rasped, his voice strangled. "I don't know!"

Gideon picked him up and slammed him back down, causing Damien to groan in pain. Blood began to pool from the back of his head, adding to the already growing stains on Gideon's floor. "Then you're going to find him. One way or another, I *will* find out where they are. If you get to them first, then I might spare your girlfriend some pain. If I get to them first, you'll be the first to watch me rip her head off. You can eat it for dinner after I lock you up and starve you for a few weeks."

Damien breathed deeply and his eyes flashed a glowing yellow. "You won't touch Whitney," he growled, his voice deeper than usual.

"Won't I?" Gideon chuckled, squeezing his throat tighter. "Maybe I'll have some fun with her before I kill her. See what's so special about her cunt that unravels you enough to betray me—"

Damien all but roared and shifted into his wolf form, his clothes ripping with the transformation. His growth into the huge, black-haired beast forced Gideon to lose his grip, and immediately, Damien was on four paws and growled at the vampire. Damien lunged at Gideon and pinned him back, snarling so aggressively saliva dripped from his now black gums and down onto Gideon's face. He snapped down at Gideon's neck and ripped into his cold flesh, but before he could take a chunk out, Gideon shoved him off and sent the wolf flying across the room.

Damien landed with a yelp and pushed himself up. The moment of recovery was enough for Gideon to get the upper hand. He was on Damien in an instant and tried to get his arms around his center so he could crush his ribs, but Damien was gnawing, thrashing, and clawing against the vampire to break free. In his rage, Damien was able to bite down on Gideon's hand and rip it off, making the immortal shout in pain and rear back from him. Damien panted heavily, the bloody hand still in his mouth. He chomped down and shattered the bones, the flesh ripping off between his teeth.

"I'm going to send you to your lovers in a goddamn body bag," Gideon grunted angrily, cradling his mangled limb. He would recover, but it wouldn't be instantaneous, especially now that Damien had all but destroyed his severed hand.

Damien barked loudly and gnashed his teeth at Gideon, then launched himself at him again. Gideon braced his feet against the ground and grabbed a fistful of wiry hair, then slammed Damien back down on the ground like before. He brought him back up, his body writhing, and slammed him down again. And again. And again.

"Why do you make me do this to you, Damien?" Gideon cried out angrily, bashing him over and over. "Why? Why? WHY?"

Gideon's hand became bloodied and covered in bits and pieces flying off of Damien. "You were my brother and you've betrayed me. You've turned against me and this is my only option," the vampire growled. "*You* did this to us, *you did*. Nobody else. This is not my fault, this is not my fault," Gideon went on. Squelching noises filled the room along with the rhythmic banging of Gideon's movements.

After a minute or so, Damien was nothing more than a twitching, gored pile of innards coating Gideon's floor.

Gideon slowly fell back on his heels, staring down at the scene beneath him. He looked down at his good hand, which was hard to see due to the blood and brains between his fingers and under his sharp nails. His red eyes flicked back to what used to be Damien, then he slowly began to laugh. Gideon brought his hand up to his face, covering the pale skin with fresh crimson liquid, and sat back fully on the floor. His laughter escalated to maniacal cackling and soon, he was on his back, roaring with laughter in a pool of his best friend's blood.

# 22

hitney stood in the kitchen of Jules and Lucinda's home, eyeing all the different ways they could make blood taste *different*. She supposed if she had been alive as long as they had, she'd get bored with the same old, same old, too. She finally uncorked one of the bottles labeled 'Blood Orange Juice' and poured herself a glass. The pun wasn't lost on her and made her smile to herself as she lifted it to take a sip.

The smile faded though when she felt a stabbing sensation in her chest, causing her to drop the glass to the floor. The shattering had all the other vampires in the house in the kitchen surrounding her: Sebastian, Leona, Piper, Charlotte, Victor, Jules, and Lucinda. Whitney clutched her chest and gripped the counter with her other hand, her face even paler than usual.

"What's happening?!" Piper squeaked as she immediately took hold of the brunette's arms. "Whitney—"

"Agh!"

Piper whipped her head to the side at the sound of a pained shout coming from upstairs.

"That was Theodore," Sebastian said. "I'll go get him."

"No, you won't," Leona said as she grabbed his arm. "What if it's *him*?!"

"I'll go," Jules said, leaving the space where she stood empty in a blurred flash of movement.

"Sit down," Piper said to Whitney, easing her down on the floor. Charlotte quickly got a hand towel hanging off one of the kitchen cabinet knobs and wiped up what she could of the liquid and glass at their feet. Not that it would necessarily hurt any of them, but she wouldn't want to sit down in spilled blood-juice in any case.

"I feel—" Whitney started, her hand still gripping her chest. "Something's wrong, something… I've never…"

"A heart attack?" Sebastian asked though he felt stupid the moment the words left his lips.

Before any of them could laugh at his blunder, Jules was hauling a practically comatose Theodore with her into the kitchen. His expression mirrored Whitney's. What the hell was happening to them?

"He won't speak," Jules said, settling him down next to Whitney. Theodore slumped against the cabinets with the brunette, his breathing shallow and labored.

"He's having a panic attack," Sebastian said. With haste, he pulled open a few different drawers and finally found a few dish towels. He ran one under the tap water, then knelt to press the cold material against Theodore's forehead. "Breathe," he instructed softly, trying to get his eyes to focus on him. He had been through this many times, but never on *this* side of the panic attack. It was fucking terrifying.

"Whitney, sweetheart," Leona said now, kneeling with Piper. "What are you feeling?"

"Empty," the vampire finally managed to rasp out. "Like I've been stabbed, like something… something's *happened*."

"Yes," Theodore agreed, his breathing still rapid. "Yes."

"Did they get poisoned?" Charlotte suggested with a shrug, her eyebrows stitched together in concern.

"You said we could get poisoned," Victor added, looking at Jules.

"You'd know if you got poisoned," the Spanish vampire countered, glancing at Lucinda. "Do you two have something in common that might have triggered this? I have never compared vampires to werewolves as far as… DNA structures go."

"We don't have *anything* in common," Theodore spat as he thunked his head back against the cabinets. Breathing heavily, he shook his head. "Other than Damien."

Leona's eyes widened and she looked between them, before moving closer to Whitney. "What *exactly* are you feeling?"

"Like someone stabbed me," Whitney repeated in a gasp, tears pricking her eyes. Her hand was still firmly against her sternum. "Like I can't even stand up. I can't think straight."

Immediately, Leona was transported back to that awful night she thought she was going to lose Sebastian. Seeing him bleed out and not knowing what to do, not being able to *move…* It was one of the most frightening moments of both her human and undead lives.

"Is Damien… Do you think he's okay? When was the last time you spoke to him?" Leona asked, stroking Whitney's hair.

The brunette shrugged and squeezed her eyes shut. "I don't know… Before Sebastian was made a vampire. Before the fight. Before we came and got you. I have been pissed at him since he told Gideon about the ball and all this shit got started."

"What about you?" Leona asked Theodore, eyeing him.

"I saw him a few weeks ago after all the shit went down between you and Gideon. He told me about the fight. That's why I came to find you all. That's the last I've heard from him."

"Do you think Gideon's done something to him?" Sebastian asked, folding his arms. "Hurt him?"

"I don't know," Leona sighed, shaking her head. "But I know when you were on the verge of death, I looked like both of them. I thought I was dying, too."

"Can we be affected by other people's deaths?" Sebastian asked, looking to Jules and Lucinda for answers.

Both women glanced at each other, but it was Lucinda who spoke up. "I have never experienced this, because Jules is still here, but I have heard from others who have lost their mates that it can be devastating to the immortal form. I did not know werewolves endured the same experience. But… considering you both have the same symptoms and share mates, I fear the worst for your Damien."

"Oh, God," Whitney choked out, covering her mouth with the hand not on her chest. "Oh, God, Dame, my love…"

"He's *fine*," Theodore reassured, his voice shaking and his eyes red-rimmed. "Damien is *fine*. Gideon wouldn't hurt him. They're best friends."

Sebastian resisted making a snide comment, knowing it wasn't the time and it certainly wouldn't help. That psychopath had no friends, despite what he led others to believe. Sebastian wouldn't be surprised in the slightest if he'd murdered his only 'friend.' Theodore had claimed to be friends with Gideon before, and now look at the state of him, of *them*. Theodore was probably lucky to be alive.

"We don't know anything for sure," Charlotte said, stepping toward them. "Whitney, let's get you fed. You, too, Theo. Then we can let you both rest and calm down. Hopefully, the pain subsides soon and we can try and figure this out. But *none* of us are going to go try and find Damien to investigate, do you both hear me?" She glared at them both seriously, eyebrows raised. "We don't need either of you getting yourselves killed. This could be a trap. We don't know. So we're going to *stay here* where we *know* it's safe, then we'll come up with a plan. But rescuing someone potentially in Gideon's clutches is exactly what led to the bloodbath that immortalized Sebastian. And we don't have any more get-out-of-jail-free cards if Gideon decides to shove his hand through one of our chests again. It's game over."

"Charlie is right," Piper said softly to Whitney. She glanced at Theodore and took pity on him. "Come on, both of you. Let's get you into a bed and I'll bring you each some food," she added, heaving both of them to stand.

"I can help," Charlotte suggested, taking Theodore from the woman's grasp. In a moment, they were gone from the room and up the stairs.

Sebastian rubbed his forehead tiredly and shook his head. "I can't believe this shit. Do you really think Damien's dead?"

"Yes," Leona said quietly, not wanting either of her friends to overhear. "I do. I'll never forget that pain I felt with you, and you didn't even technically die. I can only imagine what it would feel like if you *had*."

Sebastian pulled her into his arms and rested his chin atop her head. "I'm not going anywhere, baby girl. I promise. Gideon is going to have to rip me inside out before he takes me from you a second time."

Leona closed her eyes and nuzzled into his chest, her arms snaking around his middle. "I love you, Seb."

"I love you, too, Leona."

# 23

Whitney opened her eyes at the sound of a light rapping against her bedroom door. She shifted just enough in bed so the blankets she was wrapped up in didn't obscure her view. "Come in," she said in a weak, cracked voice.

The door opened and Theodore stood there, his face pale and his eyes sallow. His light brown hair was more disheveled than usual. He just looked exhausted. Whitney was too weak to tense at his intrusion, so she just stared at him. Theodore stepped inside and shut the door behind him, then leaned back against the large plank of dark wood.

An age passed and finally, Whitney broke the silence. "Are you going to say something?"

Theodore's eyes flicked to her, then he slowly shook his head. "I thought I was but… I find I don't know what to say."

Whitney stayed still under the covers. Only her mouth up was visible. The rest of her was merely a bundled cocoon. "I'm not in the mood to console you, Theodore. Go away."

Hurt flashed across Theodore's features and he stayed where he was against the door. "Remember when we used to be friends?"

Whitney scoffed and glared at him as best she could from her position. "That was before I found out you were fucking my boyfriend."

Theodore's frown deepened and he shook his head. "Why is it always my fault? Why does the blame never lie with Damien?"

Whitney didn't immediately respond. She knew he was right. It was partially his fault, all of his affairs with Damien, but Damien was who she should truly be angry with. Not that she could do that anymore. Damien was the one who had betrayed all their vows of exclusion and loyalty and made a mockery of their relationship. He was the one who always looked at her with those chocolate-colored eyes and made her melt with one small 'Sorry.' She was weak every time.

"Damien is dead," Whitney finally said in little more than a weak whisper.

"We don't know that—"

"Yes we do." Whitney's eyes filled with tears and she struggled to stave them off. "He's *gone*, Theo. I can't feel him anymore. I know you can't either." Whitney choked those last words out and closed her eyes, her quiet sobbing filling the room.

Theodore watched her and finally pushed himself off the door. Slowly, he approached her and sank onto the floor by her side of the bed. Resting his head back against the edge of the mattress, he bent his legs and rested his forearms against his knees. Whitney's crying shook the bed and it was several minutes before she calmed down again.

"You know," Theodore started quietly, staring up at the ceiling, his back still to Whitney beside him, "I hated you for a long time."

Whitney snorted and stared at the knotted hair atop his head. Her eyes moved over the curve of his nose and the facial features she could see with how his head was leaned back. His skin was slightly raised along his face where his scar was, and she realized this was the closest she'd ever really been to the werewolf.

"Not breaking news, I know, but… I blindly hated you just for taking Damien from me," Theodore continued. "I didn't understand why I wasn't enough. I thought perhaps it was because he didn't want to be seen with a man, or… perhaps being with a woman was easier, more proper. I hated you before I even met you," he laughed, closing his eyes as he recalled the memories. "I'll never forget the first time I saw you. The first time I saw *him* with you. At first glance, it boiled my blood in a way I never thought possible. I wanted to kill you, if only just to make him feel hurt."

"Such a gentleman," Whitney muttered, counting the strands of hair atop his head to keep herself from whacking him.

"The way he looked at you," Theodore went on, unfazed by Whitney's comment, "made my world stop. He looked at you like you hung the moon. I don't even know if he knows I was standing there watching you."

"When was this?" Whitney asked. "The first time I met you was at dinner at Gideon's. Leona invited me. You were late."

"It was the same night. I wasn't technically late, I was actually early. I saw you two strolling the grounds, arm-in-arm. You started laughing at something he said and he pulled you in close and kissed you. I had only just arrived. It was like watching a fire, I just couldn't look away from you both," Theodore murmured, his eyes still closed. His eyebrows furrowed at the strain of the memory. "When you pulled back to look at each other, he smiled in a way I'd never seen before. He held you in a way he has never held me. As if he were afraid to break you. Like you were the finest porcelain doll and even the slightest touch would shatter you. I left after that but ultimately decided to come back. I don't know why I did. I should have just kept going in the other direction."

Whitney began welling up again. She remembered that moment. It had been the *very* early 1700s and they were wandering Gideon's expansive gardens just as the evening turned to dusk. She had asked him if he had ever gone dancing and he told her she couldn't teach a dog to waltz. She had found the visual so hilarious that she couldn't stop giggling, and he'd laughed with her and kissed her chuckles away. Her heart ached so deeply in her chest, she was sure it was trying to burst from her ribcage.

"He loved you more than he ever loved me. I'm sorry for all the pain I put you through," Theodore finished, turning his head to finally look at the brunette above him. "I'm sorry, Whitney," he whispered, tears filling his eyes.

Whitney gently pushed the covers down from her face and brought her arm out from her woolen sanctuary. Gently, she placed her hand on Theodore's shoulder and gave a gentle squeeze. There was nothing she could say.

Things with Theodore had always been complicated. As Damien's partner, she had never wanted to forbid him from being with his friends. She had never wanted to control him. She hadn't even *known* about his romantic history with Theodore until she'd caught them together. It had only been a few months since she and Damien had started seeing each other, and only a few weeks since she'd met Leona. She had been fighting with the werewolf and though things had gotten heated and they'd said things they hadn't meant, she certainly didn't think they were *broken up*. Damien, apparently, had a completely different interpretation of their fight and had almost immediately fled to Theodore. Whitney had asked Leona for help finding Damien when she had gone to his cottage and he was nowhere to be seen, then Gideon had laughed both of them off and simply advised they 'check Theodore's house.'

She would *never* get the visual of Damien and Theodore together out of her head.

Leona had come with her and had screamed at both men. She had even slapped Damien across the face and in his anger, he'd shifted. Theodore, being the calm, cool, and collected immortal he was, shifted into his wolf form and blocked Damien from ripping the girls to ribbons. Whitney had been a blubbering mess filled with betrayal and Leona quickly evanesced them back to Gideon's castle where she consoled her.

She hadn't gone back to Damien until after the first time Leona escaped. He had been integral in helping them get out and she took that risk as an apology and let him back in time and time again.

"He loved you too, you know," Whitney said, removing her hand from Theodore's shoulder. "He may have come back to me, but when he wasn't with me, he went to you. You know that."

"He didn't love me the same way," Theodore sighed, turning sideways so he could lean his shoulder against the edge of the mattress and look fully at Whitney's face. "Suppose it doesn't matter much now, does it?"

"Of course it does. It'll always matter," Whitney said, pushing herself up to prop on her elbow. She was still in the same clothes as the day before when they'd both been brought to their knees with grief. "Do you think Gideon did it?"

"Yes," Theodore mumbled, his eyes darkening. "Who else could it have been? Damien is too strong to be taken down by anyone else."

Whitney shook her head sadly and collapsed back down against the pillows. "How much more can he possibly take from us?"

"More than we even realize," Theodore muttered, closing his eyes again. "I think he's finally gone crazy."

"He passed 'crazy' centuries ago," Whitney retorted, searching Theodore's anguished face. "I still feel pain. In my chest, right here," she said, pressing her fingers to her sternum against the thin, white t-shirt she was wearing. "Do you?"

"Yes. I can't stop reliving that moment. It's on a loop in my head, even when I try to block it out. It felt like I got shot."

Whitney nodded. "I don't think it will ever go away."

"Me neither." A pause. "It may dull but… it'll always be there. I've never lost someone close to me before."

"It has been a long time for me. It wasn't like this though," Whitney admitted. "Nothing has ever been like this."

"Who did you lose?"

"When I became immortal, I went back to my family. I was hurt, scared, and clueless. I should have stayed away," she whispered in a strained voice, her eyes distant. "I was also hungry. Hungrier than I'd ever been in my short life thus far. My sister was the only one at home. She was barely fourteen. Had her whole life ahead of her."

Theodore shifted awkwardly, his body going rigid.

"I went back home and opened the door. I had been in Oxford at the time, but they were still in Birmingham. Father must have been at work, and Mother had her book club with a group of women who lived within their neighborhood. Mary was home alone, knitting by the fire," she said, shaking her head. "She looked so peaceful. When I walked in, she turned and faced me… You should've seen the way she lit up. I've never seen someone jump out of a chair so fast to greet me. I was so happy to see her," she sighed, "until I smelled her. I hadn't fed yet. When I awoke after the transformation, I didn't know what had happened to me. I went straight home. I was starving and I couldn't have helped it, I know that now, but…"

"You killed her?" Theodore asked in a small voice.

Whitney clenched her jaw and fought to say the words. "Yes. I drained her right there. Afterward, I couldn't believe what I'd done. I was so… disgusted. I was going to wait for my parents to return, but then I became petrified with fear that I would kill them, too. So I left her. All alone, just pale and limp on the floor. I still remember the color of her yarn," she whispered, her eyes glossy with tears. "I still remember the way her body went still and she quit thrashing against me. I remember the flash of fear in her eyes when she went to hug me and I bit into her neck instead. I can still hear her *scream*," she said shakily. "I was a coward. I should have turned myself in. I should have done… *something*. Instead, she died alone. My parents had to find her alone, never knowing what happened. I read in the papers that the police determined it was a home invasion and someone had simply stabbed her to death. What other explanation is there when you find a poor girl drained of blood with nothing but two puncture wounds in her neck?"

Theodore regarded her thoughtfully. He did not say anything.

"My parents both died not long after that. Neither of them made it a decade after losing Mary and me," Whitney said. "Things got easier when I met Leona and she took care of me."

Theodore let out a quiet breath and then shook his head. "Damien never told me that."

"He didn't know," Whitney confessed. Theodore snapped his head to look at her. Shame flooded Whitney's features. "I was embarrassed. Guilty. I didn't want him to look at me differently knowing I murdered my own sister."

"Damien was estranged from his family. He would have understood," Theodore reassured.

"It's different," she said. "Damien had a family who didn't love him. He was glad to leave. They were eager to *see* him leave. He didn't love his family. He didn't care about their well-being. He was better off alone. My family was good. My sister was *pure*."

Theodore blinked, then turned his gaze back forward toward the wall in front of him. "Gideon was like a brother to him. I think they loved each other. I don't know why Gideon has *changed* so much."

"Has he?" Whitney asked. "He has always been cruel, ever since I've known him."

"I knew him for more than a hundred years longer than you did. He wasn't always so obsessive and vengeful. Something shifted, it was right before he found Leona. When that vampire hunter came after him. Almost killed Damien, too. Ever since then, he turned even colder than usual. He turned scared, even. Frantic. It got worse after Leona. As if he would lose everything if he lost her."

Whitney huffed quietly. "He's a piece of shit."

"He is," Theodore agreed. "Nobody's negating that. Gideon has never taken shit from anybody, but there used to always be a reason for it. Not saying I agree with his reasoning, but when he'd kill immortals, there would be a reason. They wronged him or one of us. When he killed humans, it was to feed. After Leona, he would kill just to kill. Like it made him feel better or something."

"So you're saying this is Leona's fault?"

"No," Theodore said pointedly, turning his head to glare at her. "None of *any* of this is Leona's fault. Or Sebastian's. Or yours." Whitney moved her eyes to him at those last words. "He has gone from caring for Damien like his own kin to probably killing him. That is not the Gideon I know."

Whitney shook her head. "That monster could never care for someone."

"I don't believe that," Theodore said. "Gideon was good to me for a long time, especially after Damien found you."

"Gideon has kidnapped, raped, and tortured my best friend. You'll get no sympathy from me, Theodore."

"I'm not asking for sympathy. I don't deny that he is psychotic and bloodthirsty. I'm thinking aloud."

"Keep your thoughts to yourself next time," Whitney said, turning over in the bed. "And get the hell out of my room."

Theodore let out a long breath and slowly pushed himself up to stand. He stared at Whitney's back for a few lingering seconds, then did as she asked. When Whitney heard the door click shut, her body deflated and she broke down into sobs again.

# 24

It had been a long few days of trying to make sure Whitney stayed upright.

They were comforting her in shifts, and all of them were exhausted by the very real possibility that Gideon had murdered Damien and was coming for them next. They had theorized that Gideon found out Damien saw and spoke to Theodore and that Theodore had gone to find the coven and help them. It only made sense that Gideon punished his so-called friend for that transgression.

Sebastian had been trying to delve inside the headspace of a murderous, insane vampire overlord. If it were him, he would have used Damien to find Theodore, and ultimately the rest of their group. But if both Whitney and Theodore felt as empty as they claimed, Sebastian was positive Damien wouldn't be providing any new information to Gideon anytime soon.

There was also the haunting possibility that Gideon got

the information from Damien that he needed and disposed of him so he didn't warn Theodore or Whitney. It petrified Sebastian with fear just thinking about the fact that Gideon could be closing in on them right now and they were none the wiser.

Jules and Lucinda had done their parts in fortifying the home. They had gone out to get their supplies to try and weaken Gideon, and Sebastian, being the most recent human, had been working on rigging the flashlights and other tools they had to be the best vampire-slaying artifacts he could manage. He was really trying to lean into his heritage. Perhaps it was the spirit of his ancestor guiding him to fulfill the prophecy.

Never in his life did he think he would even *think* those words. He had not expected to close out his twenties as the main character of some Anne Rice novel.

Sebastian sat in the basement training area, testing his weapons. The flashlight was good to go and his burns were still healing from when he'd tested it on himself. There was one for each of them. As juvenile as it seemed, water guns had been the best route for spreading holy water, and it worked a charm. Charlotte and Victor had found it humorous when he suggested it to Jules and Lucinda before their shopping trip, but they *quickly* stopped laughing when he shot a jet of blessed liquid at them. Now all he had to do was get the shit in Gideon's eyes and hope for the best.

That seemed to be *all* they were doing lately: hoping for the best. All of this supernatural shit was far beyond his pay grade and he didn't know how he got into it.

Well, he did, but still. Leona was worth any pain he had

to suffer.

Sebastian swiped through the air with one of his sharpened wooden stakes, wanting to be as prepared as possible if a fight was coming to their front door. He tightened his grip on the wood, then looked at one of the target dummies on the other side of the room. Bracing himself, he reared his arm back and launched the short spear at the dummy, the wood splintering through the doll's head. He smirked and nodded, then picked up another. Throwing it the same, it darted through the target's chest this time.

"Save some for the rest of us."

Sebastian turned and saw Charlotte behind him, a small smirk on her pretty face. He huffed a laugh and quickly removed the stakes from the dummy, then sped back over to Charlotte. "Just want to be prepared. How is Whitney doing?"

"She's… managing," she sighed, her eyes following her best friend as he began putting the weapons up. "But who could blame her? She just lost the love of her life. If I ever lost Victor, I don't know what I'd do. That possibility doesn't even compute in my mind."

"I know what you mean," Sebastian murmured. It was similar to the dread he felt when she and Victor confessed they wanted to become vampires. He hadn't known what to expect and thought they'd just disappear forever. He had mourned before their hearts even stopped beating.

"Are you scared?" Charlotte asked, shifting on her feet back and forth.

"Of course I am," Sebastian laughed incredulously, his voice weak. "I don't know what else we can do to prepare, but

I'm still worried it won't even be enough."

"What happened to you being all adamant that we would kill him? You seemed so confident."

"What else could I do?" Sebastian retorted tiredly, his eyes sad. "I couldn't admit defeat in front of Leona, not when she's so scared of being taken again. I had to put on a brave face. Otherwise, we'd all just be scared shitless. I *have* to convince myself and everyone else that we stand a fighting chance. Or else… what's the point?"

Charlotte nodded and eventually stepped forward, placing a hand on Sebastian's forearm to stop his meandering around the training grounds. His pacing unnerved her. "We're either all making it out of this, or none of us are. However it goes, we'll be together. Okay?"

Sebastian stopped when he felt her hand on him, then forced himself to look at her. She had always been such an optimistic person, which was why he got along so well with her. And now, being connected to her on a deeper level than he ever had before, he could feel all her emotions. He could feel her fear, her dashes of hope, her *strength*. She possessed qualities he could only dream of having.

"Together forever," Sebastian smiled slightly, before cradling her cheeks and kissing her forehead.

"That's right," Charlotte murmured, her hands curling around his wrists as he held her. "You're basically my kid now."

Sebastian looked down at her and pinched her cheeks. Always with the parental teasing. "Shall I start calling you 'Mommy?'"

"Victor might kill you himself," Charlotte giggled, pulling

back from him. "It does have a nice ring to it, though."

"I'm not into that kind of thing," he teased. Charlotte also had the *always*-needed superpower of lightening a heavy moment at the perfect time. It had come to his mental rescue more times than he could count.

"How's Theodore doing?" Sebastian asked as they ascended the steps to the main floor of the house together.

"Um," Charlotte started, frowning a little. "I don't know. I haven't checked on him today. I heard Piper knock, but she said he was probably still sleeping. Jules said some of her old alcohol got raided."

"Alcohol?" Sebastian asked with a frown. "Like, real alcohol?"

Charlotte nodded. "Yeah. She said the bottles were gifts from over the years. She just kept them. Something about *reminiscing*," the blonde shrugged, stepping in front of him so he could shut the door to the basement behind her.

"So he's passed out, not asleep," Sebastian said, arching an eyebrow as he turned to face her.

"Guess so."

"Well, we should still probably check on him," he said, wading through the living room to the staircase at the edge of the room. He took the steps two at a time, then stopped at the room Theodore had commandeered. "Theo?" Sebastian called out, knocking on the door a few times. "Theo, you okay in there?"

At no response, he glanced at Charlotte and frowned. "How long did you say it's been since anyone saw him?"

"A day," she shrugged.

Sebastian tried the handle but it was locked. "Theodore," he called out more insistently, banging his fist harder on the door. "Open up."

"What's going on?" Piper asked as she exited Whitney's room with Leona. Victor, Jules, and Lucinda emerged from their respective rooms.

"The door's locked and Theodore isn't answering," Sebastian explained. "And if he's been drinking, then… that's not a good combination," he said. All of a sudden he was a child again, trying to figure out if his parents were alive or dead in the next room.

Sebastian stepped back, then shoved his shoulder against the door, cracking the wood. Bursting into the room, he looked around. There was no sign of Theodore. He inhaled deeply and went to check every crevice a grown man could possibly fit into. "His scent is barely there," he said, vampires crowding in from outside to help him look. "He's not here."

"Where the hell is he?!" Piper yelped, her eyes wide.

Sebastian sighed deeply and ran a hand through his hair. He only needed one guess to figure it out.

# 25

heodore ran up to the familiar countryside cottage in wolf form and never stopped sniffing. It had been easy to slip out of the vampires' home unannounced during the day when they'd all been resting. Nobody had come after him yet, so he could only assume he hadn't been caught. He wondered how long it would be before they noticed he was gone.

Shifting back to his human persona, Theodore opened the door and looked around. He was naked, as was the case when they became one with their inner wolf, but he didn't care. Several lifetimes of this disease made him comfortable with his skin.

"Took you long enough."

Theodore snapped his head to a shadowed figure sitting in one of Damien's armchairs across the room. Theodore growled and shifted back into wolf-form, before snarling at the silhouette.

"Awww," the voice cooed. The shadow rose to its feet, and a hand reached out to catch Theodore by his furry throat when he jumped forward. Stepping out of the darkness, Gideon smiled sadistically and threw Theodore back into one of the bookshelves situated against the wall. The room was quite small, as was the rest of the cottage. There was a fireplace against a beige-colored wall, a grey armchair and sofa, a dark wooden coffee table, and a dark grey circular rug in the middle.

"Are we going to speak like adults or am I going to have to brain you like I did your boyfriend?" Gideon sighed, shaking some of the shed hair from his hand as if it stained him.

The impact against the bookshelf made Theodore shift back to his human form. He groaned in pain and blinked a few times, his vision coming back into focus. Gideon tossed a blanket at him and Theodore grabbed it and let it rest over his crotch. "Where is Damien?"

"Can't you listen? He's gone," Gideon said, picking underneath his sharpened fingernails.

"What?" Theodore asked dumbly.

Gideon rolled his eyes and was squatting in front of him in a blink. "I know you heard me. You didn't hit your head that hard. Surely you didn't think you'd come all this way just to find out he was safe and sound in my bed? Tell me, what did it feel like when you knew he was dead? I hope it ripped you and that fucking *whore* apart."

"I'm going to kill you," Theodore growled, but Gideon grabbed him by the throat again the second he started to move against him.

"You sound like him," Gideon said with a sympathetic smile. Leaning in close, he inhaled deeply, his nose pressed against Theodore's cheek. Sighing out, his lips hung open and his fangs extended. "I knew I smelled you at that hovel in New York. Damien stayed loyal to you right until the end, but I knew he was lying. Where are the others?"

Theodore was struggling to breathe and move, his nails not even making a dent as they clawed into the back of Gideon's hand.

"You're going to make me ask twice? You are *not* good at this," Gideon tutted, shaking his head. "Where are the others hiding? Where is Leona?!" Gideon snapped, pressing against his neck with more pressure. Theodore's skin was turning blue.

"Go to — hell," Theodore slowly managed, his eyes bloodshot.

"You're about to *know* hell," Gideon whispered darkly before they evanesced out of the cottage.

When they appeared in Gideon's castle, he tossed Theodore to the ground and the man began hacking and wheezing with the release of his windpipe. Theodore braced his hands and knees on the cold flooring and looked down, noting it wasn't smooth, but... sticky. Red. Widening his gaze, he began swiveling on the floor and eventually choked out a sob when he saw the pile of gore just a few feet away. Crawling to the remains, he immediately closed his eyes and gagged. There wasn't much of Damien's face left for him to identify, but his body was unmistakable.

"Damien," Theodore cried, unable to move anymore from where he was.

"Say hi," Gideon laughed as he came to squat by the body. It wasn't as mangled as the upper area was. He picked up Damien's lifeless, stiff arm and waved it at Theodore. "Dame lost his head when we were arguing… I used to think he was hard-headed but… apparently not," he said, poking out his lower lip.

"You are a monster," Theodore murmured, his body vibrating in shock.

"Yes I am," Gideon muttered, before dropping Damien's arm. He rose to his full height and folded his arms, staring down at the scene at his feet. "I gave you what you asked for. I showed you where Damien was. Now it's time for you to hold up your end and return the favor."

"You're going to have to kill me," Theodore laughed dejectedly, his eyes still downward at Damien.

"Don't worry, I intend to," Gideon said, clenching his jaw. "My patience only lasts so long, Selwyn. If you don't tell me, I'm going to go into that fucked up little head of yours and fish it out myself."

"Why didn't you just do that in the first place?" Theodore asked, closing his eyes again. He tried to dispel every thought he had of Spain, of the girls, of the newborn vampires, of…

"Spain?" Gideon said, raising his eyebrows. "Ah… of course."

Theodore's eyes snapped open and he lifted his head

to Gideon. "Why are you doing this, Gideon? You *loved* Damien."

"No, *you* loved him. He was amusing for a time, but his petty alliances with that band of bitches grew tiresome *very* quickly. I admit I was weak for centuries in not killing him, but… it was time. I no longer had use for him."

"You no longer had *control* over him," Theodore corrected, pushing himself to stand.

"You're right," Gideon said calmly. "In hindsight, perhaps I should have kept him alive. If only to kill him in front of Whitney. But his death led you straight to me, and you're about to lead me straight to Leona and that *vermin* she's attached to."

"You got what you wanted. Why am I still alive?"

Gideon smiled and leaned forward to grab him, shoving him down into Damien's rotting guts. He ignored his struggles and whimpers of pain and horror, then rubbed his face even further into the brains. "You're still alive because I *will it so*. I want you to *soak in* what your betrayal cost you. Damien's blood is on your hands, Theodore. He's dead because of you. And now your other friends will die because of you, too."

"Please," Theodore cried, spitting out some of the bloody remains and gagging. "*Please!*"

"You're so cute when you beg, darling," Gideon laughed heartily. He pulled him up and let him gasp a few times. His face and hair were covered with blood and brain matter, and then Gideon shoved him back down into the mush. "I want them to know *exactly* who gave them up. And let's make sure we bring a souvenir for Whitney," Gideon grinned.

# 26

"Have we considered *leaving*?" Victor asked in a panic while he helped sharpen more wooden stakes down in the basement with the other immortals.

"This is the safest place you can be," Jules said, shaking her head. "Leaving and going out in the open is a suicide mission. You can't go to New York, you can't go to New Orleans, you're going to have to stay here. At least here, we'll have our advantages that we trained for. We can corner him into one area and go at him with our full forces."

"Theodore is a fucking idiot," Piper swore as she carefully poured more holy water into the spout atop the white and blue water gun in her hand. "What did we say? *What did we say?!*" Piper hissed to herself, shaking her head. "Damien is fucking dead and he thinks he can just be the hero and go in by himself. It's only a matter of time before Gideon reads his mind and figures out where we are, and then we're *cooked*."

"Way to have faith," Whitney snapped, glaring at her.

"Arguing isn't going to help," Leona said, her voice wavering. She was also trying to fill guns up with water, but her hands were shaking so badly that she was spilling it on herself and causing welts to appear.

Sebastian frowned and gently took the container away from her. "Why don't you go help with the stakes with Victor? We can finish this," he said gently. Leona nodded and got up to join the blonde man, and then Sebastian took up her post in filling the toys. He knew everyone was freaked out, *he* was freaked out — but it wasn't going to prolong their safety any longer by bickering with each other. What's done was done and Theodore was gone. He was probably dead by now. Gideon was probably on the way, and they were fighting sooner than later.

Sebastian couldn't blame Theodore for his actions. He had practically done the same thing when Leona was kidnapped a few months ago. If he had known where to *go* the first time, he absolutely would have left without everyone else and gotten himself killed before he even stepped foot through the front door. He remembered how frantic he had been upon realizing that Leona was in danger and not coming back from her hunt. Sebastian didn't even *know* what he would have done had he found out Leona was dead. The rage inside him would not have been bridled by *anything*, vampire or not.

The only thing in their favor was Gideon's arrogance. As much as Sebastian wanted to think the psychopath would try and sneak in around the back or pop up from underground through the cement, he wouldn't be surprised if Gideon just showed up at the front door and knocked. Or more accurately, busted it down. He wasn't sure Gideon would come up with any sort of plan of action. He would probably just rely on his brute strength and supernatural abilities to get the job done for him, as he'd done countless times before. Perhaps it was the only reason he was scared of Xavier; the vampire slayer knew how to work around all his powers and get one over on him. Gideon had to rely on Xavier's human side and use Leona to prey on him. It was eerily similar now.

Sebastian tuned out everyone's complaints and verbal panicking and instead focused on not spilling Jesus water all over himself. This was perhaps one of the most ironic moments of his existence thus far: he had spent his entire human life renouncing religion and everything associated with it, had laughed in the face of anyone who worshiped a god over logic and reasoning and science, and now he was using *actual* holy water to try and kill a demon. God really *was* a better con artist than the devil.

"I'm sorry about all this," Sebastian finally said without looking up. Jules was sitting next to him while Lucinda was testing every flashlight nearby to ensure they worked.

Jules glanced up at him and shook her head in confusion. "For what?"

"For bringing all this to your doorstep. For putting you in danger. I never expected to walk into this life, with these people. A year ago, everything in my world was completely normal. There were no vampires, no werewolves, no witches, no blood curses, nothing. Just regular me living my regular life."

Jules smiled empathetically, then reached out to squeeze his knee. "If we die tomorrow, or even tonight, I won't regret a single thing."

"*Why?*" Sebastian asked.

"Why not? What is there to regret? I have lived thousands of years with the love of my life. I have seen history unfold before my very eyes. I have witnessed the rises and falls of great dynasties. I have seen technology develop and save lives. I have seen babies born. I have seen people die and pass on to the next world. I have seen laughter, sadness, joy, grief, terror, every human emotion across countless faces. I have lived a hundred different lifetimes and I wouldn't trade it all for anything. When it's our time to die — *truly die* — then we'll be ready. And we'll have lived a damn good life right up until the end."

Sebastian nodded and let her words sink in. He cut his eyes back down to his water gun and started filling it up again. Before he moved to the next one, he lifted his head once more and looked around at his friends, who were now family to him.

He had been willing to lay his life down for them as a human, and that was never truer than this moment. They were all preparing to fight against an enemy that was coming after Leona and *him*, not them. Each one of them knew the high probability that they'd lose against a monster whose powers *none* of them knew the true scope of, but nobody was shying away. *That* meant something to him. No matter what happened, he knew they were making the right choice. This had to end somehow.

Sebastian stood up to help with the preparations, but a familiar scent caught his attention. He sniffed a few times, then furrowed his brows. "Do you smell that?"

Jules looked over, then inhaled deeply. "Werewolf."

"Maybe… Maybe it's Damien!" Whitney exclaimed, her eyes sad but hopeful. She hadn't been doing much of anything like the rest of them were, but they hadn't forced her into any tasks.

Before the brunette could jump up, Charlotte grabbed her arm. "We don't know that. It could be Theodore. It could be nobody we know. If Gideon is attached to both of those boys, then he could have other werewolves we aren't familiar with. We need to stay down here where it's safe."

"But what if he needs our help? What if it *is* Damien and we just left him out there? What if Theo is hurt and escaped Gideon?"

"Escaping Gideon is not a walk in the park," Leona muttered, putting the stake she was sharpening down. "Especially after what happened with me, I doubt he would have just let Theodore go, *if* that's where he went. We can't operate on assumptions. We need to be sure there is no threat."

"That's never gonna happen," Victor scoffed, letting the stakes in his hand clamber to the floor. "Look, Whitney, I know you're worried, but this is for the good of the group."

"What if it were Charlotte, hmm? What if she went missing and you caught her scent?" Whitney snapped, her eyes welling up.

"We don't know it's Damien's scent," Charlotte reminded, not wanting things to get out of control. "It's too dangerous.

We came down here for a reason. Gideon could be using him as bait."

"We have to *check*!" Whitney cried out, slowly turning hysterical. "I know I— I don't feel him anymore, but— but what if—"

"I will go check," Jules said as she put her hands up.

"No," Lucinda immediately intervened, putting her flashlights down. In a moment, she was by her lover's side. "I don't want you to take any unnecessary risks, mi corazón."

"I'll be just fine, amor," Jules smiled warmly as she cradled Lucinda's cheek with one hand. After a moment of gently stroking her chilled skin with the pad of her thumb, the curly-haired woman traveled up the steps to the main floor.

And they waited. And waited. And waited.

Lucinda's worried eyes never left the ceiling, her fingers picking at her nails. Sebastian watched as she stressed her lower lip with her teeth. He knew that feeling of dread and fearing the unknown all too well. He had been perpetually nauseated when Leona had been stolen from them a few weeks prior. He could only hope this *was* the ending they all hoped for. Maybe it *was* Damien and he was alive and well, with Theodore by his side. Maybe they were coming back to tell them that Gideon was dead and they were all free to live their lives without having to look over their shoulders.

But of course, it wasn't.

A crashing noise upstairs and a woman's shriek made that abundantly clear in the following seconds.

27

ucinda was the first one to fly up the steps. The rest of the coven followed, arms full of their new weapons. When they got into the living room, they were met with Gideon holding Jules by the throat with one hand, and a limp Theodore crumbled beside him in the other. There was a stained bag hooked across Theodore's chest. The tall vampire looked over at the group as they emerged from the basement and a smirk slowly spread across his lips, the sharp points of his fangs barely visible.

"*There* you all are. I've been scouring the globe for you," Gideon said smoothly. Jules's struggling wasn't even making him budge an inch. "Who knows how much longer it would've taken me to find you lot had our lovely Theodore not led me straight to you. I should have killed Damien a long time ago. It would have saved me a heap of trouble."

A small, hopeless whimper came from Whitney, causing Charlotte to tighten the hold on her hand. The blonde held her close but kept her eyes on Gideon. She would be ready to jump in and protect her family at any moment.

Lucinda was rigid, her eyes glued to her mate. She swallowed, then steeled her voice. "Let her go. Now."

"We're only just getting re-acquainted," Gideon said, his voice mocking a pout. "What's your name again, beautiful? I can't seem to recall…"

Jules answered by spitting in his face. Gideon laughed under his breath and let the saliva drip down his cheek. "You've been keeping something that doesn't belong to you. I'd like it back now."

"Let her go, asshole."

Gideon turned his attention from Jules to Sebastian, who was standing in front of everyone else. Sebastian's innards turned to ice as that piercing gaze swept over him. He wondered if this was what cows and other livestock felt when they were sized up for butchering.

"So they *did* make you immortal," Gideon said. Without breaking his gaze with Sebastian, Gideon threw Jules to the ground. She quickly crawled and eventually stumbled back into Lucinda's arms.

Sebastian wasn't looking away either. He could feel Leona's grasp on his bicep, but he wouldn't let Gideon so much as whisper in her direction. "I'm going to kill you," Sebastian said. "Drop Theo."

The werewolf groaned in pain at the sound of his name. Gideon lifted him by the hair, and only then did the rest of the coven see the state of him.

He was covered in grime and blood, and his face was

swollen up to an almost unrecognizable state. His clothes were tattered and his hair matted, and there were fresh scars to join the centuries-old ones he'd sported before.

"Theo, sweetheart," Gideon cooed, stretching his arm up so he could bring the werewolf a little higher. His feet were barely brushing the ground now. "Show them what you brought. With your good arm."

Theodore didn't do as he asked. He was hardly breathing.

"Don't make me ask twice. You know I hate asking twice," Gideon warned. "Show them."

"I'm... sorry..." Theodore croaked, a thick stream of blood and saliva drooling from his busted lip.

"SHOW THEM!" Gideon boomed, causing the entire house to rattle.

Theodore slowly unclipped the bag from his body with his unbroken hand and it fell to the floor.

Gideon rolled his eyes and threw Theodore aside, the man slamming into a table and breaking it with the impact. Small noises of pain were heard from the heap of werewolf behind Gideon. The vampire kicked the bag toward the coven and it landed near Whitney. "Go on. Open it," Gideon encouraged.

Charlotte scrunched her nose at the smell. She still wasn't used to being around so much *death*. "Whitney..." she whispered, squeezing her hand again. "Don't."

"It wasn't a request," Gideon said. "Do it or Theodore dies."

Whitney wrenched her fingers from Charlotte's and took a small step forward. Sinking to her knees, she flipped up the clasped flap of the bag. A pungent stench wafted out of the bag and had Sebastian been human, it probably would have made him vomit. Whitney's hand trembled as she pulled up one edge of the bag and peered inside. She reached in and made a face at the mush she was met with. She pulled it out and realized, along with everyone behind her, that it wasn't *just* mush.

A mangled hand attached to a severed, decaying arm was inside the bag. Though it wasn't recognizable specifically to Damien, they *all* knew it was his hand.

Whitney's horrified gasp made Gideon laugh wholeheartedly. "See? Theodore told me you were worried about Dame. So I brought him to you. You're welcome."

Charlotte moved to grab Whitney's arms and hoist her up. The gore slipped through Whitney's fingers and squelched on the floor as she was pulled back to safety.

Sebastian's mind whirred. He was trying to go through every scenario he could think of in his head, but they all ended with them getting brutally slaughtered. They had their weapons, yes, but would they even be able to get more than one cheap shot at Gideon before all hell broke loose and he picked them off one by one?

Sebastian watched Gideon as the monster continued to taunt them with his monologue. It reminded him of every shitty superhero movie he'd ever watched, and how the villain always revealed a chink in their armor by prolonging the fight instead of delivering the final blow. He hoped this would be a situation where life imitated art.

Sebastian focused and tried to listen to this killer's thoughts, but it was faint. Not surprising, considering he had been alive for thousands of years and had honed in every ability he had. Sebastian was even shocked he hadn't caught him listening, or *trying* to listen.

The only word he caught was *Leona*, which boiled his blood.

"Gideon, stop this madness," Leona said, breaking Sebastian's focus. He looked at his lover and shook his head, not wanting her to engage. He also didn't want her to try to do anything stupid like sacrifice herself for the greater good. He didn't *care* that she agreed she could be bait. There was no way he would let her make a choice like that.

"You're *really* not in the position to be making demands, my flower," Gideon responded. Sebastian could see his jaw clenching.

"How many people have to die before you realize you aren't ever going to get me back? I would kill myself before being dragged back to that dungeon. You are insane. I've *never* loved you."

Gideon's eyes flashed momentarily and his nostrils flared, but everything else about him remained calm. He forced a smile and tilted his head. "How many people have to die? Shall we make that a game? I'm sure I could add…" he trailed off, his eyes scanning over the vampires, "what, half a dozen more to the tally?"

"What good am I to you if I'm miserable? Wouldn't you want someone to make you *happy*? Who's *happy* to be by your side?" Leona reasoned, her eyebrows stitched together.

"Happy?" Gideon scoffed, barking out a laugh. "What makes me *happy* is taking everything you hold dear from you and making you watch."

Leona's expression faltered and she went quiet. Not that she thought she could make him see sense, but… he had changed. He wasn't ever a kind, gentle soul in all the decades she'd known him, but this was a different, more sinister side of him that even she didn't recognize.

"Tell you what," Gideon said. "Let's make *Sebastian* decide. I think that'll be far more enjoyable for all of us."

Before Sebastian could even process those words, Gideon was a mere shadow of movement, and a small shriek made them all turn their attention to his new position in the room…

With Charlotte in a chokehold in front of him.

"This is your sire, correct?" Gideon asked, eyeing Sebastian as Charlotte struggled under his arm.

Sebastian's insides turned to molten lava and he could *feel* Victor's fear permeating next to him. He felt the same. It was borderline more powerful than the fear he'd felt when Leona had been captured and tortured. When he thought he was going to lose her.

"I'd recommend answering me when I ask a question. It's terribly rude otherwise," Gideon murmured, inclining his chin just a bit. "You see what happened to Theodore when he tried to make me ask twice."

Sebastian could hardly find his voice. A quiet 'yes' rasped from the base of his throat.

"Sorry, you'll have to speak up. These ears aren't what they used to be," Gideon teased.

"Yes," Sebastian said, this time louder and more firmly. "Release her."

"That's *not* how the game works. You're cheating," Gideon sighed, shaking his head. His tone reminded Sebastian of condescending a child. It reminded him of his father.

"Leona, come here," Gideon demanded.

Leona felt a jerk on her inhibitions and it was taking every drop of her powers not to let her legs walk to him. She swayed on the spot and clenched her hands, her fingernails digging so deep into the skin, that blood was drawn. The wounds healed instantly.

Gideon's patience tinkered down to the lowest threshold, and with a jerk of his free hand, he yanked Leona toward him without touching her. Her feet skidded across the floor and Gideon's fist was soon tangled in her red locks.

"Now then," Gideon said simply, turning his attention back to Sebastian. "Time to play. You have to choose one of them. Your maker or your lover."

Sebastian's eyes were wide and nobody around him made a sound. Not even Victor. Not even Piper. Not even Theodore in the corner. Sebastian looked between the two women frantically, white dots pricking his vision. This was not happening.

"The longer you take to decide, the more your choice will suffer. Who's it going to be?" Gideon asked, his tone icy.

"Sebastian," Leona started.

"Be quiet, Leona!" Sebastian snapped, his chest heaving with the exertion of his internal struggle.

"Sebastian," she continued, ignoring his glare. "Sebastian, it's okay. It's okay," she reassured over and over. "You're in this mess because of me. I'm who he wants. One day, you'll forget this ever even happened. You'll forget me. You'll live a long and happy life, a *peaceful* life, with the others, and you'll be set free. I will be set free from the shackles of his rage. It's *okay*."

"It's not okay!" Sebastian cried out, tears pooling in his eyes, his voice wavering with frustration and anger. "How can you *say that*?"

"Sebby," Charlotte managed to choke out. She had no airflow to cut off, but her trachea was on the verge of collapse with the force of Gideon's clamp on her throat.

Sebastian had a thousand frenzied thoughts dashing through his mind at once. There had to be a way out of this. If they could just distract him long enough to get him to loosen his grip, Sebastian could grab one of them and maybe Piper could grab another. There were more of them than him. Gideon wasn't a god. He wasn't immortal. He wasn't—

Gideon rolled his eyes and shook his head. "I'm bored," he muttered, then flexed his arm so hard that Charlotte's neck crunched. Gideon violently jerked his arm to the side and the blonde's head came with the movement, her body crumpling to the floor.

A hollow wail came from Victor, and similarly horrified noises sounded from the rest of the coven. Piper buckled against Victor, struggling to remain upright with him. Sebastian's entire body was trembling, his eyes wide as he watched Gideon toss Charlotte's severed head to his feet. She still had a look of pure fear on her face. Sebastian made a small noise that sounded like a weak inhale, as if the breath in his lungs had suddenly been extinguished.

He felt like he'd been *dismembered*.

A loud ringing noise deafened him and his senses could no longer register anything around him. Black splotches began to populate his vision and his throat felt like wet cement had been poured down it. His pale skin lost even more color and his entire body began to tremble.

White-hot *fury* exploded within Sebastian's entire core, coating every nerve ending in magma. Before, he hadn't been overly confident that even their combined strength could take Gideon down, weapons included, but now?

He was going to rip this motherfucker to shreds molecule by molecule.

Sebastian's body glowed white under his already pale skin and pulsated, mirroring an electric charge. Gideon's grip loosened on Leona for a moment as he observed Sebastian, his expression falling slack. It was enough for Leona to rip from him, chunks of hair falling to the floor. The momentary distraction allowed Sebastian to claim some much-needed leverage over Gideon, and he pounced.

Sebastian's attack wasn't graceful or thought-out; it mimicked a rugby player tackling his opponent to the ground. Sebastian roared as he locked his hands around Gideon's throat, the elder vampire screaming in agony as his skin sizzled with Sebastian's electricity. A vase nearby fell to the floor with the power of the clash and shattered next to them, large shards of glass peppering the ground.

Gideon clawed at him, using all of his strength to try and get Sebastian off him. "What are you?!" Gideon growled, some blood coating his lips.

"Death," Sebastian snarled, causing Gideon's eyes to

widen. Sebastian slammed his head back against the floor over and over.

Gideon kept one hand desperately clawing at whatever he could reach of Sebastian to try and pry him off, ripping into his back. Gideon felt around beside him with the other hand.

Victor noticed and quickly kicked the glass Gideon had almost gotten. With a stake in his hand, the blonde drove it down into the top of Gideon's hand, making the vampire cry out in pain again. Whitney and Piper followed suit and went to the other side of Sebastian, wrenching Gideon's opposite arm off Sebastian's tattered back. They pinned it down with another stake while Leona, Jules, and Lucinda did the same with both of Gideon's legs.

"No," Gideon coughed, blood splattering all over Sebastian's face.

"Get the holy water," Sebastian said, ignoring Gideon's screams. "Now!"

Leona was the one to answer the command. She grabbed one of the water guns and quickly knelt beside them. She unscrewed the cap to the water chamber and turned the toy upside down, water spilling all over Gideon's face and into his mouth. Gideon's crimson eyes turned even darker, a nearly black shade, and more blood came pouring from his mouth. His screams turned to gargled howling, as if rocks were being overturned again and again inside his throat.

Sebastian kept one hand gripped around Gideon's throat, and used his now free hand to grab one of the pinned arms beneath him. He ripped it harshly from its socket, blood pooling under Gideon's body. Sebastian threw the arm to the side and switched hands on Gideon's throat, treating the villain's other arm just the same. "Get his legs," Sebastian barked, and Victor happily obliged.

Only when Gideon was nothing more than a bloody torso and head did Sebastian finally let go of him. His mangled body twitched as volts coursed through his collapsing veins.

"What are you doing?!" Victor hissed. "Finish him off!"

"Not me," Sebastian said, shaking his head. He looked at Leona, his dark hair matted and his face stained with blood. "You're going to be the last thing he sees when he goes to Hell."

Leona's throat tightened and her stomach did somersaults. This was a scene from her dreams, one she never thought she'd get to fulfill in reality. With a nod, the redhead walked cautiously over to the now-lump that was her creator. He looked so helpless, something she had never been able to even imagine. He was suffering — which brought pure elation to every corner of her darkened soul — but it would never be *enough* suffering. If he wasn't too dangerous to be left alive, Leona had a high mind to lock him away in a cellar and torture him for the rest of eternity.

"Leona," Gideon said weakly as he stared up at her, unable to move.

She moved to straddle him, and never in her existence did she think she would ever *enjoy* doing it again. She took in the scene, never wanting to forget what this monster looked like in his last moments. She wanted him to *beg* for mercy.

"You're not going to kill me," Gideon laughed weakly. "You don't have it in you."

"You have always underestimated me," Leona said softly, searching his eyes as she peered down at him. "And that has been the biggest mistake of your miserable existence."

"My biggest mistake was not killing you the moment I laid eyes on you. Not slaughtering your puny family as you cowered in the corner. I should have raped your ugly sister and mother when I had the chance."

Leona's smile was tight and she shook her head. "Beg."

Gideon stopped with his dramatic flare and blinked a few times at that single word. "What?"

"Don't make me tell you twice. You know I hate to repeat myself," she purred.

Gideon was silent.

"*Beg.*"

He gritted his teeth at her command, a small mewl of pain escaping as electricity continued to ring through what was left of him. "Beg you? A good-for-nothing whore who's too stupid to follow simple instructions? No," he said, making a small noise that somewhat resembled a laugh. "No."

Leona tutted and poked out her lower lip, then she shoved two of her fingers into his eye sockets. Blood spurted from the intrusion as Gideon yawped in agony again. Leona twisted back and forth, then curled her nails to hook into his skull. "Changed your mind?"

"Fuck you," Gideon spat.

Leona smirked and brought her hand from his face, his eyes very *slowly* healing. "Luckily for you, I want you to see me when you die. I want you to feel me against your skin as the light leaves your eyes."

Gideon was practically seizing under her, the pain receptors in his body giving out one by one. "Please," was all he managed.

Leona's grin was feral. Unhinged. She leaned down, her lips barely brushing against his ear. "What was that?"

"P-Please, Leona," he repeated. "Please."

Sebastian and the others stayed close, but still kept enough distance to let her have this moment. It was one of the most satisfying things he had ever experienced.

Leona sat up and stared down at him, waiting until his eyes cleared up enough to focus on her. "That was for me," she said, stroking a hand down his hair, his cheek. "And this is for Charlotte," she growled, hooking her hand under the roof of his mouth. She used his teeth as an anchor and wrenched upward, the stretched skin of the corners of Gideon's mouth splitting inch by inch. Using her other hand, she braced her grip against his chest, then used the rest of her strength to tear the upper half of Gideon's head from the lower half. The chunks of flesh fell from her hand and onto the floor by the body, which was not moving. Blood merely began to pool beneath them.

Leona sat back against the floor, finally off his body. She clutched her chest, her hand still soaked in red liquid, and felt the door of the cage she'd been trapped in for three centuries fly open.

Gideon was *gone*.

28

Once the monster that plagued *all* of their existences was destroyed, Sebastian caught up with reality and looked over at the space next to him.

Charlotte's body lay in a pool of blood a mere ten feet from him and her head was…

Sebastian's eyes followed the trail of blood to Victor, cradling his wife's severed head, wailing so loud it could break sound barriers. Sebastian only just now registered how *noisy* the room was, how chaotic everything had become. Piper was next to Victor, crying just as hard. Her fingers stroked down Charlotte's white cheek, then moved up to close her eyes.

"Seb?" Leona said quietly, all of a sudden by his side. "Hey. I'm here."

Sebastian couldn't tear his gaze from his best friend's body. He blinked a few times, trying to get his mind to clear. Could vampires faint?

"Let us clean this up," Leona continued, placing a hand

on his upper arm.

That brought him out of his trance.

"What?" he asked, looking over at her. "Clean what up? She's going to be fine. We'll just put her back together."

"Sebastian…" Leona started, her expression pained.

The man registered her look of hopelessness and it reminded him of the police telling him his mother was dead and not just wounded. That she wouldn't come back. That she was *gone*. He let out a quiet laugh and shook his head. "What?" he repeated. "I told you, she's *fine*. We'll just put her head back on and she'll come back to life."

"That's now how it works, Seb."

"What do you mean? Of course it is," he said. "Watch." Sebastian walked over to Victor and leaned down, taking the head from him.

"What— What are you doing?" Victor spluttered, his eyes following his best friend.

"Bringing her back, obviously," Sebastian said. He kneeled by Charlotte's body and put her head back on her neck. He held it in place on the floor and stared down at the broken skin and ligaments. Any second now and she would be sitting up, laughing with all of them. Any second now she would open her eyes again and tell Victor to stop being such a baby.

"Sebastian," Leona said again.

"It's working, just wait," Sebastian said, shaking his head.

Ten seconds passed. Then thirty. Then a minute. Then two minutes. Then five. Then…

"Sebastian," Leona repeated, reluctant to approach. "She

is gone."

Sebastian glanced up at her and did a double-take when he saw her face. She was crying. Why was everyone crying? He looked around and saw the rest of the immortals staring at him. They all looked like those goddamned police officers.

He laughed again and shook his head. "She's fine, she's…" he trailed off, looking down at Charlotte.

It was as if he was seeing her body for the first time.

He choked out a small sob and moved his hands to her face, feeling for any sort of life. "Wake up, Charlie, it's not funny," he said firmly. She did not move. Nobody did. "Charlie," Sebastian continued, waiting for a response. He got none. His eyes moved frantically over her, then he began touching the inside of her wrists, her sternum, any place where he might feel a pulse point.

She was cold and still.

"Charlotte," he said again, raising his voice. No response. He leaned down and bit into her wrist, then leaned back. "There. Now we're even. Come on," he said, shaking his head. "You're fine. Wake up."

"Sebastian—" Leona said again, but the look Sebastian gave her when he lifted his head shut her right up.

"I said she's FINE," Sebastian snapped. "Why are you all so quick to give up? I bit her, she'll come back. Just like I did. And then this will all be behind us."

He looked down and noticed his bite mark hadn't healed. Nothing had healed. Turning his head, he looked at Piper and Victor, who were holding each other and still weeping. Sebastian looked back down at Charlotte and shook his head.

"No," he said. "No."

Charlotte was not dead. Charlotte *was not dead*.

As more time went on, Sebastian became more and more unhinged. Sobs slowly began to overtake him, to the point where he was nearly dry heaving with how much he cried.

"Charlie," he said weakly, his tears soaking her cheeks. "Please, please, *please*," he begged, his voice hollow and strained. "Come back to me, *please*. You can't die— you *can't*. You promised you wouldn't leave me. You promised you'd be here forever. In every life we'll find each other," he cried. He was braced on his hands and knees next to her. He felt empty. *Drained*. "God, *kill me*."

Arms wrapped around his middle and heaved him up. He jerked from their grip and stayed glued to Charlotte. "No!" Sebastian shouted, refusing to move. "No, I won't *leave her*!"

"You aren't," Leona said, wrapping her arms around him again. "But we need to get her cleaned up and we need to get ready to say goodbye. Looking at her isn't going to help."

"This is all my fault," Sebastian whispered shakily. "All my fault…"

"It's not," Leona said, successfully pulling him off. Sebastian was practically limp in her arms as she dragged him away from Charlotte's body. Whitney had managed to get Piper to walk out of the room with her, but Victor was still in a comatose state on the ground, leaning up against the wall. Jules and Lucinda took over the job of moving Charlotte elsewhere and preparing her body. They still had to tend to Theodore as well.

"I'm going to vomit," Sebastian said weakly as Leona

got him up the stairs. Piper had gone outside with Whitney. Sebastian slumped against the wall and braced himself, trying to find *something* that would bring him down from his panicked state. "I'm going to throw up," he repeated.

"Vampires don't vomit," Leona reassured. She slowly helped him sit down completely on the floor. Sebastian's hands shook as he brought them up to scrub over his face. Leona took them gently and squeezed. "I'm here. I'm right here."

Sebastian dazedly focused on his mate and swallowed thickly. "It's not real," he whispered.

Leona sighed sadly and rested her forehead against Sebastian's temple, her arms hugging around his torso. She did not say anything.

Sebastian started crying again. He thunked his head back a few times against the wall as tears flowed freely down his cheeks. Pressing his hand to his chest, he tried to calm down, but he couldn't. "It hurts," he whimpered. "My chest..."

"It's the sire's bond being severed," she murmured. "I felt it when I killed Gideon. That was a welcomed pain, though. I'm sorry, Seb. I wish I could take it away."

Sebastian inhaled and exhaled, but it didn't provide the same relief it had when he'd been this worked up as a human. Or maybe he'd just never actually been this worked up before. There were no scenarios, no amount of training that could have possibly prepared him for this feeling. Charlotte dying didn't *compute* in his brain. It was a sick joke.

"Victor," Sebastian mumbled jaggedly. "Vic..."

"Do you want me to go check on him? Will you be

alright?" Leona asked, lifting her head from his face.

Sebastian could only nod. Leona stared at him for a longing moment, then got up to go back downstairs. When he was alone, he broke down into sobs again, his hand clamping over his mouth.

Grief flooded him. Anger flooded him. Regret flooded him. *Guilt* flooded him.

Charlotte was dead because he hadn't been able to make a decision fast enough, because *he* had not been ready.

Sebastian gritted his teeth and blinked several more tears out. He wanted to scream, he wanted to break things, he wanted to bring Gideon back to life just so he could make him suffer even more. Victor and Whitney had lost their everythings and they all got to continue with their mates. Sebastian got to continue life with Leona. Piper still had both her best friends. Jules and Lucinda had one another.

If they had just stayed far away from any of these immortals, they'd all be fine. They'd be humans, they'd be alive, and Charlie would be there next to him telling him everything was going to be okay.

But she wasn't. They weren't human. Nothing was the same. Nor would it ever be again.

# 29

Sebastian looked down at the floor as Piper and Leona worked to scrub all the blood clean. He stared at the space where Charlotte's body had been. It had been nearly a day since the fight and Charlotte's remains were in a coffin Jules provided, waiting for closure. Sebastian's arms were folded and it felt like he hadn't moved from that spot in years. His brain felt numb. Thoughts were barely coherent inside his head. It took great effort to do anything but stare into space and dissociate.

Movement caught his eye and he could see Victor going at lightning speed to help clean up the house. It was so silent. What could anybody say? Jules, Whitney, and Lucinda were tending to Theodore's wounds. Werewolves healed quickly, but not as quickly as vampires. Plus, Gideon had done a number on him.

They had burned Gideon's remains after moving Charlotte and getting Sebastian, Victor, and Piper out of the room. Nobody was taking any chances on him rising from the dead to terrorize them again.

Sebastian watched Victor busy himself. He had never seen him this way. Was this what *he* looked like when his two best friends had to calm him down from a manic episode? No wonder they had been so concerned about him over the years.

Victor was going throughout the living room, into the kitchen, down to the basement, up the stairs, in, out, in, out, up, down, up, down. He was moving so fast that even Sebastian's head began to spin.

When Victor went upstairs again, Sebastian followed him. When he got up there, it was quiet. All the doors were open…

Except one.

Sebastian walked to the closed door — Victor and Charlotte's chosen room — and turned the knob. Opening it, he saw Victor standing in the middle of the room, his back to the door. Sebastian stepped inside and slowly shut the door with a click behind him, staring at his friend in concern. It looked like he was holding something.

"Vic," Sebastian said slowly. "Take a break."

Silence.

Sebastian frowned and felt uneasy. "Victor…?"

Slowly, the blonde turned to him, and Sebastian's eyes lowered to the stake Victor had pressed against his chest. Tears streamed down the older vampire's cheeks, his sobs getting choked in the back of his throat. "I can't live without her."

"Victor," Sebastian said, not moving. "Look at me. Look

at me."

Victor's light eyes shifted, his knuckles whitening with the tight grip he had on the piece of wood.

Sebastian had been in this situation more times than he was comfortable admitting, though the roles had always been reversed. He shook his head, tears pooling in his eyes. "I can't live without her either, bud, but…" he trailed off, not even knowing what else to say. Charlotte's death had rocked him, and it still was difficult for him to even process that it had actually happened. He was still waiting to *wake up.*

"But what?" Victor cried out, gritting his teeth. Tears continued streaming down his cheeks and dripping onto the floor. "This is *your fault*! You're the reason she's dead."

Pain and anger both stabbed Sebastian right through the chest. He was *just* enough in the right state of mind to remind himself that Victor was grieving and couldn't possibly mean that. He had to stay calm. He thought about the vitriol he would spew to both Victor and Charlotte when *he* was teetering over the edge all those times in the past. "This is not my fault," Sebastian said shakily, trying to keep it together. It still *did* feel like his fault, no matter how much Leona reassured him otherwise. Couldn't he have done something to save her? Couldn't he have bought them a little more *time?*

It also disgusted him with guilt that he had been on the verge of picking Leona to die over Charlotte.

"She's dead, Bas," Victor sobbed. "My Charlie is *gone.*"

"She's not gone," Sebastian said, his dam finally bursting. Tears flowed freely down his cheeks and he shook his head, a few drops flying to the floor. "Charlie is *not gone.* She will never be gone. She's right here," he said, pressing a hand to his chest. "Give me the stake, Victor."

"No," Victor said, pressing it against his chest even more. It made Sebastian flinch. "I want to be with her. We're meant to be together *forever*."

"Killing yourself isn't going to bring her back or take you to her," Sebastian said. "I can't lose *both of you*."

"It's always about *you*," Victor snarled.

Sebastian swayed on the spot as if he'd been struck. Ash grew in his throat and he blinked a few more tears from his eyes. "Give me the stake, Vic," he finally whispered, taking a step forward. Then another step. Then one more. "I cannot lose you both."

Victor stared at him for what felt like an eternity. His eyes were red-rimmed and glossy, his cheeks moist with his grief. His expression turned from sadness, to anger, and then finally... to something so peaceful, it made Sebastian's intestines turn watery.

Sebastian moved so quickly that it had to be instinct. As Victor started to plunge the stake the rest of the way into his chest, Sebastian grabbed it and tugged it from him, then crushed it with his hand. As splinters dropped to the ground, Victor's knees buckled and he went down with them. He sobbed violently, barely bracing his hands against the floor. Sebastian was immediately on the floor with him, holding him so tight in his embrace. Both men cried against each other, their bodies wracked to the core with misery.

Sebastian felt delusional. The pain in his entire soul was so dizzying, there was a part of him that wanted to join Victor's journey into oblivion.

"Charlie did not die in vain," Sebastian said, his voice thick. The words 'Charlie' and 'die' put together in a sentence were foreign to him. It was like he was speaking a different language, one he wished he never learned.

"What are we going to do, Bas?" Victor asked weakly, slumped against his friend.

"I don't know," Sebastian answered honestly. He didn't. He had *no clue*. "But I do know, after all the times Charlie pulled me off the edge, that she wouldn't want you to suffer the same fate she did."

"We chose this life to be together forever. My forever begins and ends with her," Victor said, his sobs starting up again. "I don't *want* forever unless she's by my side. I cannot live in a world where she does *not*."

"We have to," Sebastian said.

Charlotte's funeral was as beautiful as a funeral could be.

They had taken her coffin to the backyard of Jules and Lucinda's property. She was surrounded by plush greenery, beautiful flowers, and the scene was illuminated by the bright moon above them.

They had discussed whether to take her to New Orleans, New York, or just leave her in Spain and have the ceremony there. Leona had been the voice of reason for Sebastian and Victor, who both wanted to return home and do it at the Labasques'. She had explained it would draw too much attention to them, given they were wanted for the murder of Charlotte's neighbor. That was yet another thing they had to deal with, and Leona knew telling Victor and Sebastian that they wouldn't be returning to New Orleans any time soon was too much of a blow in the middle of this tragedy.

They were going to burn the coffin and her body, the only true way for a vampire to be memorialized. Sebastian had begged any higher power that would listen to bring her back somehow, to let them reattach her body and get her back, but… it couldn't be done. She wasn't going to wake up.

Sebastian spent a long time next to her coffin. He traced the smooth surface of the enclosure, tears still steadily streaming down his cheeks. He hadn't *stopped* crying in the last two days.

"Sebastian," Leona said gently from behind him. "It's time."

He sniffled and stood to his full height, then nodded at her. Taking her hand, he went to sit in some of the chairs they had set up. They joined Victor, who was still a wreck. Piper, Whitney, Theodore, and Lucinda were sitting in the small row behind them.

"The end is not something most of us imagine enduring. We have all faced loss, grief, pain, but… losing a light like Charlotte is an especially egregious blow," Jules said from her position in front of them. She had volunteered to handle most of the funeral, knowing Victor wouldn't be able to. Losing Lucinda was something she couldn't fathom, and she wouldn't wish this burden on *anybody*.

"I first met Charlotte when Piper and Whitney brought

her and Victor to us for training many months ago. They were humans when they came. I have never seen someone, a mortal, no less, be so excited to be somewhere that meant death to her old life. Charlotte never wavered, never seemed frightened, and always had an answer for everything. It was easy to see why Piper and Whitney had chosen her to come into their coven. I could sense how much she grounded Victor. It's not often I see two people together who actually *belong* together. If a human has a mortal mate, most times, they'll grow to forget them as their immortal life takes over. Their old flame will burn out and they'll move on to be with one of their kind. But watching the energy she shared with Victor made me realize separation was not an option for them. It would be a crime."

Victor broke down into harsh sobs again, and Sebastian wrapped his arm around him and folded him into his chest. Jules looked concerned, but Sebastian nodded for her to continue. Everything she said was true, and there was no way to sugarcoat the fact that Charlotte would be missed by all.

"Charlotte's death should never have happened. It was the result of an insane, murderous snake who will never have the chance to take anyone we love from us again. Though she is gone, her spirit remains with us. We have our memories with her, our stories, and everything she has taught *all* of us along the way. Grief is the ultimate price we pay for love, and given how devastated we all are, it shows that Charlotte was loved more than *anything*."

Sebastian nodded and hung his head, his emotions taking over. Leona gently rubbed his back but stayed silent, wanting him to have his moment with his grief. He leaned against Victor and held him even tighter.

"Would anyone like to say something in Charlotte's honor?" Jules asked after several moments of silence.

"I will," Leona said, standing. The sound of her voice made Sebastian lift his head, and he watched her tearfully as she went to stand in Jules's place. She sighed shakily and clasped her hands together. "I did not know Charlotte as well as some of you do," she started, her eyes moving to the two broken men in front of her, "but I can tell you the impact I've seen her make on the people I love.

"The night I met Charlotte is the same night I met Victor and Sebastian. Bringing in more people to our coven was not something we ever thought we'd do. At least, *I* never thought it. It was nearly impossible to trust anyone else outside our circle. But when Piper and Whitney came to me, telling me about a couple that would be a perfect addition, I was skeptical. Even walking in, meeting them… I was skeptical. How could I trust these two strangers? How would I know they wouldn't turn their backs on us and try to kill us someday?"

Leona sighed and tilted her head. "Then, I got to know Sebastian. I saw the way his eyes lit up every time he talked about Charlotte. When I asked about his history with her, he spoke to me like he was explaining how sunshine warms the body. Hearing how much she meant to him, and how he'd do anything for her, made me want to keep her close and protect her from harm. I failed in doing that. I'm sorry," she said, looking right at Victor. "I'm so sorry," she repeated emotionally. Guilt had been devouring her, but she wasn't going to focus on it at the moment. She *couldn't*.

"There is nothing I can say or do that will make either of you forget what happened and feel better," she continued, shaking her head at both men. "But you both were so *lucky* to have someone that special in your lives. Charlotte possessed qualities that do not come regularly to *anybody*. She brought us all together," she said, looking around. "All because she treated my best friends, my *sisters*, like they were just a regular group of girls she could bring into her life. She — *Both* she and Victor never once felt fear around us. They were only fascinated and receptive to the life we were thrust into. Piper and Whitney told me they felt immediate sisterhood with Charlotte, and after just a few times in her presence, I agreed. I felt like I had known her my entire existence. It was difficult to remember a time *before* her. And Victor. And Sebastian. Our family was complete with you three," she said, her voice hitching. A few tears escaped and she swallowed the rest of her cries down. "I'm so sorry."

Piper and Whitney both stood up to go to her, but Victor was the one who got there first. He wrapped his arms around her and hugged her tight as Leona dissolved into sobs.

"Leona, it's alright," Victor said quietly into her hair.

"It's my fault," she cried softly, clutching him for dear life.

"You didn't kill her. *He* did. It's not your fault," Victor said. "It's not Sebastian's either. It's *his* fault. He did this to us. To her."

Leona continued crying, letting out all her pent-up frustration into the lapel of Victor's blazer.

After a few somber minutes, Leona eventually went to

sit down at Victor's gentle urging. He stood at the front, his eyes puffy, and looked at his friends. His throat tightened and all of a sudden, he wasn't sure he could move. He became paralyzed.

Sebastian saw this and got up, steadying him before his legs gave out again. He held him upright and stared into his eyes. "Let us carry you, Vic. Please. You never let me do anything on my own, now it's my turn to hold you up."

Victor's shoulders sagged in relief and he nodded. Leona got up again and helped Victor back to his chair.

Sebastian remained at the front and held a hand in his trouser pocket. Words were escaping him, and he understood why Victor hadn't been able to do it. Nobody was *forcing* him to either, but... he had to say *something*.

"I met Charlie on the first day of college at NYU," Sebastian started, his eyes glued to the coffin nearby. "I was scared, nervous to be in this big new city, despite having Victor by my side the entire time. We went to go get lunch on campus the day we moved in. We were hungry, tired, and I think I probably was a little *too* mean that day."

For the first time since everything happened, Victor laughed.

"Victor told me to go find us a spot to sit while he went and ordered our food. I think he just wanted to get away from me," he smiled wistfully. "I rounded a corner, and as usual, was not paying attention, and slammed right into the prettiest girl I had ever seen. Her tray of food went everywhere. Down her shirt. In her perfect blonde hair. On my clothes. The floor. It was a disaster. I briefly considered flinging myself from the top of the building. Or just dropping out and changing my name."

Laughter came from everyone at this point. He was glad. He was laughing, too.

"But she didn't yell at me or hit me in the head or push me onto the floor — all of which she would have *absolutely* had every right to do. Instead, she just laughed and said, 'Oops,'" he smiled, shrugging one shoulder as he did the impression. "Victor came back with a tray full of food and I thought he was going to drop it and add to our pile," Sebastian said, eyeing his best friend. "When I tell you the world stood still when those two locked eyes..." he trailed off, shaking his head. "Victor was *always* a player in school. All the girls loved him, and there were times I couldn't even keep his girlfriends straight. But he just *transformed* when he saw Charlie. Admittedly, the first thing that went through my teenage brain was that all shots I had with this girl just flew out the window... in addition to spilling ranch dressing all over her hair," he said, unable to stop a small laugh. Leona was *very* amused. "I was pretty much forgotten the rest of the day while Victor went to clean Charlotte up."

He remembered it like it was *yesterday*. God, they had been so young, so naive. He didn't know how much their lives would change just from that encounter.

"We were all inseparable after that. The amount of times I was comfortable with being a third wheel is actually pretty embarrassing," Sebastian said with a blush, making Victor laugh again. Sebastian brought his hand from his pocket and wiped at his eyes, feeling tears approaching again. "Charlotte pulled a side of myself out of me that I never even knew existed. She helped me stay focused in school, she nurtured my passions, and always had time to listen to whatever sad story I had to vent about that day. She *always* had enough energy for me. She never acted like I was a burden. She never told me she was too busy. She always made time, even when I knew she didn't have it. That's how I knew she and Victor were soulmates. This girl, this *woman* was the person that made my best friend happier than I'd ever seen him before. I loved her endlessly for that. And I loved her endlessly for how happy she made me, too."

He paused in his speech and clenched his jaw, trying to keep his emotions in check. Once he started sobbing, he wouldn't be able to stop. "Charlie understood me in a way that nobody else did. Not even Vic," he said shakily. "She wasn't just his soulmate, she was mine too. We were all meant to be together. Stay together. Forever. We made a pact after the last final of our freshman year that we would never leave each other. Really, it was just us being sad that we were going separate ways for the summer, but that pact went so much deeper and we knew it. When the girls came along, I was terrified. I thought my lifelines would be cut from me. The world felt like it was caving in beneath my feet and I was in a never-ending freefall. Charlotte came over and explained to me how much she wanted this life. How much you three meant to her and Victor. She *convinced* me to give Leona a chance, to give *all of this* a chance. She *saved* me," he said, his voice garbled. "She made the choice nobody else could and kept our promise. She made sure I didn't leave her. And I couldn't save her," he finished quietly. "I couldn't save her and I'm sorry, Victor, I'm so *sorry*."

Sebastian brought his hand up to his face and cried into his palm, his entire chest heaving as he wept. Arms wrapped around him and he didn't know who they belonged to, but he didn't care. He welcomed the embrace, the support, because he was going to collapse otherwise.

"You did it, Sebastian," a soft voice reassured, one Sebastian recognized to be Piper's. "Come on."

Sebastian walked back with her and reclaimed his seat, Leona and Victor both leaning into each of his sides. Blankly, he blinked a few times as Jules went back up to the front to close out the ceremony.

"When you're able, I ask everyone to stand and gather around Charlotte," the woman said solemnly.

After a few minutes, Victor and Sebastian both helped each other up, and the rest of the coven followed. They gathered around the coffin and Sebastian watched as Jules began lighting torches for each of them. A panic overtook him and he tensed, causing Leona to look at him immediately.

"Sebastian?" she murmured softly. "Seb?"

"I can't do this," Sebastian whispered. "I can't…"

"You don't have to," Leona reassured, then she squeezed Victor's arm. "Neither do you. Let us take care of it."

Victor was a similar shade of green and leaned on Sebastian, both of them backing off from the group. Victor turned his back to the coffin and shook his head. "I can't watch, Bas, I *can't*."

"Let's go inside," Sebastian urged, gently pulling him with

him into the house. They went far away from any window, despite being able to hear the ignition of flames. He sat with Victor on one of the still-in-tact sofas in a sitting room near the front of the house and held him close.

It was time to start again.

# Epilogue



"Uncle Sebby, *pleaaase?*"

Sebastian looked down at the blonde child who was giving him the most *intense* puppy-dog eyes she could muster. A small smile spread across his lips and he rolled his eyes. "You're a spoiled brat, you know that, right?"

He melted at her little giggle and he wrapped the girl in his arms, then launched them up to one of the balconies. She squealed in delight and held close to Sebastian, her eyes whirring frantically to take in all the scenery from above.

"Sebastian! Lottie! For the *last time*, I told you not to fly around like that!"

Sebastian looked down at Victor on the ground, who was seething. The girl and Sebastian shared a knowing look, then laughed softly together. "Alright, alright," Sebastian conceded with a sigh. "We'll come down."

"Do *not* drop her," Victor warned.

"When have I *ever*?" Sebastian retorted, before coming back down to the ground with the girl. Lottie ran up to Victor and wrapped her arms around him, hugging him close as the man picked her up.

"Don't be mad, Daddy," she murmured, hiding her head in his neck.

"I'm not, sweetheart. Never at you," Victor said quietly, then eyed Sebastian. His harsh gaze softened, and he eventually shook his head. "Your uncle is such a bad influence on you."

"The worst," Sebastian smirked, stepping forward to kiss the girl's head, then Victor's. "Has Leona started on dinner?"

"The woman can burn water. That's why I came out here to get you. She needs help," Victor said.

Sebastian smiled to himself and walked past them to go back inside.

In the kitchen stood Leona, carefully perusing a page in a recipe book. Sebastian stilled and just admired her. He never tired of her beauty, and any chance to look at her was one he was thankful for.

Sensing his presence, Leona slowly flipped a page and didn't look up. "Take a picture, it'll last longer."

"Maybe I will," Sebastian responded, walking up to her. He wrapped his arms around her from behind and looked down at the recipe. "Don't you think a six-year-old wants something *other* than tuna casserole?"

"What's wrong with that?"

"What's *wrong* with it is that someone who hasn't properly

eaten human food in hundreds of years is trying to cook a child dinner. Step aside," he said, moving to nudge her with his hip. "Let's just do spaghetti."

"She had spaghetti two days ago."

"Yes, and now it's all gone, therefore she needs more. The girl would eat pasta for every meal if we let her."

"Which is *why* she needs something *healthy*."

"She can have some fruit juice with it," Sebastian teased, pecking her cheek. "*Someone* has to be the fun parent around here. She's got four other immortals who watch her like a hawk."

"Don't act like you don't have eyes on her *all the time*."

"Still," he said, getting out a few pots so they could get started. "Spaghetti it is."

Leona stared into Sebastian's now dark caramel eyes and shook her head, a small smile ghosting around her lips. His eyes had changed after the fight with Gideon, and finally, he was the Seb she had fallen in love with. He looked like *himself*.

"Whatever you say," Leona laughed, grabbing the pasta from the pantry.

Fifteen years had passed since the fight with Gideon and Charlotte's death. It had been difficult to return to normality after that, and they had done a *lot* of work behind the scenes to get their affairs in order. The easiest route had been to let the world believe that Sebastian and Victor had died with Charlotte. The Labasques and Charlotte's family, the Baldwins, had mourned and grieved over all three of them. They had gone with Victor's original plan of a plane crash and it stuck. It made it easier to not produce body doubles for them. Jules and Lucinda had helped stage the wreckage. They had returned to Louisiana to hijack the small plane Victor kept in a warehouse just outside of New Orleans in Metairie. The missing plane had garnered attention. The crash happened in the Atlantic Ocean. Sebastian and Victor had been the only ones inside the small aircraft and had jumped out while in a nosedive. Their speed allowed them to swim far enough way to not get crushed by the machinery.

Piper had helped clear Charlotte's name before the crash. The police were still trying to figure out who killed her neighbor in New York. It had been important to Sebastian that Charlotte wasn't remembered as a wanted fugitive or murderer. She deserved to be remembered in all her wonderful, bubbly glory.

It had been difficult for Sebastian and Victor both to actually go through with faking their deaths, more so for Victor. They both had close relationships with the Labasques and Baldwins, and knowing they were about to find out they'd lost all their children was enough to depress both Sebastian and Victor. Leona had assured them it was better this way, *kinder* to the families to allow them to mourn and move on. She had also reminded them that in a few short decades, they would all be dead and the vampires could come out of hiding.

Returning to New Orleans was not an option, nor New York. The coven had agreed to find a new place to live: England. It was far away from their old lives, and Leona now had the chance to reclaim her heritage and enjoy being back home. Sebastian and Victor welcomed the change in scenery, and Whitney and Piper were both equally as excited to come back to their roots.

Theodore came and went as he pleased from their new home. It was difficult to be around him and vice versa. Nobody held a grudge, but… without Damien, he had no real reason to hang around. Sebastian wished him well. It was always nice to see him, all things considered.

Jules and Lucinda were still at their home in Spain but visited regularly. Though they had been long-time friends of the girls, Sebastian and Victor had grown to love them fiercely.

Leona had always maintained ownership over her family's estate from the 17th century. By today's standards, it wasn't anything overly large, but they had had plenty of time to build onto it and spruce it up. They had lots of land, trees surrounding them, and eventually, had turned it into a place they could be proud to call home. The house was two stories with small balconies attached to every upstairs room. The awnings above the balcony were all engineered in a way that kept the sun shaded no matter the time of day. Victor and Lottie often sat together to watch the sunset.

Eight years after Charlotte's death, Victor had decided to focus his energy on something greater than his grief. He had suggested adopting a child, something he and Charlotte had always wanted to do. She had never been able to carry children, and they had agreed together that instead of finding one to adopt or going through countless operations that might not even work, an eternity together was their best choice. And if they wanted a child afterward, they would have all the time in the world to find one. Now, without Charlotte, Victor thought it only right to keep that plan of hers.

It had been a conversation full of mixed reactions. Leona and Sebastian had been all for it, but Whitney and Piper were more reserved about bringing a child into a den of vampires. Victor had never intended to turn the child at such a young age and had assured them that if his baby wanted it when they grew older, then they could talk about it. Whitney and Piper eventually got on board and helped with the process. There was *slight* glamouring involved with the adoption process, Whitney posing as Victor's wife. They had gone into the situation under aliases, given Victor's identity had to remain a secret for a long time. Whitney was the most gifted with altering people's perceptions, so she was the natural choice to help him with the task.

Victor had found a woman who was pregnant, but choosing to give up the child upon birth. He bonded with her, wanting to know more about her, about what the child would be like. He had asked questions about the father, but the future mother hadn't given him many details. Victor understood it to be a one-night stand.

When he asked what she intended to name the child, given she was fairly far along by the time he had met her, she didn't hesitate with her answer.

"Charlotte."

Victor had been rather stunned, thinking it was some prank set up by his friends. How could this woman possibly…?

He hadn't been sure if it was an insane coincidence or Charlotte giving him a sign, but either way, he had taken it as a green light and went full speed ahead with the adoption. Lottie was born and surrendered to Victor, and the coven raised her as a family ever since.

It had been quite difficult at times to do so, given all their differing opinions. The girls had much different ideas of parenting than the boys had. Sebastian had to keep reminding them that their ways of doing things were more than outdated, and soon enough, their house had been filled with practically every baby book ever written. Sebastian knew more about child development than any other topic on the planet now.

He liked to think they were happy. There were times, even now, when they would grow sad over those they lost. Whitney would cry over Damien, and they would *all* cry over Charlotte, but... then their little girl would come bounding in and make everyone laugh and forget about the sadness creeping into their bones.

There were many instances when Sebastian and Victor would sit with Whitney or Theodore and just... talk about death, about *grief*. They were the only ones who understood what Sebastian and Victor were feeling. Sebastian hated thinking about Charlotte in the past tense, purely because it still didn't seem real. He wasn't sure it would ever seem real. Being without her left a part of him hollow and it would never replenish.

When she died, their bond was severed. Charlotte could always make his cacophonous mind dissolve into the most blissful silence, but now the silence was deafening him. He was *empty* without her.

Navigating the storm of mourning with Leona was difficult for him. His first reaction to intense trauma like this was to shut everyone out and keep his distance from those who cared about him. Usually, Victor and Charlotte were always able to bring him back to life, but… Victor was drowning in the same sea of sadness he was. When the dust had settled after the funeral and when they began deciding the next steps, Sebastian retreated into himself. He had merely gone along with everything and Leona and Piper had made all the big decisions. Whitney and Victor were content to do as they were told, too.

Sebastian was beyond thankful they had the support system they did with the adult vampires and now Lottie. Sebastian never put any of his woes on their daughter, but she was such a light in a pit of darkness. She had no idea. They had told her about Charlotte, as well as her 'real' mother. They had told her where she got her name, about the force of a woman she never got to meet. If Sebastian thought too long about it, he broke down. They had explained their 'conditions' to her and had all agreed homeschooling would be safest. She was getting to the age where they wanted to ensure she was socialized and made friends. They were *slowly* beginning to relax and feel at ease with going out in public, but usually it was Piper, Leona, or Whitney who took Lottie to meet up with friends in nearby towns. They went to 'mother-daughter' support groups to find new children to bond with. It was still too soon for Sebastian and Victor to wander around freely. Even with the adoption, they had to be careful with how much he went out in public. They could never be too careful.

Sebastian did not think time would heal the wound Charlotte's death tore within him. Leona even still got sad about her family dying, and they all died of natural causes. None of them had been *ripped* apart. He *knew* Victor would never really recover. Lottie was a great distraction, but there were days when one of them had to take over parental duties because he just couldn't get out of bed. For the most part, they all saved face around the little girl, never wanting her to feel like she was a burden or that *anything* was her fault, but they all leaned on each other when they needed it.

Sebastian wasn't sure he would ever move forward with children with Leona, or if they would even ever get married, but...

All he knew was that this was his family, the one he was always meant to have.

And nothing would ever break them apart again.

**End of Book Two.**

# About the author

Kerrigan Bailey Casimir is a former journalist-turned-author with a passion for romance and all things weird. She grew up in Panama City Beach, Florida, but moved to New Orleans, Louisiana in her twenties with her wife, Amber. Though she has a background on the sandy beaches of the Florida Panhandle, she grew up attending Saints games and exploring the French Quarter in New Orleans with her family.

An Ole Miss graduate (Hotty Toddy!), Kerrigan has dedicated most of her life to honing her craft and delving into the nuances of storytelling. She started her literary journey by writing fanfiction with her best friend, Becca Prince; that love for stories led her to a career in journalism, where she was trained in formal writing, photography, videography, and auditory storytelling.

Outside of the writing realm, Kerrigan can be found running around New Orleans with a camera in her hand, capturing all the best moments for tourists and locals alike. When she's off the clock, she enjoys a yummy cocktail and dinner with her wife, and coming home to all her animals.

Kerrigan's debut series, containing *Bloodlust* and *Bloodstained*, is a love letter to her best friend, Becca, who tragically died May 15th, 2023. Kerrigan has taken some of their stories they created together and carefully woven them into Sebastian and Leona's tale of love and misery. Her relationship and writing style are prevalent within her works of art and can always be traced back to the unbreakable bond she had with her platonic soulmate.

Connect with Kerrigan on the Internet and social media through her website, kbcasimir.com, or on Instagram and TikTok at @kbcasimir to stay updated on future projects and her current work.

# Acknowledgments

Hello to my friends, family, and readers — as usual, this would not be possible without you!

Before anything else, I want to shout out my beloved, Amber, for always grounding me and keeping me on the path I'm supposed to be on. Amber, you are every facet of my muse and you helped me see colors when I thought the world was black and white. This is *all* for you, every second of every day. I love you in eternity, my angel.

Next, I'd like to thank my mom, Wendi, for being my biggest cheerleader behind Amber. You're the best "momager" a growing author (and kid) could have and so much of my success is down to you. Thank you for believing in my dreams, pushing me to keep going, and catching spelling mistakes my editor or I miss. You're the real MVP.

Thirdly, huge thank you to my closest friends, Nathan, Ashley, and Shelby. You have carried me across the finish line when my legs gave out more times than I can even begin to count. I would be lost without you and you have been invaluable to me over the years, but especially through 2023 and 2024. You always listen to my problems, even when you have problems of your own, and always make time for my nonsense. Thanks for helping me get my spark back.

As always, even though this part is really just for me, I want to thank Becca. As I'm writing this, it has been over a year since I lost you and I'm only just now starting to learn to walk and breathe again. You are in my thoughts always and

I miss you every second of the day. I see you in everything. I hear you in everything. I hope you're sleeping well. Can't wait to see you again.

And lastly, but not leastly, I want to thank you, the reader. Thank you for taking a chance on my little series I used to cope with grief. You have transformed this story into something that started as just for me, into something I can tell my kids about someday. This dream would *not* be happening without your support, and I thank you, thank you, thank you from the depths of my heart. You make me want to keep going.

Cheers,

Kerrigan xoxo